THE PACT

Amanda Wes

Inspired by a true story

Red Deer Press

For Xan, Maddy & Lewis

Published in Canada by Red Deer Press, 195 Allstate Parkway, Markham, ON L3R 4T8. Published in the United States
by Red Deer Press, 311 Washington Street, Brighton, Massachusetts 02135. All rights reserved. No part of this book
may be reproduced in any manner without the express written consent of the publisher, except in the case of brief
excerpts in critical reviews and articles. All inquiries should be addressed to Red Deer Press, 195 Allstate Parkway,
Markham, Ontario, L3R 4T8.

www.reddeerpress.com   rdp@reddeerpress.com

Red Deer Press acknowledges with thanks the Canada Council for the Arts, and the Ontario Arts Council for their
support of our publishing program. We acknowledge the financial support of the Government of Canada for our publishing
activities.

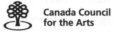  

Library and Archives Canada Cataloguing in Publication
Lewis, Amanda, author
    The pact / Amanda West Lewis.

ISBN 978-0-88995-544-8 (paperback)
1. Youth—Germany—Juvenile fiction. 2. Radicals—Germany—Juvenile fiction. 3. Propaganda, German—Juvenile
    fiction. 4. National socialism—Juvenile fiction. I. Title.
PS8623.E96448P32 2016   jC813'.6   C2016-901150X

Publisher Cataloging-in-Publication Data (U.S.)
Names: Lewis, Amanda West, author.
Title: The pact / Amanda West Lewis.
Description: Markham, Ontario : Red Deer Press, 2016. | Summary: "Exploring the radicalization of youth through the
    lens of Nazi Germany, protagonist Peter Gruber responds to propaganda and posturing while trying to
    understand conflicts of personality, culture, duty and morality" – Provided by publisher.
Identifiers: ISBN 978-0-88995-544-8 (paperback)
Subjects: LCSH: Germany—History—1933-1945 – Juvenile fiction. | Nazis—Germany – Juvenile fiction. | World
    War, 1939-1945 – Youth – Germany – Juvenile fiction. | BISAC: JUVENILE FICTION / Historical /
    Military & Wars. Classification: LCC PZ7.L495Pac | DDC [Fic] – dc23

Interior design: Karen Thomas/Intuitive Design International Ltd.
Cover design: Richard Gokool
Top front cover image property of Hans Sinn, used with permission.
Interior photos courtesy Hans Sinn

Although this work centers on historical events, this is a work of fiction. Names, characters and incidents are products of
the author's imagination and are used fictitiously. Any resemblance to actual incidents of persons, living or dead, is entirely
coincidental.

Printed and bound in Canada
10 9 8 7 6 5 4 3 2 1

I begin with the young. We older ones are used up. We are rotten to the marrow. But my magnificent youngsters! Are there any finer ones in the world? Look at these young men and boys! What material. With them I can make a new world. My teaching will be hard. Weakness will be knocked out of them. A violently active, dominating, brutal youth—that is what I am after. Youth must be indifferent to pain. There must be no weakness and tenderness in it. I want to see once more in its eyes the gleam of pride and independence of the beast of prey.

~ Adolf Hitler

Darkness cannot drive out darkness; only light can do that. Hate cannot drive out hate; only love can do that.

~ Martin Luther King, Jr.

Prologue

Years later, he would wonder if it had all begun with Eugene.

Could Eugene have made a difference?

Can the fate of one person change the fate of the world?

Part One

Chapter One

Hamburg.
May 1939

... and it's dark and I'm cold. Shivering. I think my teeth are chattering. I feel around for something solid. I hear Eugene laughing. I can't breathe. My throat swells up. There's no air coming in. I try to grab but can't move my arms. I see Eugene's face. He's smiling. I try to scream for help. I'm flailing but not moving. I can't breathe. I hear horrible gagging sounds coming out of my throat. The water closes over my head and Eugene's face is all distorted. I make myself breathe in ...

There is a soft light coming down the hall from the nurses' station. Through the window in his door, Peter sees the matron moving in her slow way, going in and out of his line of vision, sometimes carrying a cup.

It's early, Peter thought to himself. *Before sunrise.* Although it was always quiet and dark in his room. He listened to his breath. In. Out. There wasn't much of it. It was hard for him to swallow. His throat wanted to close in on itself.

A drop of sweat followed the curve of his ear and lodged itself in his eardrum, distorting the sound of his breathing. The sour smell of pee reached his nose just as he realized he was wet. He wondered which nurse would be on duty this morning. Sharp-faced Krankenschwester Helga, with her angry, reproving eyes? Or doughy Eva, who softly placed sugar cubes on his tongue as she clucked around, changing his sheets?

It would be hours before anyone came in. Hours of dim light. Stillness. Wet.

"He must lie quietly, Frau Gruber. You must make him lie still."

The wet pee had made him cold. He felt around the bed for a blanket. The weight was comforting. He wished he had a book. He tried to remember the opening of The Treasure of Nugget Mountain. He could see the words on the page in his mind and imagined he was reading himself a bedtime story. He drifted ...

... I'm on the dock, Gunter beside me. I feel sun on my back. Is my shirt off? The rough planks are swaying under me. I look down and see Eugene's face, distorted through the water, his eyes wide, staring at me, far above him. I try to reach into the water. But I'm frozen. I try to scream for Gunter to help but my mouth is locked shut. I watch Eugene watching me fade away from him ...

His mother is sitting beside the bed. A huge book rests on his legs as he struggles to wake up.

"It's by a Russian. Leo Tolstoy. There are lots of battles."

Peter looked at the heavy leather-bound book in his hands. *War and Peace.*

"The doctor says it is all right for you to read, now that your fever has broken."

His fever might have been gone, but clearly his mother expected him to stay in bed for a long time yet.

"Thank you." He said it because it was expected. He tried to keep the disappointment out of his voice.

Peter wished she'd brought him his copy of *The Treasure of Nugget Mountain.* It was worn through from the number of times he'd read it, but he'd happily read it again. He looked down at *War and Peace.*

"Frau Seligman gave it to me, for you."

The "Fraus." Frau Seligman, Frau Teitlebaum, Frau Rosenberg. Rich women with huge houses that his mother cleaned. They often sent things. Dumplings. Apple cake.

"She said it was a late birthday present."

His tenth birthday had come and gone in a haze of fever. He and Eugene had shared the same birthday. Their mothers had met in the hospital when they were born.

"The Russians are good strategists," his mother continued. "And the main character has the same name as you. Peter. Pierre."

Peter opened the book to a page at random.

"Pierre was right when he said that one must believe in the possibility of happiness in order to be happy, and I now believe in it. Let the dead bury the dead, but while I'm alive, I must live and be happy."

Peter wrinkled his nose. "Doesn't sound much like a war story to me. Sounds like a girl's romance."

His mother laughed. It was good to hear her laugh.

"Well, war starts with love. Love of your country. Love of your family and of a desire to protect them. But it's usually born in hate."

"Two sides of the same coin?"

Two sides of the same coin was a game that Peter and his mother played with each other. One of them picked a situation and the other had to see it from the other side.

Momma: Herr Ziebauer says if we don't pay our rent on time, he'll put us out on the street. I told him I just needed a couple of days, but he is an angry man, without a speck of compassion.

Peter: Herr Zeibauer says if we don't pay our rent on time, he'll put us out on the street. That's because Frau Zeibauer is sick and needs expensive medicine, and they don't have enough money for groceries to feed the baby Zeibauers, and if we don't pay them right away she might die, and all of the babies will die and there are others who can rent the apartment and get him the money he needs right away, so it is with regret that he will put us on the street, but he is too angry and upset about his dying wife to show any compassion to us."

Momma, laughing: "You win ..."

Peter's fingers traced the ridges of the book's embossed leather binding.

"I know it's big," said his mother, "but it will help to pass the time ... The doctor says you'll be here for at least four more weeks."

Four weeks. Too long. Much too long, thought Peter, looking up at his mother. She needs my help now. He suddenly regretted his reaction to the book. He hated seeming ungrateful.

Krankenschwester Helga pushed open the door. Peter hid the book under his covers. He knew she would probably disapprove or, worse yet, burn the book because it was contaminated with his germs.

"It is time for Peter to rest," she said sternly. His mother stood. Peter imagined his mother grabbing the book and smashing the nurse across the face. But, of course, she just smiled sweetly and said, "Of course, Krankenschwester Helga. I hadn't realized it was so late."

His mother leaned down and planted a small kiss on the top of Peter's forehead. Krankenschwester Helga looked as though her mouth was full of lemon juice.

"I will see you tomorrow after work. Remember there are always two sides to the same coin."

... In the moment that I can no longer see Eugene, I fall into the water. I feel his hand on my ankle. He's pulling me down, trying to climb over me, pulling himself up. I struggle for breath. My throat is burning. I look up through the water. I see Eugene and Gunter on the dock looking down at me. I reach for them but they make no movement. I'm sinking. Gunter leaves. Eugene's eyes get faint, black ...

Chapter Two

Hamburg,
June 1939

War and Peace was awful. Peter skipped large sections. There were too many characters. He tried making lists to keep them straight but it was too much work. There were ridiculous details and there was hardly any story. Did Tolstoy really need to describe every brass button on every uniform?

Each day his mother brought him more Russians—*Fathers and Sons, The Brothers Karamazov,* short stories by Chekhov. She said that the Fraus were getting rid of their libraries. He accepted their beautifully bound volumes, even if he didn't understand the stories. They were so hard to read. But he had nothing but time as he lay in the hospital, so he read them slowly. He thought maybe the short stories might be easier.

A still August night. A mist is rising slowly from the fields and casting an opaque veil over everything within eyesight. Lighted up by the moon, the mist gives the impression at one moment of a calm, boundless sea, at the next of an immense white wall. The air is damp and chilly. Morning is still far off.

Chekhov was incredibly gloomy.

A dead body, covered from head to foot with new white linen, is lying ...

"Peter?"

Gunter was standing at the door, his dark curls wild against his pale face. "Can I come in?"

It had always been Peter, Eugene, and Gunter. Gunter, Peter, and Eugene. They had their favorite places on the dock, and always sat in the same spot to watch the sunset.

Peter wouldn't sit in Eugene's spot any more than Gunter would sit in his. Peter nodded as Gunter stepped into the room.

"Your mother told me you were getting better. She said you were reading. I thought you'd want this." Gunter handed over the familiar worn red volume and, for the first time since the accident, Peter allowed himself a small smile. He turned the copy of *The Treasure of Nugget Mountain* over in his hands.

It is certainly true that no man knows what the future holds for him. When I, Jack Hildreth, newly graduated from college, won the consent of my uncle and second father, whose namesake and heir I was, to go West to see life, I little dreamed of the experience that lay before me.

"I saw Sören." Gunter's voice brought him back into the room. "He said he saw the whole thing."

Peter pictured Sören's tall frame and lanky blond hair. He was a regular client, a sailor from a Norwegian ship. He gave Peter pickled herring in exchange for cigarettes.

"What did he say?" Peter asked quietly.

"He told me to tell you to get better quickly. Hermann's taking over and he's a pig."

Peter gave a small snort despite himself. "No. I mean what did he say about what happened?"

Gunter frowned. "You don't know?"

Peter shut his eyes. The diphtheria had taken over his body almost immediately. "That harbor is full of germs," the doctor had told his mother. The fever had wiped out all memory. It wasn't until later, after the fever had broken, that his mother told him about Eugene.

He took a deep breath. "I know what happened," he said, "but I don't remember how it happened."

"Well," Gunter hesitated. "He said he saw you and Eugene running out to the dock. Saw Eugene slip on the wet wood and fall into the water. He saw you jump in after Eugene. He dove off the bridge to try to reach you both."

Peter didn't remember jumping. He remembered going to the dock that day. He remembered Gunter saying he couldn't go because he had an aunt in town visiting, and his father made him stay home.

"I should have been there," Gunter said softly.

Peter felt Gunter's dark eyes search his face. He shrugged. "It wouldn't have made a difference." He closed his eyes.

Suddenly he opened them again.

"What did Sören say about Hermann?"

Peter and Hermann were the same age. They'd gone through elementary school and Hort, the afterschool program, together. Peter had only been to Hermann's apartment once, but Hermann's mother had turned him away at the door. "I'm sorry, Peter, but you really can't come in," she'd said. "Your mother ... well, you understand." He didn't understand. It was after that visit that Hermann had called him a fatherless bastard. Peter never went back.

"He's taking over all your contacts" Gunter said. "You know no one wants to deal with Hermann. They don't trust him. He's so loud and clumsy. Sören says clients have been caught in the middle of a sale because the police could hear Hermann's voice from blocks away. But with you in hospital, they need to get their cigarettes and schnapps somewhere."

Peter had started his business when he was little. He'd begun by trading Frau Cressman's cream puffs for a piece of bacon or two. He'd quickly built up a stash of black market goods—mostly cigarettes and nylon stockings—that he traded for food. He had a good eye for trade. He knew instinctively who to trust and who to avoid. Word had gone around the shipyards that Peter's nylons were the best quality, always sure to please a girl. And his cigarettes were fresh—he took care never to trade in tobacco that was dry, or worse, cut with sawdust. Food on the ships was abundant, far better than anything you could find in the shops, and sailors sought Peter out with choice cuts of meat, bits of sausage, eggs, and even cheese. It didn't hurt that Peter was young, blond, with a big smile. The biggest smile in the school—his teacher had actually measured it once. He knew people liked him.

"I went to see him," Gunter continued. "He was bragging about trading a pair of nylons for a whole chicken and a carton of cigarettes." Gunter struck a pose, his shoulders thrust back, his head to one side, his mouth a crooked smile. "'I tell you, this stupid sailor was desperate for nylons to give to some girl. What an idiot.'"

Peter snorted. Gunter was always a good mimic.

Hermann was taking over. Here he was lying in a hospital bed, useless, and Hermann was working the docks. It made him furious. Hermann's family wasn't poor—they could get the food they needed. His father had a shipping business and Hermann always bragged about how, when he grew up, he'd sail the world on his own boats. He bragged about everything. But for Peter, the black market business meant that he and his mother had almost enough to eat. For Peter, it was the one way he could help.

As if reading his thoughts, Gunter said, "Your mother came over for coffee. She's all right. She just wants you to get better."

It was all too much to think about. Peter closed his eyes again. The next time he opened them, Gunter was gone.

Then finally, after five weeks, several re-reads of *The Treasure of Nugget Mountain*, and a few chapters of fat Russian novels, it was time to go. "You're not contagious anymore, and you'll probably get better rest and food at home," the doctor told him. But he had to wait until the end of the day to leave, until his mother finished work, so she could help to carry all the books. Krankenschwester Helga sniffed and tutted and said that a boy his age should be able to go home without waiting for his mother to pick him up. Krankenschwester Eva surreptitiously popped an extra sugar cube into his pocket. "For the road," she said in a whisper.

He saw the trunk the minute he walked into the apartment.

"It was your Opa's. Tante Elsa sent it down from Eutin."

The words hung in the air.

"I didn't want to tell you while you were in hospital."

Peter hadn't seen his grandfather in over a year. Not since they'd gone to the house in Eutin for Oma's funeral. Opa had scowled at the shiny black coffin. It had looked much too small to contain the fierce energy that had been his grandmother. "It was supposed to be me in there," his grandfather had cried. "Shush, Papa," his mother had whispered. Peter had watched his grandfather fold in on himself. That was the phrase that came into his mind. He folded in on himself.

Now Peter looked at the large trunk on the floor between them. He turned to his mother expectantly. They had an agreement that they would be honest with each other. It meant that, on her side of the coin, she told facts as facts. "I'm not going to sugar-coat this for you, Peter," was one of her favorite expressions.

"He hung himself. In the space where the stairway goes up to the second floor. Tante Elsa and Gerta were at the market."

The room went very quiet. The air felt heavy. The trunk sat between them.

"Tante Elsa has asked you to stay with her in Eutin. Just for the summer. She has Gerta, of course, but she says she needs a young man in the house to help out. She sent Opa's wristwatch for you to have ..."

Peter looked at the watch in his mother's outstretched hand. The large, cream-colored face was held by a soft brown leather strap. He'd been fascinated with it as a child and loved hearing Opa tell the story about how Oma had bought it for him when he was heading off to the Prussian war, and how, when he was at the front, he listened to it ticking at night and thought of it as Oma's heart beating. "I saw it every time I loaded a Krupp six-pounder," he'd said. "I thought of Oma as the cannonball soared through the air and landed on those bastard French heads," he'd laughed.

Peter tried to imagine loving someone else so much that you would kill for them. And then to kill yourself because you missed them. He thought of Nicholas in *War and Peace*, fighting a war and dreaming of Sonya. That was romantic and noble. But there was no glory in hanging yourself because you were tired of life. What Opa did was just sad and small.

Peter had heard that people who were hanged pissed their pants when they died. He wondered if Tante Elsa had had to clean up her father's pee.

He looked at his mother and then down at the watch in his hands. As if reading his thoughts, she said, "I'm fine." She took a deep breath. "It hurts, but he was so unhappy."

Peter let his grandfather's sadness fill the room. "It's

harder for Elsa," his mother continued. "She was always closer to him. Funny, I was so jealous of her when we were children. Then, when she went back to look after Oma and Opa, after your Onkel Berthold died ..." Her voice trailed off.

Peter tried to imagine his aunt and his mother as squabbling sisters. He thought it would be fun to have a brother. But he couldn't imagine sharing his mother.

"Now she has the farm to look after." His mother looked him full in the face. "I can manage here. It's Tante Elsa who needs your help. And your cousin Gerta needs some company, too. It's lonely for her to be in the country all year long. Besides, it would give you a chance to get back your strength."

It was the beginning of June. His teacher, Herr Neitmann, had said that there was no point in coming back to school for just the last three weeks. Peter thought of the train ride to Eutin. It was a slow train, but it never took longer than two hours and, when he got off, there'd be the smell of green. Tante Elsa lived just outside of town, past golden fields of sunflowers. He thought of the cooling breeze off Lake Keller, far from the slippery docks of the canal.

He looked at his mother. She'd lost weight since he'd been in hospital. She looked pinched, gray. He'd do anything he could to help her. Even stay with horrible Gerta and morose Tante Elsa. He'd put his life on hold. Hermann would have a field day.

Chapter Three

Eutin, in Wagrien, Germany,
August 1939

My big toe traces the bump at the front of the chair seat. I slide it along the sharp curve of polished wood. I feel calm as I step forward into the black space.

Immediately, the rope bites into my neck. My hands automatically fly up. I claw at it, trying to loosen it so I can breathe. My body is swinging in the air. I thrash my legs backwards to try to find the chair. My face is swelling. Pee shoots out, drenching me.

"Give me back my watch!" Opa yells below me. His outstretched arm is just bones, shreds of black flesh dripping from them. His face is the grimace of a corpse. I scream but no sound comes out. I rip at the rope with all my strength. It breaks and I start to fall ...

Peter gasps and wakes with a start. He feels like he's been falling. He's cold, damp, and smelly. He thinks he might have wet himself. What has he been dreaming? He has a vague sense of unease as he drifts back to sleep ...

"Herr Neitmann has recommended you for Gymnasium!"

Peter and his mother were sitting on the hill behind Tante Elsa's house, looking out over a field of late wildflowers. He'd spent the long summer days bringing in firewood and repairing the chicken coop. He'd helped his aunt polish every inch of her house. He moved her heavy wood furniture and helped her to reorganize the house while Gerta had made new curtains. He'd slept in Opa's old room and filled it with his Russian books. He'd left *War and Peace* back in Hamburg, but Chekhov was finally starting to make sense.

"Gymnasium. Such a privilege! I'm so proud of you!"

Peter felt his heart sink. Gymnasium. The elite schools were known for giving the best education. Going to Gymnasium was a "ticket to success." Gymnasium was where boys like Hermann went. Yes, it was a privilege, and for him— a boy without a father, without a family, without money—it was unheard of. It would be hard work. A lot would be expected of him.

"But I didn't finish school last spring," he said. "I'm behind, because of the diphtheria," he added, trying to remind her of how sick he'd been. He didn't want to change schools. He wanted things to be the same as they'd always been. He wanted to spend a little bit of time at school and a lot of time on the docks, making trades.

"Herr Neitmann says you'll catch up easily," she said breezily. "He gave me a copy of his letter of recommendation." She handed him a thin paper with the unmistakable imprint of typed carbon-copy blue letters.

To the Members of the Committee:

I am writing to you to recommend my student, Peter Gruber. Herr Gruber has all of the qualities necessary for an excellent Gymnasium student. He is strong, both physically and mentally, and consistently demonstrates good judgment. His work ethic is exemplary and he has a willingness to learn and to strive for what he knows to be right. Most importantly, he has shown himself to be very resourceful and is a decisive leader, respected by his peers.

It is my understanding that Herr Gruber will require a scholarship in order to attend Gymnasium. It would be my hope that the committee will award him such a scholarship, as I believe he represents all that is worthy in the German character. He is a most deserving student, who embodies the future of Germany.

With respect,
Heinrich Neitmann

Peter read the letter three times. Herr Gruber? Was that who he was? He smiled slightly at the words "very resourceful." Herr Neitmann was a customer. Last year he'd given Peter six eggs and a pound of lard for a pair of nylons for his wife's birthday.

"They've offered you a scholarship because they know that you don't come from a rich family. They know that you do not have a father."

Peter did, of course, have a father. Both he and his mother knew that. But they didn't know where he was now, and he certainly wouldn't be paying anything for Peter to go to school.

He felt his mother's eyes search his face for any sign of hesitation. He took a breath and smiled at her. He saw her relax. She touched the watch on his wrist lightly.

"But we have to fill in the application form and … you must be worthy of this honor, of the scholarship."

Peter looked up into his mother's face. "I thought that being poor meant I was worthy," he said with a wry grin.

"Peter, it's serious. Not only do you have to be strong and smart to go to Gymnasium, but your family must be pure. There can't be any weakness. Any weakness in your blood," she said with emphasis.

Weakness in his blood. It was a phrase he'd heard in Chancellor Hitler's last speech on the radio. He wasn't sure what it meant. Was diphtheria a sign of a weakness in his blood?

"We must give information about your background," his mother continued. "Three generations. Names, places of birth, occupations. And causes of death."

Causes of death.

Gerta had shown him the rope. It was stored in the barn.

"Oma died of pneumonia. Opa died of a heart attack. You understand, don't you? Opa died of a heart attack. He was a strong man."

He imagined Opa safely in bed, dying in his sleep. It was better to think of him that way.

"Yes, Mother. I understand. Opa was a strong man."

His mother had always told him to be truthful with her, but they both knew that sometimes the truth was elastic.

"I loved this spot when I was a little girl. I used to come here with your Opa, to watch the sun set. I remember sitting here with him when he told me he had to go away to fight in the Great War."

Peter gazed out over the fields dappled with late afternoon sun. He tried to imagine Opa as a young man, going off to war. He looked down at Opa's watch. It felt natural to wear it now. When he took it off, tan lines were clearly marked on his wrist. It made him feel connected to Opa, to a time when Opa was strong. He didn't really understand what it would feel like to have a father, let alone lose one, but he knew it must be hard for his mother. He smiled at her gently.

She put an arm around Peter's shoulder and gave him a small squeeze. "And I've brought you a new Russian. Goncharov," she said, brightly changing the subject. Peter repressed a sigh. "The book's called *Oblomov*. It's a comedy about a man who is very lazy, slothful. He's so indolent that he stays in bed all day," she laughed. "You can tell why the Russians decided they needed a new government—the rich were very fat and privileged, like Oblomov."

Peter had studied the Russian Revolution in school. He'd done a project about how the common Russian people were poor and starving while the aristocrats were rich beyond everyone's belief. He'd learned about how the people took over the country, killing the Czar, his family, and all of the rich nobility. The poor people had been in charge ever since.

"It seems we're to be great friends with Russia," his

mother continued. "The Führer has signed a non-aggression pact with the Russians. They've promised not to attack us and we've promised not to attack them. So it's good for you to read these Russian writers, to understand her people."

A non-aggression pact. Peter didn't know why two countries needed a pact not to attack each other, unless they had been thinking of attacking each other.

He opened the slim book. There was a picture on the title page of a boy reading inside a kind of castle. He imagined himself sitting and reading in his own private castle. He'd sit there re-reading *The Treasure of Nugget Mountain*. The Russians were always hard work.

"And Gunter sent you a book, too. Or at least his father did. Herr Schmidt came over especially to bring it," his mother said.

His mother handed him a small paperback book. *A Farewell to Arms* by Ernest Hemingway.

"I'm not sure it is suitable," she said stiffly. "But Herr Schmidt was insistent. He said it is very rare. It's fine for you to read it while you are still in Eutin, but don't bring it back to Hamburg."

Peter opened it.

"It could be worse," Passini said respectfully. "There is nothing worse than war."

"Defeat is worse."

"I do not believe it," Passini said still respectfully. "What is defeat? You go home."

Peter felt a twinge of anger. Another book about war?

"I've also brought you Chancellor Hitler's book, *Mein Kampf*. Herr Neitmann said that you will be expected to have read it before starting Gymnasium. He thinks you will like it. He says it makes you proud to be a German."

Peter looked down the hill to the fields beyond. He watched the cattle grazing slowly in the afternoon sun. It was strange to hear his mother talking this way. The last years had been really hard. Not just for him and his mother, but for everyone. There were no jobs and hardly any food in the shops. Crippled soldiers from the Great War begged on the street corners. On the radio, he'd heard the Führer say that France and Great Britain were responsible for German poverty.

But all of that seemed a long way away. Peter had enjoyed a summer of being pampered in the countryside. Tante Elsa kept a cow and a few chickens, so they always had butter, cheese, and eggs at every meal. He'd let himself forget how hard it was in the city, and how his mother had to struggle every day just to get something to eat. He'd filled his stomach and grown over the summer—his pants were short and his shoes pinched badly.

"You'll have to have new clothes for the fall, for Gymnasium," he mother said. It was uncanny the way she read his thoughts. "We'll be given extra money to get you a new uniform."

She sounded so hopeful. The Führer talked about renewal. Maybe things would start to get better.

"What about Hort?" Peter asked, suddenly remembering.

"Will I still be able to go?" His Hort group was like a large family, the only family he had. He went every day after school and all day on Saturday. He'd been in the same group for four years, hiking and playing "Knights and Horses" and "Trappers and Indians."

"No, you'll be moved to Jungvolk." She held her hand up as he started to argue. "It's compulsory for all boys once you turn ten." She must have seen the disappointment in his eyes, because her face softened. "It's like Hort," she continued, "but with new games, new skills. You learn how to shoot a rifle, how to skin a rabbit."

Peter had heard about Jungvolk from Franz, next door. Franz had just turned fourteen. He'd be going to Hitlerjugend—HJ—this year. He'd bragged about shooting real bullets from real guns. Peter thought about Opa shooting his Krupp six-pounder.

Maybe things would get better. He'd go back to the city, pick up with the business, and he'd learn to shoot a rifle. He'd become soft, living in the country, and he was ready to go back. Maybe going to Gymnasium and Jungvolk wouldn't be so bad.

Peter spent his last two weeks in Eutin helping to harvest his aunt's garden. He made sauerkraut and pickles with Gerta, stacked hay bales, and helped to get everything ready for the coming winter. In the evenings he read. "You've always got your nose in a book," Gerta complained. Reading was an escape from the sadness of the house, but he didn't really like the books his mother had brought him. *A Farewell to Arms* was a love story and a war story, but was morose and he didn't finish it. *Oblomov* wasn't as funny as he'd hoped. In fact, it was really depressing. *"When you don't know what you're living for, you don't care what you do,"* Oblomov said. Peter wondered if that was true.

Mein Kampf, on the other hand, never raised the question of what he was living for. It consistently reminded him of his duty and responsibility as a good German.

Chapter Four

Peter had never been to Poland. There was a boy on his street, Janusz, who had come from Poland. Janusz wore glasses and recited poetry. He was always talking about Warsaw. He'd shown Peter a photograph of his home there, but to Peter it just looked cold, dark, and dull.

When Peter dreamed about travel, it was to the Wild West in the United States of America. He would ride with the Indians, like Old Shatterhand in *The Treasure of Nugget Mountain*. The vast open prairies, freshly killed buffalo cooking over an open fire—that was the life for him! He couldn't imagine ever wanting to go to Poland.

But apparently Poland was important. Important enough to fight over. The Führer said that Germany needed to take back the land that had been given to Poland twenty years ago, after the Great War. Peter had never understood why the British had given Germany's land away. What would it feel like to be told that you suddenly lived in a different country? To go to sleep at night living in Germany and wake up in the morning living in Poland, learning another language, eating different foods, wearing different clothes?

He thought it made sense to take the land back. But he wasn't sure it made sense to fight over it.

The whine of a siren broke through his thoughts. He was happy to be back in Hamburg, looking out at the city from the front window of Herr Ballin's plumbing shop. The street outside was unusually quiet. There were only a few people, walking quickly, with their heads down. "Today's just a test," Herr Ballin was saying beside him, through the scream of the siren. "They're building shelters, just in case. But nothing's going to happen, at least not today. Just a bunch of saber rattling."

Peter pictured soldiers with long sabers, like in *War and Peace*. Could they rattle them as they were marching?

The Ballins didn't have any children of their own, only old Oma Ballin, Herr Ballin's mother, who lived upstairs. Peter loved visiting Oma Ballin. She gave him tiny cups of strong ersatz coffee and sometimes they shared a Kopenhagener filled with delicious marzipan. Oma Ballin cut the pastry into tiny pieces so it seemed like there was lots to go around.

Oma Ballin never said much, but when she did, she always said something that Peter needed to think about. He suspected she'd be very good at "Two Sides of the Same Coin," although he'd never played it with her.

"What does Oma Ballin think about the war?" Peter wanted to know before he talked to her. He didn't want to upset her.

Herr Ballin sighed. "This will be hard on Mutter Ballin," he said as he continued to look out the window. "There was so little food during the Great War. She fed her babies, me and my sister, before she fed herself. I'm not sure she can face another war."

Peter's heart sank. It seemed impossible that there could be less food. For the last two years he'd been able to help a bit, but there was still never enough.

"What will happen?" he asked softly.

Herr Ballin turned to look at him. "What will happen is what always happens. The rich will get richer, the poor will get poorer. The smart ones will find a way to survive. Don't look so glum," he said, reaching over to pat Peter's hand. "You're resourceful. You always have been. You'll survive this war."

Herr Ballin stood up and turned from the window. He flipped the store sign over to read *Closed*.

"Peter, please ask your mother if she would be so kind as to join Frau Ballin and me for supper this evening." The Ballins often invited Peter and his mother to join them for supper on Friday nights. He knew that they saved up their best food for Fridays. "You, too, are welcome, of course." Herr Ballin was always formal. It was a kind of game that he and Peter played.

"Certainly, Herr Ballin," said Peter, responding formally with a bow. His heart was still heavy but he managed a smile. "You are most kind. We are honored."

Peter left the plumbing shop and walked down the hall to his apartment. He could hear the sound of the radio before he reached the door. His mother had bought a radio while he was in Eutin. The government was selling them cheaply and she said it was company for her while he was away. "With a radio you can hear the truth," she'd said. "You can hear the Führer's words as he says them. It brings the whole world into my kitchen."

"It is a lie when the outside world says that we only tried to carry our revisions through by pressure."

The familiar voice of the Führer grabbed Peter as he walked into the room.

"I have, not once but several times, made proposals for the revision of intolerable conditions."

His mother looked up, her face worn and sad.

"For two whole days I sat with my government and waited to see if it was convenient for the Polish Government to send a plenipotentiary or not."

"What does it mean?" asked Peter. "What is a plenipotentiary? And why didn't Poland send one?" Peter's mother waved at him to be quiet.

"I therefore decided late last night, and informed the British Government that, in these circumstances, I can no longer find any willingness on the part of the Polish Government to conduct serious negotiations with us ..."

The Führer's voice rose to a crescendo. Peter could hear murmurs and sounds in the background. Peter knew Herr Hitler was speaking to hundreds, perhaps thousands of people in the Reichstag, the Parliament, and to many more thousands, probably millions, who were listening to the radio, just like him.

"I will not make war against women and children. I have ordered my air force to restrict itself to attacks on military objectives."

Peter looked at this mother. He watched as a slow tear slid down her face. He had a sudden image of the twists and turns of the River Elbe winding through Hamburg, as though it was a tear moving through the country.

Chapter Five

Hamburg.
Saturday, September 2, 1939

"What do you mean, you don't have a job?" Peter cried. "Why did they fire you? I thought you were good! I thought they liked you!"

He saw his mother stiffen. Once upon a time she'd been a typist. She'd only started cleaning houses two years ago because there were no other jobs.

"I was doing a very good job. Frau Teitlebaum and Frau Rosenberg wept when they told me they could no longer pay me to clean their houses. They said they weren't sure how long they'd be living in them. They're getting rid of everything—not just their books—and they said they might have to move away, to leave Germany."

Peter had heard that a lot of the Jews were leaving Hamburg. He didn't really care, except when they were the ones his mother worked for.

"Don't worry," his mother continued. "Something will turn up. It always does."

But Peter did worry. He was annoyed by her attitude—how could she take it so lightly?

She smiled. "Two sides of the same coin: The Fraus' husbands come home and tell their wives they have lost their jobs and they must cut back on expenses and—"

"I don't want to play two sides," Peter barked. "There's only one side. You don't have a job and we don't have anything to eat." He turned away from her and stormed down the hall and out of the apartment.

The minute he was on the sidewalk, Peter regretted yelling at his mother. It wasn't her fault that Frau Teitlebaum and Frau Rosenberg couldn't pay her to clean their houses any more. But he could still remember living with Frau Cressman when he was five. He'd had to live with her for a whole year. His mother was working but she made so little that she couldn't afford to keep him at home. So he lived with Frau Cressman. He hadn't seen much of his mother that year.

Frau Cressman was a fat, spongy woman who pinched his cheeks and called him her "darlink." "I don't have children—you are my only darlink. You be my darlink forever, yes?" She fed him cream puffs every day, until he began to hate their puffy sweetness. He'd sneak cream puffs out of the house and trade them to the neighborhood boys for bits of sausage, trades that eventually became the start of his black market business. He remembered Frau Cressman's rancid smell and his stomach turned.

He wouldn't let that happen again. He wouldn't leave his mother. He'd help, somehow.

He headed for the port. It was time to get back to work.

Peter had always spent as much time as possible either looking for treasure in the muddy banks when the tide went out, or helping to load crates onto wagons and trucks when the tide was in. He loved the smells. The dense fug of rotting vegetation. The dark bitter pinch of roasted coffee. The heavy sweat of men hauling crates. All of it made him feel at home.

Usually the docks were bustling with activity. But today was uncannily quiet. The ships looked empty. There were no stevedores moving crates. The warehouses stood open but there were only a few deliverymen slowly loading goods onto trucks. It looked more like a painting than a working port.

Peter's eyes searched and immediately found Gerd's hunched and wiry figure. Gerd had fought in the Great War and he dragged his left leg as he heaved boxes onto the back of his wagon. Peter fell in beside him, hoisting a heavy wooden crate and sliding it into place as he'd been shown. The sour, slightly rotten smell of cabbages filled his nose and his whole head.

"Hey, Peter! Where you been? I heard you were sick, almost dead," Gerd laughed. "Then I heard you were livin' the life in the country, gettin' fat and stupid." He wiped sweat from his forehead with a dirty cloth. "Looks like it was the country, and fat and stupid," he grinned a mouthful of brown teeth.

"Yeah, I've been livin' the life of luxury, Gerd. Eggs, cheese at every meal. Bacon! When's the last time you had a slab of bacon, Gerd? Gettin' fat and stupid sure feels good!" Peter easily fell into Gerd's way of talking. He'd known Gerd since as far back as he could remember. Some of his happiest days had been spent on Gerd's wagon, making deliveries throughout the city.

Gerd was the only wholesaler who still had a horse. Everyone else had converted to trucks long ago. "I know. It's crazy," he'd told Peter. "I could get more done, go a lot faster. But Willy and me, we been together a long time. He's good company. And hay's cheaper than gasoline." Peter had been frightened of the horse when he was a child. Willy had seemed so big, his huge hoofs threatening Peter's small feet.

But now, as Peter patted his neck, the horse seemed to have shrunk. He took an end of a carrot out of his pocket— he'd swiped it from the kitchen table last night out of habit— and offered it to Willy, keeping his hand flat. The horse's breath was warm and wet as he sniffed Peter's hand. *Does he remember my smell*, Peter wondered? Willy stretched out his fat horse lips and pulled the carrot piece into his mouth. Saliva dripped out of his mouth as he crunched.

"You're spoilin' him," Gerd said, pushing another crate of cabbage into the wagon with a grunt. "Pretty soon you'll be makin' your own dinner out of carrot tops."

Peter dug his fingers into the horse's fur, just under his mane, where it was soft and greasy. He inhaled the heavy horse smell.

"Where is everybody?" Peter asked as he stroked the horse's broad chest.

"Took the day off. No one knows whether to stay or go. No one knows nothin'. If it comes to war, they'll be no more ships, no more crates." Gerd pushed a crate toward the back of the wagon. "You know Hermann took over your business, yes?"

Peter nodded. "Yeah, but I thought maybe I could get it goin' again. Should be enough for both of us."

Gerd snorted. "The sailors, they deal with Hermann now. I know, I know," Gerd waved Peter's objections away. "He's a liar and a cheat, and he's loud and a braggart. But he's got quite a stash. Ain't nothin' you want that Hermann don't have, they say."

Peter's heart sank. "But they know they'll get a good deal from me. They know I deal in quality," he whined.

"Peter, you weren't here. New men, they don't know. Times change. And now ..." Gerd looked pained.

"What?" asked Peter.

"Ships are goin' to have a hard time getting in and out. These," he gestured to the last crate, "last of these for a while, I'll bet." Peter leaned over the box and curled his fingers under the wooden slats. The tangy sweet smell of oranges flooded his body as he hefted the crate up. "The English, they'll make sure we don't see anythin' like this."

Peter pushed the crate onto the wagon. "No, the only food they'll let through'll be potatoes," Gerd continued. "Rotten potatoes at that. Mark my words, Peter. If this war comes, it makes skeletons out of us all. Even you, Mr. Fatty," he said, poking Peter between the ribs.

"Will it be like last time?" Peter asked seriously.

Gerd cocked his head and looked at him.

"Will they poison people with the yellow gas? I heard that the gas killed all of the crops and there was nothing to eat. And people couldn't breathe. Will it be like that?" Peter tried to keep the panic out of his voice.

Gerd leaned against Willy and his eyes grew serious as he looked out over the river. "Depends," he said. "Depends on the French. Depends on the English. The Führer doesn't want war. But if they say war, you can bet they're goin' to make us pay for it. Just like last time. We lost the war, but we had to pay everyone a lot of money. French got rich, English got rich, Americans got really rich, while you and me, Peter, we got really, really poor."

Peter couldn't imagine being more poor than they were now. His mother out of a job. His black market business taken over by a loudmouth, cheating braggart.

"You won't remember, but Americans, they used to come here all the time just to have parties. They ate up all the good food, drank all the best champagne, and ran around in fur coats with nothing underneath. Those were some pretty wild parties!" Gerd chuckled as he pulled himself up and onto the wagon. He gathered up the reins.

"You comin' with me today?"

Peter shook his head. His mind was too full to sit quietly on the wagon. He needed to walk, needed to think things through.

"Suit yourself. Here, take this," Gerd threw an orange down to him. "You can tell your grandchildren you ate one of the last oranges in Germany."

Chapter Six

Hamburg,
Monday, September 4, 1939

France and Great Britain officially declared war on Germany on Sunday, September 3.

Peter expected things to change but, aside from the occasional siren and the sound of hammering as people built air-raid shelters, being at war didn't feel much different from being at peace.

Peter didn't want to go to Gymnasium. He was worried that it would be really hard work. After all, it was for the best students in Germany. He didn't think he was that smart. Sure, he was good in his German and English classes, and pretty good at sports, but he was terrible at math. He wished it didn't mean so much to his mother.

Of course Hermann would be going, but he felt better when he heard that Gunter and Otto would be there, too. They'd lived in the same neighborhood and been friends of Peter's all their lives. They could walk together in the mornings just as they used to. It would be like old times.

Except that Eugene wouldn't be with them. *Eugene probably wouldn't have had the marks for Gymnasium*, thought Peter. *They wouldn't have offered him a scholarship.*

He was a bit surprised about Otto getting in. Not that Otto wasn't smart—Otto got some of the best grades in the school. But he was small and thin and was always drawing and daydreaming. At Hort, he'd been Peter's partner for Knights and Horses, and he was great when he was sitting on Peter's shoulders. But Peter didn't think that Otto could handle all of the physical training at Gymnasium. Where Peter would fly over hurdles on the track, Otto was always one of the last, his short legs constantly knocking down the rails.

Gunter got along with everyone. He was good at school, good at Hort, good at sports, just generally good at everything. He'd breeze through.

Gunter's father often invited Peter over for dinner and Peter always made sure to bring something, even if it was just a bit of extra sausage. Gunter's sisters were older and teased Gunter all the time. Their mother had died when Gunter was five, but they talked about Frau Schmidt all the time, as though she were just in the next room. Gunter was without a mother, Peter was without a father. He sometimes fantasized about their parents marrying and Gunter and Peter being brothers. But deep down, he knew that would never really happen. Herr Schmidt still loved and missed his dead wife, and Peter knew that Gunter's mother's family was paying for Gunter's Gymnasium fees.

At Gymnasium, they started each morning with a salute to the portrait of Chancellor Hitler. "The Führer is making Germany strong," said his new teacher, Herr Birkmann, "and if we work together, Germany will be a great nation again. That is why you have been selected for Gymnasium. Never forget that you are the future of Germany."

Gymnasium wasn't at all like he'd thought it would be. Class times were shortened, so there was more time for exercise, and everything they studied connected up with everyday life. Peter was fascinated to read about the Beer Hall Putsch in his history text book. He didn't know that Chancellor Hitler had been put in jail for leading a rebellion in 1923. He looked forward to the ceremonies on November 9 to honor the martyrs of the rebellion. They'd march in a special parade that day. For the first time, he started to enjoy school. He never felt bored.

In German class, Herr Birkmann assigned them a new book, *The Poisonous Mushroom*. Peter read the first page and thought it was childish. It wasn't an adventure, like the Karl May books, and it certainly wasn't as well written as the Russians he'd been reading. But he'd had to read it because Herr Birkmann said there would be a test.

In math class, Herr Birkmann stood in front of the blackboard, tapping his pointer at a list of numbers. "From now on, all of your school work will have practical applications," he said. "Today for math, you are going to analyze a budget."

Peter turned to Otto beside him. Math had always been Peter's worst subject. Otto had spent hours trying to explain math problems to Peter. Otto nodded very slightly. Peter knew he'd help him out.

"It is very simple," Herr Birkmann continued. "Every year the government spends a lot of money to look after people living in hospitals. Many of them have incurable hereditary diseases and will never get better. We will analyze this budget and see how this money could be better spent."

A sudden memory flooded Peter's mind. He was on a class trip. He must have been about six years old. They were in a hospital for people who were mentally and physically unfit. There were cripples missing one or both legs and people who were blind and deaf. A woman was talking to herself. She had spit flying from her mouth. Her eyes were crossed. A man was screaming and smashing his head against the rough wall, blood pouring down his face and into his eyes. Another man was thrashing on the floor, foam spilling out of his lips. Herr Neitmann had said the man was having some kind of a seizure.

"Every day, a cripple or blind person costs six Reichsmarks for food, housing, and medicine." Herr Birkmann's sharp voice brought Peter back to the present. "A mentally ill person costs four Reichsmarks, a criminal three and a half. Compare this to a worker who has three Reichsmarks a day to spend on his family." He turned to write numbers on the blackboard.

"Question number one: If there are 50 cripples, 28 blind people, 35 mentally ill people, and 63 criminals, how much money do they cost the state? And question number two: How many days could you support a valuable worker with the money that is being spent on the people in the hospital?"

Herr Birkmann finished writing and put the chalk down. He turned to face the class, brushing off his hands.

Peter quickly wrote the numbers in his notebook, fighting to push the image of the man having a seizure out of his mind.

Otto suddenly jumped up beside him. "Eight hundred and twenty-eight and a half Reichsmarks," he shouted. "That would support a worker for two hundred, seventy-six days and about six hours. Almost two-thirds of a year."

Peter mentally weighed the man with the seizure against his mother feeding them for months. He shook his head. Something about the image seemed all wrong.

"Very good, Herr Brandt," said Herr Birkmann. Otto beamed as he sat down beside Peter. *He may be the slowest on the track*, thought Peter, *but he's always the fastest in math class.*

"Now, we combine math with biology," said Herr Birkmann. "Open your textbook, *Short Ethnology of the German People*."

Peter hefted the shiny new textbook onto his desk.

Herr Birkmann gestured to a boy standing at the back of the room. "You, Jakob, come to the front."

Everyone turned around to look as Jakob quietly made his way to the front of the class. Jakob Gluzman had been in Peter's elementary school, but Peter didn't know where he went to school now. He was surprised to see him there.

"In *The Poisonous Mushroom*," continued Herr Birkmann, "we read that you can easily tell a Jew by his face. What are some of the characteristics you should look for?" Herr Birkmann scanned the room. "Yes, Herr Kramer?"

Hermann stood and thrust out his chest. He'd grown a lot

over the summer, and was easily six inches taller than anyone else in the class. He recited from the text. "One can most easily tell a Jew by his nose. The Jewish nose is bent at its point. It looks like the number six. We call it the 'Jewish six.' Many Gentiles also have bent noses. But their noses bend upwards, not downwards. Such a nose is a hook-nose or an eagle nose. It is not at all like a Jewish nose." He sat down with a smug smile.

"Good, Herr Kramer. Yes, the nose is a starting point. But there are other things as well." Herr Birkmann picked up the long wooden pointer beside the chalkboard. "You see here," he continued, pointing to Jakob's face. "A Jew has a large jaw that projects forward. He has a low, sloping forehead, fleshy lips, and hard shifty eyes. These are not Aryan characteristics. This is not German. Also," he moved the pointer to Jakob's ear, "the ears are handle-shaped and the distance between the ear and the top of the skull is small." Jakob stood as still as a statue. "The Aryan race, the white race, is dolichocephalic. The Jew's brain, like the Gypsy's and the Negroid's is brachycephalic." Herr Birkmann wrote the words on the board and Peter dutifully copied them into his notebook.

"The Aryan has a large brain. The dolichocephalic brain averages 220 cubic centimeters. The Jews, Gypsies, and Negroes are all short, broad-headed races with brains that average 190 cubic centimeters. A smaller brain means less intelligence. Races with a brachycephalic brain are inferior by every standard."

Peter looked at Jakob's head. Jakob looked straight ahead.

Peter didn't even see him blink. *I always thought he was one of the smart ones*, thought Peter.

"Biology teaches us that reproducing with weakness breeds more weakness," Herr Birkmann continued.

All eyes in the room were on Jakob. But Jakob's face was a blank.

"It is pointless to create inferior people," said Herr Birkmann. "Science is a tool that we can use to help us to build a better society. You are the future and the future is yours. You must make the decisions that will build a better future."

Herr Birkmann paused to let the statement sink in. Peter knew that they all had to be strong and healthy, and work for the good of the country to help win the war. *When we win this war*, thought Peter, *there will be enough food for everyone*.

Herr Birkmann began to hand out tape measures, protractors, and sheets of paper. "This is where our biology class combines with our math class. Geometry. I want you to measure the facial angle of your seating partner." Peter felt Otto shift slightly in the seat beside him.

Herr Birkmann turned back to Jakob. "The facial angle is formed by drawing two lines—a horizontal line from nostril to ear, here to here. Use a piece of chalk to draw this line on your partner's face, like this." Herr Birkmann drew a white chalk line across Jakob's face. "Then look to find the vertical line from the upper-jawbone prominence to the forehead prominence. Draw this line." Herr Birkmann drew the second line on Jakob's face. "According to Camper's craniometry, the ideal, that of the ancient Greeks in Sparta, is a 90-degree facial angle, here. Most Aryans will have an 80-degree angle. Negroes, Jews, and Gypsies will have somewhere between 70 degrees and 58 degrees—the latter being the angle of the orangutan," Herr Birkmann concluded with a chuckle.

Jakob had not moved a muscle. Without picking up a protractor, Herr Birkmann pointed to the angle that he had created on his face. "You see? This facial angle is approximately 65 degrees. Proof that his brain is smaller and therefore less intelligent than yours."

Peter watched carefully. From where he was sitting, the lines that Herr Birkmann drew didn't seem particularly accurate. He also couldn't really follow how the facial angle had anything to do with brain size.

"Measure your partner's facial angle, using chalk and your protractor. Then, measure your partner's head. First, measure the circumference, around here, so." Herr Birkmann wrapped a tape measure around Jakob's head. "Then measure the distance from the eyebrows to the hair line. The distance between the eyes. The distance from each ear, over the top of the skull. The distance from the base of the skull to the bridge of the nose. Write all the measurements on your chart."

Herr Birkmann turned to Jakob. "You may go now," he said, turning away to fold up the measuring tape. Jakob walked stiffly to the door. He left the room, the chalk marks still along his face. *Perhaps he doesn't go to school anymore*, thought Peter.

"I'll go first," Otto said to Peter, with conviction. He drew a chalk line from Peter's left nostril to his ear.

"It tickles," said Peter.

"Be brave and strong," Otto said. His voice sounded strained. Then he drew a line from the corner of Peter's jaw, up to his forehead. "Looks like about 85 degrees to me," he said, measuring with his protractor. "Clearly you are a genius," he said jokingly. "Although I can't really be sure."

As he stretched the cloth tape measure, Peter was aware that Otto's hands were moist with sweat. He watched him recording the numbers on his chart, and saw the chart get messier with each addition. He went through the list, finishing as he held the tape measure from the base of Peter's skull to the bridge of his nose. Peter could feel Otto's hands trembling.

"What is it?" he asked. "What's wrong?"

"I don't know if this is real science," Otto muttered.

"What do you mean?" whispered Peter. "It's all in our textbook. It must be right."

"My uncle told me that there is no such thing as race, and that you can't prove anything about a person by their physical characteristics. He says that there are people who are saying these things, using them to prove things that aren't true."

Otto slowly handed Peter the tape measure. Peter started to make the marks on Otto's head, but Otto was sweating so hard the chalk didn't stick.

"I don't want you to do this," Otto said quietly. "I don't believe in it and ..."

"What?"

"I ... I ... the measurements might show something."

Peter looked at Otto.

"I don't think they will," Otto continued defensively. "I don't think they can. I don't think it works like that, but ..."

"What?"

Otto cleared his throat and murmured, "My father was Jewish." He let the words sink into Peter's mind and then continued all in a rush. "It doesn't make any difference, because you are only a Jew if your mother is Jewish. But ..." He looked at Peter searchingly.

Peter was dumbfounded. Otto had been his friend since the early days on the docks, before they even went to school.

"But your name," began Peter. "Otto Brandt isn't a Jewish name."

"My mother re-married when my father died. I was raised by my stepfather as his son. I am a German," he continued defiantly. "A pure German." He put emphasis on the word pure. "I never even knew my father. He died before I was born."

Otto continued, and Peter distinctly heard a note of pride in his voice. "My father fought in the Great War for Germany. He was very young. He was given a medal. But his lungs never recovered from the yellow gas." Otto paused. "These measurements mean nothing," he added.

Peter didn't know what to do. Otto was his friend. He'd eaten at his house. Otto had always been the smart one, the kind one. Otto's mother had given Peter delicious little pastries to take home to his mother. He even played Aryans and Jews with Otto, and it never mattered which team either of them was on. They just fought to win the territory. But what if he took the measurements and found something, a weakness, an inferiority that he was supposed to expose?

Herr Birkmann was working his way down the row of

boys, looking over the measurements. Peter had to make a decision quickly. He knew that if Otto was revealed to be a Jew, he'd get kicked out of Gymnasium. Peter wouldn't see him anymore, wouldn't go to his house, wouldn't share books. But if Peter was caught lying, the punishment would be harsh. At the very least he would be strapped. More likely he would be expelled from Gymnasium.

"I've always been bad at math," he said quietly. He wrote down 80 degrees for Otto's facial angle. He copied the measurements that Otto had written down on his own sheet, adding an extra three millimeters to each one for good measure.

"And so you can see," said Herr Birkmann, summing up, "we can use math to tell us who is weak and who is strong. Food and resources are wasted on people with disease, with illness, or with weakness. The weak will always become weaker. Better to help the strong become stronger. Remember, weak becomes weaker. Strong becomes stronger. The choice for our country is clear. Heil Hitler!" he saluted, his arm raised to the Führer's portrait.

Peter jumped up with the rest of the class. "Heil Hitler!" they repeated.

Chapter Seven

Hamburg,
September 1939

I'm sitting on a tiny chair in front of a blackboard. Eugene's in front of me. He's taller, towering over me like a giant. He's dripping. The only sound is the plunk of water as it falls off him and onto the concrete floor.

The drips from Eugene splash back onto me, soaking my feet and legs. "Stay still," he says. He raises his arm and starts to draw lines on my face. I try to stand and his other hand pushes down on my head, pinning me to the chair.

"Stay still!"

I feel the chalk in his hand move across my skull, over my face. Herr Birkmann's voice is booming, "Forty degrees! Forty degrees! An imbecile! Less than a chimpanzee, less than a Jew!" There is laughter growing, getting louder and louder all around me.

I try to speak but Eugene forces his fat, waterlogged fist into my mouth. I gag. I'm going to throw up. I can't breathe. I thrash, try to pull his hand out but his other hand has a vice-like grip on the back of my head. He's holding me at eye level, staring into my eyes, holding me as though I was a tiny wiggling fish. I'm running out of air, panicking. He rams his fist down into my throat and I choke and ...

He's disoriented. A cold gray light seeps in through the ragged curtains. He hears his mother softly snoring in the next room. For a minute he thinks he's back in the hospital. He listens ... he closes his eyes.

Peter was nervous about Jungvolk. Winning at the games would be more important than when he'd been at Hort. There would be boys coming from all over Hamburg, competing to be noticed.

Peter and Otto had won a lot of Knight's Fight competitions in Hort. Peter's shoulders were strong. He was sure-footed and could manoeuver quickly. Otto was thin and wiry but his arms were strong. He had a knack for getting his hands under another "Knight's" shoulders and pulling him off his "horse."

But now that they were in Jungvolk, Peter wondered if he should find a new partner. He liked Otto, but maybe he should work with someone else. The incident in biology class had unnerved him.

Fifty boys filed into the field at the edge of town, where they were gathering for their first Jungvolk weekend. Peter scanned the crowd to see who he knew. He wanted to show off his skill as a "horse," and hoped there would be new boys from other programs, stronger boys, better challengers. A warm, light mist hid some of the boys from view.

"Looking for your little friend? The one with the piggy eyes?"

Peter turned to see Hermann, grinning a smile full of malice. Hermann was the same age as Peter, but his stocky, muscular build had always made him look older. Over the summer Hermann had outgrown his clumsiness.

Hermann was sneering at him. "This is the big league now. No one here is going to be impressed with you and your little sidekick."

Peter turned to walk away. He knew Hermann was baiting him.

"You think you're special," taunted Hermann behind him. "Poor little you. Had to go to hospital, too sick to go to school. Not that it bothered me! I made a killing this summer!" Hermann laughed as he followed on Peter's heels. "But I guess you'd already made your killing. I mean, what really happened to Eugene?"

Peter stopped in his tracks. He felt a hot rush of adrenalin flood through his body. His heart started pounding.

"Eugene slipped. Ask anyone," he said quietly.

"Ha. That's not what I heard," Hermann was behind him, spitting the words quietly in his ear. "I heard he was taking over your business and you got rid of him so you didn't have to share."

Peter spun around. "You're a damn liar and you know it! Eugene was my friend. He had nothing to do with the business. The docks were my territory, my business. He knew that, you knew that. You just took it over when ..." Peter stopped short. Sickness was a sign of weakness.

"Yeah, when you were sick. You weakling. You make *me* sick. You murder your friend and then run away to the country for months and fatten yourself up on butter. Look at you. You think you are a fit specimen for Jungvolk? I bet they kick you out by the end of the day."

Peter clenched his fists. If Hermann was looking for a

fight, he'd be happy to give him one. They were practically nose to nose. Peter could smell the stale onions on Hermann's breath. He saw Herman's sidekick Kurt standing poised beside him. Two mouths curled into smiles filled with malice.

"Okay, Jungvolk," a voice behind him bellowed. "I am Scholl. Your new group leader."

Hermann's eyes slid from Peter. He moved away and positioned himself at the front of a group of boys that Peter recognized as belonging to one of the other Horts that they had competed with last year.

"Look at me when I am speaking to you," the voice that was Scholl shouted. Peter slowly turned to see a boy about fifteen years old, walking stiffly in front of the groups. Scholl was short, shorter even than Otto, but he looked like a fierce ball of energy. His uniform was crisp. Hard muscles defined his legs below his short pants.

"A lot of you probably think you are good at the games," Scholl continued. "I am here to tell you that you are not. You know nothing. You are here to train, not to play games. You are here to fight, not to make new friends," he said with a sneer.

Peter saw Otto out of the corner of his eye. He suddenly hated himself for thinking of abandoning him. He might not be at Jungvolk to make new friends, but he didn't have to give up on old ones. His body was still tense from Hermann's insinuation. He tried to consciously slow his breathing.

"Germany is at war," Scholl went on. "Our enemies are weak, spineless, and stupid. It is your job to build your body and your mind to show them your superiority. You are here to fight and to win. To fight for the Führer, and to win for the Fatherland. Starting today, you will fight to win!" Scholl's sharp face scanned the group.

"Sieg Heil!" Scholl's arm shot up at a 45-degree angle to his body, his wrist stiff, making a sharp straight line down to his shoulder. He clicked his heels together.

"Sieg Heil!" Peter and all of the boys answered.

"Capture the Flag is a war game," shouted Scholl. "It is a serious business. In Hort you wore little paper armbands to distinguish your team. It was a polite tea party—you ripped off the enemy's armband and asked him nicely to go to 'prison.' Ha!" Scholl snorted. "You are not here to be polite. You are not here to be nice. You are here to win."

Scholl was handing out strips of cloth. "Tie the cloth on your arm. If you see an enemy, you tackle him. You hold him on the ground until a referee comes to bring him back here, to the Prisoner of War camp. Red team uses the north end of the wood, blue team the south."

Capture the Flag had been one of Peter's favorite games at Hort. He had a knack of being able to move on the edge of the field without being seen. He could get behind enemy lines and, while the sentries were expecting an attack from the front, Peter would quietly grab the flag from behind. He could race away and hide before anyone realized it was gone. He loved the strategy, but most of all he loved the thrill of the chase. Peter tied on his red armband as he walked with his team into the woods. He heard the starter pistol and headed toward enemy territory.

The mist had turned into a light rain. It made the ground

slippery under Peter's feet. But it muffled sound and Peter easily got into position. He was excited and nervous as the game began. As an offensive player, he didn't need to worry about tackling anyone. He just had to use all of his senses to stay alert to the defensive players who could bring him down at any moment.

Peter's job was to get behind the guards while Otto moved in parallel along the other side of the field. Otto's job was to create a distraction so Peter could scoot across sideways, slide into the cave, and grab the flag.

He crept quietly through a thicket, far from where they thought the enemy's flag was being guarded. He carefully poked his head out. He could see the hill about fifteen meters away. He scanned the field and saw a weak spot on the far side, a place where he could hide and watch the guard's movements but not be seen.

"Arrrhgh!" A war cry went up behind him and Peter only had time to turn his head to see Hermann flying through the air. Suddenly he was flat on his back in the mud, the air knocked out of him. He began to gag and gasp.

"Ha! Got you now, you pissy little traitor. It's about time you were taught a lesson!"

Peter struggled to breathe. He thrashed, trying to flip over onto his stomach, or free his arms so that he could push Hermann away. But Hermann was sitting on his hands and pounding on his head.

"This will teach you to come into my territory!" Hermann spat on Peter's face as he punched.

"Hit him, Hermann!"

"Stupid bastard!"

"Knock him out of the game!"

Peter realized a crowd of enemy players had gathered around them. Hermann was using both his fists, pounding Peter's head from side to side. The metal taste of blood spread across his tongue. The pain jolted through his body. He squirmed to try to free his arms but they were pinned under his body. Hermann's face was contorted with anger. As he leaned forward to snarl, Peter felt his opportunity. He jerked his hands into position and squeezed Hermann's testicles as hard as he could.

"ARGHHHHH!" Hermann screamed and fell backward, giving Peter enough time to bolt to his feet and turn to face Hermann.

"You cheating BASTARD!" Hermann spat through clenched teeth, his eyes exploding with fury like a mad bull.

"He may be a bastard but he got you where it hurts!" Someone laughed. The crowd circled closer and Peter could feel the blood lust.

Suddenly there was a scream in the distance. "The flag's gone!"

Immediately the boys raced off in different directions, searching for their enemy, leaving Hermann writhing on the ground. His eyes never left Peter's face.

Scholl ran up and stood between Peter and Hermann. "Okay, Peter. You're caught. You've got to go to prison."

Peter didn't mind being out of the game. He'd done his job well. The fight had distracted the enemy, and Otto must have seen his advantage and grabbed the flag. With luck,

Otto had enough of a head start to make it through no-man's-land and home. Peter's heart started to slow and he turned to follow Scholl.

"You are dead, you fatherless bastard." Hermann's voice cut into his back like a knife.

Victory had come at a price.

Chapter Eight

Hamburg,
June 1940

... reaching down into water, black and thick like molasses. Searching, trying to find something. Stretched out as far as I can. Something pulling me back, away from the edge. I pull harder. It's important to find it. But someone is laughing and I can't reach the water anymore. I turn and it's Hermann's face, his mouth laughing, huge long teeth coming at me. I can't move. His teeth start to sink into my cheek, slicing through the skin. I feel his teeth in my mouth. I'm trying to shout, to push him off and ...

Peter startles. What is he trying to find? If he can remember, maybe he can sleep.

After the fight, Peter knew the best thing he could do was to stay out of Hermann's way. He wasn't going to try competing with Hermann for any bits of trade on the docks. He concentrated his efforts closer to home, doing odd jobs in the neighborhood in return for the occasional soup or loaf of bread.

So far, things weren't that different from the way they had been before the war. They'd been poor then, they were poor now. Tante Elsa welcomed him in Eutin on holidays, giving him milk, cheese, eggs, and pickles to bring back with him to the city. His mother found the occasional odd job cleaning. When there wasn't enough money for the rent, Herr Zeibauer accepted payment in eggs from the farm. Peter's heart always sank when he handed over the perfect little eggs that he had gathered from Tante Elsa's brown speckled hens. He was hungry all of the time and he resented putting his dinner into Herr Zeibauer's hands.

Then it was winter and Tante Elsa's old hens ended up in the stew pot. She was raising new young hens, but they weren't laying eggs yet. She traded the milk and cheese for money to buy grain and hay. They lived off fall sauerkraut, pickled beets, turnips, and potatoes.

Peter took to chewing on bits of old paper. Somehow it made him feel a little less hungry.

When spring came, Peter and his mother searched the park for any trace of wild leeks. They monitored patches of the bright green shoots daily, trying to wait until they were big enough to pick. But one day they arrived at the park to find all of their carefully tended patches gone. Apparently they weren't the only ones hoping for a free meal. They went home to rubbery old potatoes, imagining how good they would have tasted with a bit of fresh green leek.

In school, there were celebrations on the day Denmark surrendered, and then again when Norway, Holland, and Belgium surrendered. Peter watched as Herr Birkmann re-drew the map at school to include all of these new countries as part of Germany. It seemed as though each day his country got bigger, while old countries vanished. He thought about the people who woke up to find themselves living in the new Germany. Their countries were gone, but they'd never be real Germans, ethnic Germans. Herr Birkmann was very clear about that.

But to Peter, these were just places with exotic names. They sounded even more cold and forbidding than Poland, although he'd heard Belgium had good chocolate. He wondered if it meant they'd get more food now. Chocolates from Belgium, pastries from Denmark, fish from Norway?

He thought he probably dreamt about food. Except he could never quite remember his dreams. He was aware of waking to fleeting sensations, and then nothing. If he could remember dreaming of eating and of being full, maybe he'd feel a bit better.

But at least Chancellor Hitler's voice on the radio was encouraging:

"The struggle that begins today will decide the fate for the German nation for the next thousand years. Do your duty now."

Posters lined the walls of the school:

That we live in this great age is a gift of fate; that we may fight with Adolf Hitler's Greater Germany is the greatest joy of our existence.

And:

Talkativeness shows a need for attention, whereas modesty is silent.

The war demands silent fulfillment of duty.

And:

One's appearance is the mirror of the soul.

An essential characteristic of the Hither Youth must be to be proud but not arrogant, free but disciplined and clean.

Peter practiced being silent. He tried to remember to clean his nails every day. It was the least he could do to help win the war. There'd be lots of food when the war ended, and it would probably end soon. The British had all but given up—they'd run away from France and a lot of them had been killed in a place called Dunkirk. Herr Birkmann had laughed about it, saying that the new English prime minister, a man named Winston Churchill, was a clown. Mr. Churchill was a nasty-looking man with a squashed face like a bulldog. Otto drew a picture of him as a dog with a huge white face and a big red, dumb-looking smile. Herr Birkmann put it up on the board and gave Otto an A in art.

But as the seasons changed, so did the mood of the war. Mr. Churchill was apparently in a fighting mood. In September, he started dropping bombs on the outskirts of Hamburg. Peter and Herr Ballin sat together, looking out the front window of the plumbing store into the night sky. Flashes of light sparked through the sky as anti-aircraft fire sent tracer bullets through the air.

"Got one!" Peter said as a plane exploded across the night sky. It was like watching a movie or the fireworks at New Year's. In the distance, he saw fires on the ground where bombs had hit their mark. The port? The shipyards? The Führer had promised to bomb only military targets, and Peter assumed that the British would also follow the proper rules of war. If *War and Peace* had taught him nothing else, it was that war was a civilized necessity, and that there were rules to be followed. The British could bomb the port and the warehouses, but not where there were people. Here, in the center of the city, they would be safe.

The light show only lasted a couple of hours. By the next day, Peter had almost forgotten about it, until Franz knocked on their door to tell them what to do in the case of an attack. It was the first time Peter had seen him in his Hitlerjugend uniform. His straight brown hair was clipped short and his boots were gleaming with polish. Peter was impressed. Franz had always seemed a bit dull.

"When you hear the Kleinalarm, it is a warning that there are hostile aircraft in the area, and you should be ready to take cover. The second alarm is the Fliegeralarm. It is fifteen short, four-second wails. That means you will have twenty minutes until the first bomb hits. You have to quickly get to the shelter in the Pressehaus."

"But I thought that the British weren't targeting the city center," said Peter. "They are supposed to just hit the factories, aren't they?"

Franz snorted. "The enemy is not playing by the rules. All civilians are being targeted. You must be ready at all times. Heil Hitler!"

Peter returned the salute. "Heil Hitler!" He looked at Herr Ballin as Franz went down the steps to warn the people next door. Herr Ballin shrugged and went back to serving a customer, explaining to him that he could make a new washer for the man's faucet, but the tap might still leak a bit.

... I'm running in molasses. It's hard to move my legs, hard to breathe. My breath is screaming at me. There's a violent sound—a siren wailing. It shatters my eyeballs and they fall out of their sockets. I try to grab them as they fall, to shove them back in, but I can't see. I feel something melting in my hands and realize it is my eyes, dripping through my fingers. The siren is ripping through my brain but I'm blind. I try to call out for help, but I can't move my mouth. I ...

"Peter. Peter, wake up." His mother is shaking him urgently. "We have to go to the shelter. You must help with Oma Ballin."

Peter stood up immediately and started to search for his clothes.

"No," his mother said. "There is no time. Put on your bathrobe and your slippers and go upstairs to get Oma." His mother pressed a flashlight into his hands. He stumbled up the steps to Oma's apartment. She was waiting for him at the door.

"I won't go," Oma said defiantly. "If they are going to bomb my home, what is there for me to live for?" Her face looked hard and pale in the beam of his light, but Peter could see she was trembling. Her wrinkles looked razor sharp. A small drop dangled at the end of her nose.

"Oma, I need you to come with me. Please. I cannot go without you." The siren's wail filled every corner of the hallway. Short, four-second blasts. Repeated over and over.

"Mother, you must hurry," Herr Ballin called from downstairs. "We don't have much time!"

Peter looked at Oma.

"Please," he said gently. He put her hand on his arm and started to guide her down the stairs, lighting their way with his flashlight. Herr Ballin stood at the front door of the building. Frau Ballin was beside him, holding a basket. A corner of a dry loaf of bread stuck out from under a napkin. "Come, Mother Ballin, we must hurry."

On the street, siren blasts bored into his mind like a headache. Peter, his mother, and the Ballins walked the two blocks to the Pressehaus as quickly as they could. The building belonged to one of the biggest publishing firms in the city, and the ground floor was filled with large black printing presses, crates of books, and the greasy smell of printer's ink. They made their way to the basement. There were about thirty people there already, most of whom Peter recognized from the neighborhood. Outside, the siren was still wailing, but the sound was muffled by the thick concrete walls.

Franz was at the door and checked their names on his list as they came in. "Right. You lot from Neue Gröninger-strasse can sit over there, beside the Neitmanns." Peter looked over and saw his old teacher, Herr Neitmann and his wife. Two young children were sitting on her lap. Like him, they were in pajamas. He wondered if his eyes were as wide as theirs. He began to guide Oma Ballin across the room.

"Hey. What do you think you are doing?" Franz's voice barked behind him. "You can't come in here. Get out. There's no place for you here!"

Peter turned and saw Jakob and his family standing at the entrance to the shelter. Jakob's father stood slightly stooping, his head tilted to the side. Jakob's older sisters stood straight and tall. One of them carried a basket. Jakob's mother held a small child by the hand. Peter noticed they were all fully dressed in their street clothes, not in their pajamas. Their clothes were immaculate. Jakob's father was a tailor.

"We are from Brandstwiete Street. We are on the list," Mr. Gluzman said patiently.

Franz smirked. "I don't care if you are on the list or not. No Jews allowed."

Peter felt the ground vibrate under his feet. The bombs had started to fall. They were a long way away, but they were definitely falling on the city. Oma Ballin clutched his arm tightly.

Mr. Gluzman moved a couple of steps further into the shelter, his family taking small steps beside him. Franz stood, blocking his way, his legs spread and his fists closed. Peter recognized the fighting position from his training at Jungvolk.

"Don't be ridiculous, Franz." Herr Neitmann said from the other side of the shelter. "Of course they must come in."

"I will not have them in my shelter," hissed Franz.

"It is not *your* shelter, Franz," said Herr Neitmann, calmly standing. "And we are not going to send them out to have bombs dropped on their heads."

There was another rumble. The bare electric bulb hanging in the middle of the room flickered. Franz spun around to face Herr Neitmann.

"You are no longer my teacher, Herr Neitmann. The Führer—"

"—The Führer is not here in this bunker."

A slight, almost imperceptible gasp went around the room. The ground shook.

"Herr Gluzman," Herr Nietmann spoke straightforwardly, without any show of emotion. "There is room against that wall for your family." He gestured to a vacant spot.

There was a pause when no one moved. Peter could hear small explosions outside, probably caused by tracer fire. Herr Gluzman gave a tiny nod to Herr Neitmann and led his wife and children to the far side of the room. Peter looked away before he caught Jakob's eye.

"I'll report you for this," Franz hissed at Herr Neitmann.

"It is bad enough to be fighting the French and the British," said Herr Neitmann, to no one in particular. "We do not have to fight each other as well."

"The Jews do not belong in our air raid shelters!" Franz shouted.

"There is no law forbidding them to be here," said Herr Neitmann calmly, "and until there is, or until they have somewhere else to go, we must allow them to shelter in here."

The Gluzman family stood quietly together. Their faces were impassive. Peter looked from them to Herr Neitmann to Franz. The ground shook. The light flickered. No one spoke.

Peter and Jakob had played together as children. He thought about the chalk marks on Jakob's face.

A memory suddenly zipped into Peter's mind. Frau Gluzman is standing in front of him smiling, handing him warm bread, fresh out of the oven. He must have been about four years old. She places the shiny braided loaf, wrapped in a towel, in his arms. "Challah. For you and your mother. That you may have better luck this year."

The memory of the sweet, yeasty smell of the bread filled his mind. He looked over at his mother. She was staring straight ahead. When had "the Gluzmans" become "the Jews"?

It was silent in the shelter. The bombs had stopped falling. The wail of the "all-clear" siren cut through the night. Peter instinctively reached for his mother to help her to her feet.

"Thank you," she said, her face a mixture of relief and thoughtfulness. "Back to bed. We should be able to get an hour or two of sleep before morning."

They emerged from the shelter into the smell of smoke. Peter looked around. There were no electric lights on, so the street was unnaturally dark. But in the light of the almost full moon, he could see his ghostly neighborhood intact. As far as he could tell, all of the buildings in the Altstadt were safe. He walked with his mother and the Ballin family through the still streets, the sound of their feet echoing off the silent buildings. He could hear the distant scream of sirens as fire trucks raced through the western side of the city. Exhaustion began to overtake his body. The strangeness of the air raid began to fade into the realm of sleep as he sank into his familiar bed.

Chapter Nine

By October, air raids had become part of normal existence. Peter couldn't remember what it felt like to get a full night's sleep.

But today was a perfect autumn day. There was a bright crispness in the air as he headed to the Zoll Canal.

One of Peter's responsibilities in Jungvolk was to help the war effort by collecting scrap metal and delivering the state paper. He was responsible for all of the Altstadt and it was long slow work that took up most of the weekend. When Herr Birkmann found out that he didn't have a bicycle, he berated him.

"It is your duty to have a bicycle! You'll get twice as much done in half the time. You must have a bike," he growled. "Go to see Herr Weber. He has bicycles to sell."

Herr Weber was Franz's father. He had a second-hand business and sold everything from clothing to lampshades to mattresses. Peter had visited him last year to trade some sausages for a pair of shoes that almost fit his mother. They were fine if she wore extra socks. Recently, Herr Weber and Franz had moved from the neighborhood and gone to Barmbek on the other side of the Osterbek Canal. With so many people selling everything and leaving, Herr Weber had needed more space for the business.

Franz's father had been born with a clubfoot, so he dragged his leg as he walked. Peter assumed that was why he hadn't been in the army during the Great War. Now that Franz was in Hitlerjugend, maybe he was doing duty for both of them.

Peter knew he could find Franz patrolling the dam where the Alster Lake fed into the Osterbek. As he walked up, he saw Franz standing outside the patrol box, smoking and laughing with one of the other HJ members.

"Yeah, my father's got a great bike," Franz told Peter. "Because you're a friend, he'll probably let you have it for two Reichsmark. Smoke?"

Since Peter had stopped his business, he had no access to cigarettes. He didn't really miss them, but standing beside Franz and smoking in the fall air felt right. He could almost forget there was a war on.

"I don't have any money," Peter said, trying to pitch his voice lower so that he sounded older. "Would he trade? I've got some great pickled beets."

Franz snorted. "Everyone's got pickled beets. No, it's got to be cash. It's a great bike!" Franz added.

"But I don't have any money," repeated Peter. "I can't make money because I don't have a bike. And I can't get a bike because I don't have money." Peter was annoyed that his voice sounded so whiney. He took a deep drag on the cigarette.

"Come on, Peter. I know you can get something together. One Reichsmark. He'll sell it for one. You can come up with one. You're resourceful." Franz was pushing. *His father probably needs the money as much as I need the bike*, thought Peter. *One Reichsmark is a good deal.*

Herr Ballin was always telling Peter that he was resourceful. Maybe Herr Ballin would loan him one Reichsmark. He could pay him back next week.

The next day, with the borrowed Reichsmark in his pocket, Peter went over to Gunter's. Gunter was really good at bicycle repairs, and Peter wanted his opinion on the bike at Franz's apartment. He also knew Gunter liked to go for the music Herr Weber played.

Gunter was cleaning his bike chain when Peter arrived. Bike parts, grease, and dirty rags were strewn all over the cracked linoleum floor. "I'll be finished in a minute," Gunter said as Peter came into the room.

Gunter's apartment was a chaos of old newspapers, piles of books, and dirty tea cups. Gunter's father was sitting deep in a worn armchair by a small coal fire, scowling over a paper. Peter thought about the book Herr Schmidt had loaned him so long ago. *A Farewell to Arms*. He didn't have the heart to tell him he hadn't finished it. He'd left it back in Eutin, with the Russians.

"It can't last," said Herr Schmidt throwing down the paper. "We've been taught to think, to read, to discuss our thoughts.

No one is going stand by and have their rights taken away." Herr Schmidt waved the paper in the air. Peter looked more closely and saw that it was a French paper. How on earth had Herr Schmidt gotten that? It was subversive to read any paper that wasn't German.

As if reading his mind, Herr Schmidt turned to him and swished the paper under his nose. "The Social Democrats are the party of social justice. With the defeat of France, they're in exile in London. They may be our only hope."

Peter turned to look at Gunter. Gunter was greasing his bike chain, avoiding his eye.

"We have to get back to a democratic system, where people can vote, and vote this madman out of office." Herr Schmidt smacked the chair's arms angrily as he stood up. Small explosions of dust flew as he left the room.

Peter was really uncomfortable. They'd been taught at Jungvolk to tell their group leaders if anyone, including their parents, spoke against the Nazi Party. This was just the kind of thing they were supposed to report. He decided to pretend he hadn't heard what Herr Schmidt said.

"I love going to Franz's," Gunter said loudly. Peter could tell he, too, was trying to pretend he hadn't heard what Herr Schmidt had said. He followed Gunter as he wheeled his bike out of the apartment. They bumped it down the stairs together.

"Last time I was there, Herr Weber played me a record called 'Summertime.' The cover had drawings of Negroes dancing but it was sung by opera singers. I didn't really understand it, but Herr Weber said it was about Negroes in

America and what it was like to be a slave. I've never heard anything like it. If I'd had a record player, I would have bought it. If I'd had any money! Get on."

Ever since they were little, Peter and Gunter had traveled the streets of Hamburg together, Peter standing on the axles of the back wheel and expertly balancing as Gunter sped around corners. Gunter pushed off and Peter grabbed onto the seat.

"I'm telling you, Peter, their voices gave me goosebumps. I felt like they were singing just to me." Gunter looked over his shoulder at Peter with a grin.

Gunter headed toward the Alster. The army was busy constructing a huge fake city on top of the lake. Sheets of wood and metal were being painted to look like streets and buildings, in the hopes that the enemy would drop their bombs there, where they would sink harmlessly into the lake. Peter thought it was a crazy, wonderful scheme and he loved his city for trying to fool the smug British.

They turned from the lake and headed over the Mundsburger Dam, then zig-zagged through the streets of Barmbek. As Gunter cut through the park to get to Elsastrasse, Peter noticed a skinny dog lying on the grass. It raised its head weakly to watch them pass. He looked at the huge milk-filled teats, flies buzzing around them. No puppies in sight. Nobody would want puppies. No one could look after them.

Peter had his eyes on the dog, so he didn't see the man come across their path.

"A crust of bread? A Reichsmark?" The man called out to

them as they swerved to pass. His face was hollow and his cheeks were covered in a rough stubble, a patchwork of brown and gray that extended all the way down his neck. He was wearing a black suit—Peter could tell that it had been a good suit once—but it hung on him as though it had made a mistake.

Peter thought about the Reichsmark in his pocket, the one he needed to buy the bicycle.

"Time and unexpected events overtake us all. Ecclesiastes 9:11," the man called out to them. "God dignifies us by letting us choose our own course!" The man was shouting at them as Gunter pedaled faster down the alley.

"The whole world is lying in the power of the wicked one. John 15:19!"

Gunter turned the corner and headed up Elsastrasse.

"Jehovah's Witness," Gunter called back over his shoulder. "My father spent an afternoon at the park, years ago, before the war, trying to argue with him. I was so embarrassed. It doesn't do any good. They never listen. They don't discuss. They just quote scripture. Always Old Testament. Really, they are just Jews."

Peter wasn't sure he followed this logic. Jews were a race, and their religion was a part of their race, wasn't it? Jehovah's Witnesses were just people who went to a different church. Weren't they?

"They won't do the salute. They won't fight. My dad told me that guy was in jail for two years because he wouldn't stop being a Jehovah's Witness and he wouldn't join the army. When he got out of jail, his wife was dead and his children had been sent away to live with other families. He went kind of crazy after that. He should be put away somewhere."

Peter had heard of Jehovah's Witnesses but never actually seen one. He couldn't understand why someone would rather go to jail and lose everything, than just stop going to church. He couldn't imagine any God who would want that.

Franz and his father lived on Weidestrasse. The air in the hallway of the apartment building was heavy with a sour smell, a kind of smell that made Peter feel slightly sick to his stomach. There were dirty papers in the hall, all crumpled and thrown about. They walked up a flight of stairs and down the dark corridor to Franz's apartment. They could hear the sound of a woman singing.

"What took you so long? You're lucky he didn't sell the bike to someone else," Franz said as he opened the door. He looked out of place in his uniform, standing stiffly among the old baby carriages, umbrellas, suitcases, and piles of books that lined the hallway.

"... J'ai deux amours, mon pays et Paris ..." sang the voice.

"Who's that?" Gunter asked Franz as they wove through the obstacle course to get into the apartment.

"Josephine Baker," said Franz. "An American. A Negro." His lip curled as he said the word.

"We're not supposed to listen to any jazz, not even *white* Americans, let alone a Negro woman singing in French," Peter said quietly.

"Tell that to my father," said Franz angrily.

Peter had never heard a voice like it before. He hadn't learned French in school, but it didn't matter that he didn't understand the words. It was like she was singing into his ear, his ear only. It made his back feel soft.

"J'ai deux amour

"Mon pays et Paris ..."

"I have two loves, my country and Paris," Gunter sang, swaying his hips provocatively.

Peter couldn't help laughing. "Since when do you speak French?"

Gunter shrugged. "That bit's pretty easy. I don't understand the rest."

"Well, if you know what's good for you, you'll forget all of it," growled Franz.

If it had been treasonous to hear this before the fall of France, Peter could only imagine the punishment now. He assumed it was illegal to even own the record. He looked at Franz's grim face. He wanted to just get the bike and get out.

"Come along, Pierre. Let's take a look at this *bicyclette*," said Gunter, wiggling his hips as he walked down the hall. "Thank you, Franz," he called over his shoulder.

The hallway opened out into a dining room of sorts. On the table sat mounds of serving dishes, candlesticks, plates, table linens, jars, pots, and bowls. Everything was dusty and dirty. Two of the candlesticks were broken and, even at a distance, Peter could see cracks in several of the dishes. In one corner of the room was an old sofa that looked like it had sprung a leak. Straw and horsehair were jutting out of the top. Pushed against the sofa was a collection of bicycles and bicycle parts. Extra wheels without tires, chains, and seats were piled around the floor.

Herr Weber was sitting on a piano stool with a stack of records on his lap. "So what do you think of this Josephine Baker? Dangerous, yes?" Herr Weber glanced over at Franz scowling in the corner of the room. "Yes, too dangerous, perhaps. Maybe *Porgy and Bess* is better for your young ears. If I remember correctly, you've got a fondness for that one." Herr Weber grinned at Gunter as he unfolded himself and stood up crookedly.

"Lawrence Tibbett's a white man, so I think you're safe listening to him singing 'Summertime.'" The top of Herr Weber's head grazed an old chandelier as he clumped across the room. Dust settled on his shoulders.

"Here," he said, moving a pile of records from the lid of the phonograph and handing them to Gunter. "Take a look through. I got them yesterday. Frau Goldberg gave them to me to sell." Gunter hesitated. "It's all right, they aren't going to arrest you for looking," he said, pushing them into Gunter's hands. He turned to Peter.

"So, you need to get a bicycle. About time." Herr Weber gestured behind him as he turned to put a new record on the phonograph. "That is the best one I have. Two Reichsmarks."

Peter's heart sank. Franz had said one Reichsmark. He only had one, and that one had been hard to come by. It was all Herr Ballin had.

"I ... I only have one."

Music flowed from the phonograph's tiny speakers. Peter's attention was immediately drawn to the deep voice. He'd taken English all through school and the voice was slow enough for him to just make out the words.

Summertime, and the livin' is easy
Fish are jumpin' and the cotton is high

"Well, then you can't have the bike," Herr Weber shrugged.

Your daddy's rich, and your mamma's good lookin'
So hush little baby, don't you cry.

Peter couldn't stop the music from coming into his mind. The lyrics seemed to be about him. He'd been told his father was rich. Gunter said his mother was good looking. He dragged his attention back into the room. He was there for a bicycle. He shouldn't be listening to this American jazz music. He tried to appeal to Herr Weber's sense of patriotism.

"Herr Weber, I need the bike to do jobs for the Party—checking for incendiaries after raids, distributing Party papers, collecting tin. Herr Birkmann said that if I don't start working for the Party, they'll question my loyalty. One Reichsmark today, the rest on account?"

"Hmmm. Well, I don't suppose anyone else is going to come by with a better offer today. But you have to pay me the rest after the next bombing raid. If you do the night duty putting out fires on the street, you can make a Reichsmark easily."

One of these mornings
You're going to rise up singing
Then you'll spread your wings
And you'll take to the sky
But until that morning
There's nothing can harm you
With your daddy and mammy standing by.

Peter didn't relish the idea of extra work at night. He frequently did the day shift, but that only earned him fifty pfennig. The night shift paid more. One night and he could pay off his debt to Herr Ballin, another night and he could pay off his debt to Herr Weber. Not that he wished for more nighttime raids.

He handed over the coin.

Herr Weber pushed a bike forward to Peter. "Here, this is it. Just needs a bit of grease."

Peter looked at the bike in Herr Weber's hands. It had been blue once, but the paint was mostly chipped off now. Like the other bikes, it had no tires. Rubber was one of the things they had to collect for the war effort. Instead of tires, the wheels were covered in heavy-looking black tape. Layers and layers of tape.

"There's no seat," said Peter.

"Seat is extra," said Herr Weber.

"You'll get used to standing and pedaling, like the rest of us. Looks great to me," said Gunter, barely looking up. "Hey, look at this. *That* is Josephine Baker." He handed Peter a record cover.

"Whoa!" Peter almost dropped it. He was shocked. A beautiful woman stood posing, wearing a small jeweled top with beads flowing over it. Below she wore only feathers. Her middle and all of her long legs were totally exposed. Her hips were thrust forward and she looked out with a cheeky, sexy smile. Large plumes of ostrich feathers fanned out behind her. Peter had never seen anything so exotic, so disturbing. He read the record sleeve.

The Black Venus

The two of them stared at the picture. "Say, Herr Weber, how much for this Josephine Baker record?" asked Gunter.

"One Reichsmark. But you don't have a record player, Gunter."

"I don't have a Reichsmark, either. But if I did, I would buy it just to look at it!"

Herr Weber laughed. "You come back when you have one. It will probably still be here. I don't think anybody else would risk buying it!"

Franz stood motionless, glaring at his father as Peter and Gunter maneuvered the bicycle through the crowded hall, along the dark corridor and down the steps. Peter was glad to get out into the fresh air and the warm fall sunshine. He put the bike onto the street, swung his leg over and pushed off, standing as he pedaled.

"You look great!" Gunter called after him. "But I think it would have been more fun to have the record!"

"Yeah, and completely illegal," said Peter as the bicycle bumped erratically down the road, pitching from side to side. He backpedaled to brake and came to a stop, standing on his tiptoes to balance over the center bar. Suddenly his heart felt light. He felt a freedom he hadn't felt since the war began. He pushed off and began pedaling. He could go anywhere.

Chapter Ten

Hamburg.
November 1940

It wasn't long before the October sunshine faded into a November gloom that seemed to go on forever. *"Time is out of joint,"* Peter said to himself. It was a line he liked. He remembered reading it when they'd read *Hamlet* in school. Shakespeare was the only English writer they were allowed to read. The days were gray and cold; the nights were darker gray and colder, just like the somber nights at the beginning of that play.

Peter was exhausted. He was awake most nights, either sitting in the bomb shelter, or lying in bed, waiting for the alarm to tell them to go to the bomb shelter. Night after night, he'd stumble over to the shelter in his pajamas and huddle with his neighbors by the light of an oil lamp. Together, they'd listen to the planes flying overhead. He spent a couple of hours after each raid, shoveling sand on small incendiary bombs so that they didn't start fires.

He saw bodies pulled from the rubble daily. The city was being pummeled.

"A cup of coffee, Frau Gruber?"

Gunter's father's hand was poised above a scuffed coffee pot. Peter knew it wasn't real coffee, not the way coffee used to be. It wasn't even as good as Oma Ballin's ersatz coffee. It was dry-roasted chicory and something else. Sawdust, he assumed, judging from the way it smelled. He remembered the coffee he used to get from the sailors, the coffee he traded for nylons.

"Thank you, Herr Schmidt. That would be nice."

They were here to talk about the evacuation, the Kinderlandverschickung. Peter and Gunter were scheduled to leave with their class next week. They were being evacuated to the south—Neumarkt in Oberpfalz. They'd be leaving the war behind, leaving everything behind, including his new bike.

Gunter's older sisters, Brigit and Charlotte, were going with their Bund Deutscher Mädel group, the BDM, to Warthegau the next morning. The girls were carefully folding clothes into a suitcase.

"It's a dangerous trip," Peter's mother was saying, lifting the cup to her lips. "The English are bombing the train tracks—they'll be totally exposed and could get hit en route. At least here we have shelters. And who is going to look after them in Neumarkt? The school tells us nothing." Peter noticed a slight tremor as she lowered the cup.

"They will travel at night," Herr Schmidt said reassuringly. "The odds are with them because they'll be on small tracks, not major routes. No one will be able to target them.

And once they get there, they will be safe. Neumarkt is a sleepy little backwater—there is nothing there. No one would bother to waste bombs on it."

"What about Warthegau, Papa?" asked Charlotte. "Is it a 'sleepy little backwater,' too?"

"Please don't say it is. I can't bear the thought of being stuck out in the country for months," said Brigit.

"You'll be out of the way of the bombs, and that's what matters," said their father.

"But what will we *do* there?" whined Brigit.

"You'll do just what you do here," said Herr Schmidt. "Go to school and study. Go to BDM and learn how to be a good German. The only thing you won't be doing is spending night after night in a bomb shelter."

Since the last time he'd been at Gunter's, Peter didn't know what to think about Herr Schmidt. He felt on edge. He didn't know what he'd do if Herr Schmidt started talking about the Social Democrats again. He wasn't sure he'd be able to ignore him. But Gunter's father seemed supportive of the government's evacuation plans.

He was looking forward to leaving the city. His mother had become very possessive lately. The war had made her nervous and he felt like he couldn't breathe. She always wanted to know what he was doing and where he was going. He could look after himself.

"What's more," continued Herr Schmidt, "they'll stay with families in the countryside who have a lot more food than we do here in the city. These boys will come back fat and lazy if they aren't careful," he said with a laugh.

Not lazy, thought Peter. *I won't let myself get complacent again, like last summer. I have to stay alert.*

"But they're not even twelve years old yet. How long will they have to stay away?" his mother asked.

"No one knows," replied Herr Schmidt softly. He refilled her coffee. "But I'm sure it won't be long. This madness can't last."

Peter wondered which madness Herr Schmidt was referring to. The war? The enemy bombings? There was something about his tone that made him wonder what Herr Schmidt thought of Chancellor Hitler.

His mother sipped her coffee thoughtfully. She looked over at him with the barest hint of a smile. "You could certainly use some meat on those bones."

Peter thought about that phrase. Meat on his bones. When was the last time he'd had a bit of meat? He looked down at his skinny gray arm and remembered the tan lines that he used to have around his grandfather's watch. He'd traded the watch for a beautiful ham roast for his mother's birthday last summer. She'd been shocked and upset, but they lived off that meat for a week. Then they'd made pea soup from the ham bone and lived off *that* for another week. But the food, like the watch, was long gone now.

Perhaps Neumarkt would be like Eutin, with rolling green pastures and the smell of wildflowers pervading the air. Well, maybe not in November. But still, it would have to be better than the flat damp of Hamburg.

"Maybe Peter will fatten up and meet a pretty country girl," said Gunter with a grin. Brigit and Charlotte laughed.

Peter felt his face go red. "And you'll—"

WWWOOOOOOWWAAAAAA

Peter was cut off by the scream of the siren.

"The middle of the day?" his mother said, putting her cup into the saucer.

"Might be just a test," said Herr Schmidt. "Still, we should go."

His mother stood and straightened her dress. "Peter, we'll have to run. Our shelter is blocks away. It will take us at least ten minutes to get there."

"There's room in ours," said Herr Schmidt. "We're in an office building, just down the road. You've got your identity cards? Good. Charlotte, Brigit, let's go."

Charlotte made a face. "I hate sitting in that stuffy cellar."

"Well, at least it's daytime and we've got proper clothes on," Brigit shouted over the roar of the siren, "It's embarrassing having to go there in our nightclothes."

"I don't see why you're complaining," said Charlotte. "At least you have a pretty nightgown. I have to wear mother's old one and it looks like a bag."

"Girls. That's enough." Herr Schmidt's tone silenced them immediately.

WWWOOOOOOWWAAAAAA. Four seconds of siren blast.

WWWOOOOOOWWAAAAAA. Another four seconds.

Peter's mother quickly gathered up her handbag and buttoned her jacket. Gunter pocketed his deck of cards. "We'll need something to do. I'll teach you how to play poker."

The six of them walked swiftly into the bleak street and headed toward a large office block.

"Our shelter is one of the safest places to be, from what I can tell," Herr Schmidt said as they made their way through the front door of the building. "The only way that a bomb could reach us in here is if it came down into the center of the building, into the courtyard. A ridiculously hard shot by any stretch of the imagination. To actually hit the building, it would have to travel sideways."

They followed a stream of people and walked through the courtyard to the other side of the building, before going down the stairs to the cellar.

"Identity cards." A Hitlerjugend guard stood at the doorway to the shelter, checking everyone who was entering. Peter handed his card over and the guard passed it back without comment. The room was filled with office furniture, tables, and chairs for about thirty people. Gunter sat down at one end and began shuffling his card deck.

"Have you ever played seven-card stud? We can use matchsticks for betting." Gunter took a small box of matches out of his pocket and began breaking them in half.

This shelter had an entirely different feel from their nighttime cellar. It was almost like a party. Many of the people had walked down from offices in the upper part of the building. Peter could hear them talking about their jobs—they were working for some kind of government planning office and talked about building by-laws and permits. Charlotte and Brigit sat together, whispering and occasionally giggling. Peter turned his attention to the cards. A two of hearts, two of spades, and a queen of hearts in his hand. A ten of hearts showing on the table. Possible flush?

He picked up two matchsticks. His hand was poised over the table and—

WHAM!

The door blew open.

Dust and debris flew everywhere.

A force swept through the room.

Blackness.

A moment of incomprehension. Silence. Then everyone started talking at once.

"Matilda!"

"We've been hit!"

"Simon! Frederick!"

"I'm over here!"

"Brigit?"

"A light, somebody!"

"Charlotte!"

"AHHHH! NO! Get me out of here!"

"Viktor?"

"Gunter!"

"Is anyone hurt?"

"Rudi!"

"Agatha? Karolin?"

Peter realized he was still holding the broken matches. He flicked them against each other and two small flames broke through the blackness. He could see the outline of the Hitlerjugend guard standing where the door had been. The dim light of the matches showed a gaping hole. But everything looked crooked. The room began to come into focus and he saw that he was lying on his back, still sitting in his chair.

The match flames crept toward his fingers. The heat startled him and he dropped them just as another match flared up across the room.

"Find the emergency candles!" someone yelled.

The light across the room spluttered and caught. Shadows swung wildly in the room. The air was thick with dust and smoke.

"GET ME OUT OF HERE! GET ME OUT OF HERE!"

Someone was screaming.

Peter could see the guard holding a candle. "Is someone hurt?"

"AHHHHH! AHHHH! AHHHH!"

There was a scuffling and banging at the other side of the room. Peter rolled out of his chair. He was unhurt, just disoriented and startled. He knew the drill from Jungvolk. He got to his feet and went to the guard, who handed him a second candle, lighting it from his first. People were slowly getting to their feet, looking around and holding each other. He saw Charlotte and Brigit dusting each other off. The banging persisted.

"GET ME OUT! PETER! PETER! WHERE ARE YOU? PETER, ARE YOU ALL RIGHT?!"

Suddenly Peter realized that the panicked voice was his mother's.

He crossed to the other side of the room in two strides. A heavy oak table had flipped over against the wall.

"I'm here, Mother. It's all right," Peter called out with more reassurance than he felt. His mother had been thrown backward and was wedged between the table and the wall.

Gunter was already at the other side of the table and together the two of them lifted it up and turned it over.

"We've been hit! We've been hit!"

Peter bent down to look in his mother's eyes.

"Are you all right, Momma? Can you stand up?"

He put his hand on her arm. He could feel her trembling. Her whole body was vibrating.

"Frau Gruber? Frau Gruber? Can you hear me? Are you hurt?" Herr Schmidt was crouching beside Peter.

"We've been hit. Peter? Peter?"

"Yes, I am right here, Mother. I'm fine."

"Peter, we've been hit."

"Yes, I know, Momma. You're all right. It's all right."

"The bomb didn't hit us directly," said Herr Schmidt. "It seems to have exploded in the next room. A storeroom, I think."

"We must leave the building right away," said the guard loudly. "The stairs may not be stable. Follow me and watch carefully where you step. You—Peter—you bring up the rear. Make sure everyone gets out."

Herr Schmidt turned to Peter's mother. "Do you think you can walk, Frau Gruber?"

Peter's mother clutched his arm. She was still trembling but she slowly nodded her head. Herr Schmidt and Peter gently lifted her to her feet. Peter thought she was more shocked and scared than hurt.

"Mother, you go with Herr Schmidt and Gunter. I'll follow you out." She meekly allowed him to pass her hand over to Herr Schmidt's arm.

"Are you all right, Gunter?" asked Charlotte as they started to move out of the shelter.

"I'm fine, Lottie. Although if my face looks anything like yours, I suspect I've ruined my chances of any social engagements for the rest of the day," Gunter replied with a grin. Charlotte smacked him on the shoulder.

"Hey, it's bad enough being shot at without you beating me up as well!" he said.

"I guess this means a really extended lunch break," joked one of the workers.

As the last person walked through the doorway, Peter turned back to look at the destruction. The door had been ripped off its hinges and smashed into the far wall. Chairs and tables were flung every which way. The shelves of tinned food had collapsed. A thick layer of dust covered everything. But everyone had been able to walk out. Although there were a few cuts and bumps from flying furniture, it seemed that everyone was unhurt.

He stepped into what was left of the corridor. A huge mound of rubble blocked most of the path. The wall had caved in and parts of the ceiling had fallen. The bomb had hit the room right next to theirs. All that was left was a pile of plaster and wood lathe. A storeroom, Herr Schmidt had said. Peter hoped so. He hoped that there was no one in there. They would not be walking out.

Peter followed the line of people moving slowly forward in single file. Nothing looked familiar; nothing made sense. But luckily the concrete stairs were intact and, by the time they got up to the ground floor, the building looked almost normal.

They walked out into the courtyard into a peaceful autumn day. The sun had come out. It seemed impossible. Daylight. The first sunshine they'd had in weeks. How long had they been down there? He glanced at his watch. Three-thirty. He and his mother had gone to Gunter's at 2:00. It felt like a year had passed since then.

As he crossed the courtyard, Peter looked back to see the hole in the side of the building. How could the bomb have come down at that angle? A ridiculously hard shot, as Herr Schmidt had said. It didn't just stretch imagination, it defied it.

He turned to find his mother waiting for him. She threw her arms around him and held him tightly.

"I will miss you when you are in Neumarkt," she said. "But it will be easier for me, knowing you are safe. That is all that matters."

Peter stepped back awkwardly. He looked at his mother. Her dress was torn. Her hair had come unpinned. She was covered in a fine layer of plaster dust. For the first time, Peter wondered if it was *he* who should be worried about *her*.

Chapter Eleven

Neumarkt,
November 1940

It was night and the windows of the train were painted black, so Peter couldn't see where they were going. He opened the window of the train compartment just a crack and drank in the sweet musty smell. The clacking of the train filled his ears and he let his mind wander.

He hadn't been frightened by the bombing raids in Hamburg, but he was glad to leave the noise and chaos behind. He'd miss his mother, but he felt mean because he knew he wouldn't miss her very much. He was excited to be traveling. He was happy to leave the ghosts of Hamburg and Eutin behind.

He closed his eyes. The swaying of the train made him feel dozy. His mother had cried at the station. She'd given him a present—a small black box camera she'd got from Herr Weber. "It's just a cheap one, but you can take pictures to show me when you get home," she'd said. Then she'd burst into tears. It was horrible. Embarrassing. He'd stiffened up, turned on his heel, and walked briskly to the compartment. He hadn't looked or waved as the train left the station, although he knew she was there watching. He regretted his behavior already, but there was nothing he could do now. Best just to get on with things. He'd write to her once he was settled. If he could get a stamp. If there was a post office. He'd stowed the camera in his rucksack.

The rough fabric of his new uniform scratched across his chin. He opened his eyes. His face was colorless, reflected in the dark window. He listened to the sound the train was making, and wondered if they were crossing a bridge. He knew they'd be crisscrossing the River Elbe as they clattered through the heart of Germany.

He couldn't believe that the Gymnasium was paying for this trip. It was more like a holiday than school. He even had a camera to take snapshots, like a tourist. *The war is giving me a chance to have an adventure*, he thought guiltily.

Neumarkt was tiny compared to Hamburg. The streets were cobbled and the buildings were hundreds of years old. In Hamburg, most of the buildings had been rebuilt after the Great Fire of 1842. Going to Neumarkt was like stepping back in time.

They were staying at the Cloister St. Joseph. The Nazi Party had prohibited religious services, but the nuns at St. Joseph's were going to take care of the Gymnasium boys. He carried his case from the train station to the gate of the walled cloister and waited with the rest of the boys until two stern-looking nuns in long black habits opened the gate.

It creaked on its hinges, a sound that made Peter immediately feel claustrophobic. He'd been free to come and go as he liked all his life. There were rules now that he was in Gymnasium, and he knew that he would always have to appear to be following them. But he wasn't going to change his ways.

Instinctively, he looked to see how difficult it would be to get out once they were shut in. The big iron lock would be easy to pick. An old apple tree grew beside the wall, easy access to climb over. He took a deep breath as he followed the nuns into his new home.

As it turned out, things were a lot more relaxed in Neumarkt than at school in Hamburg. The mornings were dedicated to schoolwork, particularly in studying the history of the Nazi Party. They spent most afternoons hiking. The woods that surrounded Neumarkt were thick and lush. Peter loved the wet, earthy smell and the squelch of the dead leaves and soft moss under his feet.

There were fifteen boys in his group. Otto and Gunter were with him, and so was Hermann, but Peter made sure to stay clear of him. Scholl was in charge of them, even though he was only sixteen years old. He said he was heading off to the SS Training camp in the spring, and told them that he'd been promised an officer's commission. But even Scholl was different in Neumarkt. He loved to be outdoors and seemed to like playing more than giving orders. He set up obstacle courses for them in the woods. At the end of the day, he'd march them down to the river and then they'd all jump in, splashing and shrieking together. The cold of the water was jarring, but clean and clear. It was nothing like the brown, sludge-filled canals of Hamburg. Peter pushed the thought of the dock out of his mind. Any residue of fear wasn't allowed.

On Sundays, Peter, Otto, and Gunter had free time to explore on their own. Sometimes they just sat on a hill and talked or read.

Ever since Peter helped win Capture the Flag by grabbing Hermann's testicles, Otto and Gunter had teased him.

"Herr Gruber is the reigning King of Gymnasium!" Gunter laughed.

"We bow down as your loyal subjects," added Otto. "But we follow you in secret, because there is no place for royalty in the new Germany," he whispered conspiratorially.

And thus they became an official secret club, and called themselves the SFGBS—Secret Federation of Gruber, Brandt, and Schmidt. They reported on overheard conversations between the teachers, the group leaders, other students, the nuns. They made up a secret code and filled a journal with notes. Peter liked having a private life, away from the rest of the Jungvolk.

They left the cloisters separately on Sunday morning, making sure they weren't followed. Peter liked heading out before everyone finished breakfast. He edged his way across the dining hall, picking out some hunks of bread that the nuns put out for their meal. The nuns were stern but they made excellent bread. He popped a few pieces in his rucksack and headed toward the gate.

"Where are you heading so bright and early, pretty boy?"

Hermann stood in the shadow of the dining hall door. His redheaded sidekick Kurt was beside him.

Peter kept walking. He started to think about his route, wondering if Hermann would follow him.

"I'm talking to you, skinny legs."

"In case you haven't noticed, Hermann, you are not my group leader or my commanding officer."

"Ouch, that hurt," said Hermann sarcastically, putting a hand to his heart. Kurt gave a small snort. "Are you such a bully with your little friends? Or do you treat them with a softer touch?"

Peter hesitated. His back was to Hermann.

"Don't forget I know where you come from. I know you're a harbor rat, a bastard without a father, who only got into Gymnasium as a charity case."

He felt himself stiffen involuntarily.

"You cheated at Capture the Flag. You're nothing but a cheat," Kurt called out in a whiney voice.

A fleeting image from the fight flashed across Peter's mind. Had he cheated? Was it an unfair fight? A sliver of doubt slid under his skin.

"I just defended myself," he said as he continued walking. "You're the one who attacked." He heard the lack of conviction in his voice.

"It was a game, pretty boy. I was playing by the rules of the game. I could have beaten you to a pulp with one hand. But you stepped outside the rules."

"Water under the bridge. Give it a rest," Peter said with

a confidence he did not feel. He reached the gate and pulled open the heavy iron bars.

"You're right," Hermann called after him. "Beating you up wouldn't be worth my time."

Kurt sniggered.

Peter took a long, circuitous route to their meeting place under a copse of aspen trees in a field at the edge of town. He walked through the quiet streets of Neumarkt, past the empty Cathedral, and crossed the courtyard in front of the triangular Rathaus. It looked like a cake with its thirteen chimneys instead of candles decorating the steeply sloping roof. A woman walked past him in a long, tattered brown coat, flicking her eyes over his casual clothing. On Sundays he wore nothing that identified him as one of the Kinderlandverschickung, but in a town of this size, everyone knew who was an outsider.

Peter had heard hatred in Hermann's voice. Why? Because of the Capture the Flag game? No, it came from before that. Hermann had been a bully for as long as Peter could remember, but he'd never known why. Peter just wanted to get through school, make a bit of money on the side, and eventually travel the world. What had he done to deserve Hermann's wrath?

He dug his hand deeply into his pocket and came out with one of the pieces of bread. He put it to his nose, inhaling the smell of rich molasses and tangy caraway. He tore a corner off and rolled it between his fingers before popping it in his mouth, an old habit from when he was in hospital and his mother fed him tiny bread balls, making a game to try to get him to eat. He felt a sudden pang of missing her. He was so far from the war here, it was hard to believe there were still bombing raids and that she might be in danger.

He rounded the corner of the Rathaus and walked down the long, quiet, cobbled street toward the town's gate. A dog sleeping in a doorway lifted its nose to sniff the fresh bread as he passed. He tossed a tiny bread ball over his shoulder and walked on.

The sun was shining. It was a perfect fall day. Hermann could choke on his own bile for all Peter cared.

By the time Peter got to the copse, Gunter and Otto were already there.

"What took you so long?" said Gunter. His mouth was full of bread and it sounded more like he'd said "Wff dook oo s'gln?"

Peter plunked himself down and began on his bread in earnest.

"Had to avoid detection. Hermann. Took a winding road." Peter liked the poetry of "a winding road." He liked picturing himself on the journey.

"You weren't followed?" asked Otto, slightly nervously.

"No. I'm sure. What's that?"

Otto was slowly unwrapping a handkerchief. He peeled back several layers but even before Peter could see what it was, he could smell it.

"An orange! Where did you get that!?"

Otto was grinning from ear to ear.

"One of the nuns. She's quite taken with me. She says

that if she'd had a child, she would have wanted him to be just like me. Don't know where she got the orange, though. Do nuns use the black market?"

"Everyone uses the black market. Wow. I haven't seen an orange in over a year, not since the last shipment in Hamburg."

Otto broke into the peel and started tearing it off. The smell was overwhelming. Peter felt his eyes water. He watched as Otto carefully took off the peel and broke the orange into ten segments.

"Three for each of us," said Otto, "and one extra. Maybe if we plant it we'll get an orange tree." He laughed as he carefully placed the segments in Peter and Gunter's hands.

"Thanks, Otto," said Gunter staring down at the bright sticky pieces in his hand. "You are a true friend."

Peter slipped a segment into his mouth. For a moment he didn't bite into it. He just let the texture and aroma sit there, filling his brain with orange goodness. Then, when he couldn't wait any longer, he bit down. The juice exploded in his mouth. Had oranges always been this sweet?

"Oh, Otto," he sighed.

They sat there, making the segments last as long as they possibly could, silently chewing and swallowing.

"She must really like you. Maybe you could get her to adopt you, just while the war is on, so we all get better food." Peter looked down at his empty hand. He cupped it over his nose, inhaling the last of the smell, and licked off all traces of the juice.

Otto was staring guiltily at the last segment. "There's not

really enough to share ..." he said. It sounded more like a question than a statement.

"It's all right, Otto. I'm full up now. What about you, Gunter? You all full? I honestly couldn't fit in another bite," said Peter with a grin.

"Yeah, Otto, really. I'm feeling as fat as an old sow. Couldn't fit in another crumb. You better finish it off," said Gunter as he stretched out and lay down under the trees. "I don't suppose either of you has a cigarette?"

"No, the nuns don't seem as willing to share their cigarettes!" laughed Peter.

Otto stood up. "Well, if you two will excuse me, nature calls."

Otto headed past the copse and out of sight behind the side of the hill.

"Would you have shared?" Gunter was still on his back, looking up through the dappled trees.

"What?"

"Would you have brought that orange to share with us? I'm not sure I would have."

"Yeah, of course I would have shared it," said Peter slowly. He could tell that his voice didn't sound convinced.

"Naw. You're just like me. You'd think twice. Otto's different. He doesn't even have to think about it. He just does it." Gunter sounded wistful. "I hope he survives this war," he said quietly.

"He's got a better chance than either of us, if the nuns keep giving him treats," laughed Peter.

Suddenly they heard a yell from the top of the hill.

"Hey! Come here! You've got to see this!" Otto was waving at them.

Peter and Gunter leapt up as Otto disappeared over the other side. They raced to the top.

There was a cluster of large boulders, overgrown with wild hop vines and grasses, but they couldn't see Otto anywhere.

"Here! Over here!" Otto's voice sounded distant. Peter ran down the hill and began scanning the woods beyond. He darted in and out of the trees.

"Otto? Where are you? Are you all right?"

The canopy of fall leaves above him dappled the ground and made it hard for him to distinguish shapes.

"Not that way. Over here!" Now Otto's voice came from behind him. He turned around expecting to see Gunter, but now he was nowhere to be seen.

"Otto? Gunter?"

Peter began to double back over the hill. As he passed the boulders, he could hear laughter. He looked closely. The undergrowth partially obscured a large dark hole. Cool, dank air seeped from the opening. Suddenly he realized that Otto's broad smile was beaming at him from behind the foliage.

"Hey!"

"Took you long enough. So much for your tracking abilities," Otto laughed. Peter could now see Gunter beside him.

"Come on in. You won't believe the size of this. I think it goes all the way through the hill. It can be our hideout." Gunter's voice was high-pitched with excitement.

Peter pushed aside the vines and stepped into the cool of the cave. The earth was hard packed, and a rock opening narrowed to a smaller tunnel at the back. It was the size of a small room. It was perfect.

"How far back have you gone?" asked Peter.

"Not far. It's really dark back there," said Otto. "But we can come back later with flashlights and explore. There might be treasure!"

"More likely just a bunch of animal bones," said Gunter.

"But still, it's a great place," said Otto, looking for reassurance.

"It's perfect," said Peter.

"It's ours. The SFGBS. For our meetings," said Gunter.

The next day, when they were heading out for the Jungvolk afternoon hike, Peter saw Otto put his sketch-book in his rucksack at the same time as Gunter picked up his flashlight. They didn't want to wait until next Sunday. They wanted to explore the cave now. Peter grabbed his camera and slipped it carefully into his rucksack. He wanted a photo of their new "headquarters."

Halfway through the afternoon, there was always a break. Everyone had a bit of bread, a hunk of cheese, and a flask of water. After the break, there was sometimes a game of Capture the Flag, or maybe Knights and Horses. But the games were pretty informal. No one would miss them if they weren't there for a few minutes.

At break time, Peter sat at the outer edge of the group. After a few minutes, he stood up and went into the woods, as though he was going for a pee. He walked quietly behind the group, curving around to get to the other side of the clearing. From there it would be about a five-minute walk to the cave.

The afternoon sun warmed Peter's arms. The dry grasses gently scratched his legs as he walked through them. He enjoyed the feeling of walking not marching.

Summertime, and the livin' is easy ...

The line from the American song ran through his head and he was immediately back in Franz's apartment. He felt as though that was years ago, yet it was only last April. He wondered if Franz was still in Hamburg or if he, too, had been evacuated somewhere. Last he heard, the Hitlerjugend were being trained to shoot the anti-aircraft FLAK guns. There was a big FLAK tower being built over near St. Pauli. Franz might be at the end of an anti-aircraft gun, protecting Hamburg. Protecting his mother.

"Da-da-hm-hm-hm, da-da hm-hm da early ...." Peter hummed the tune softly to himself. He came over the crest of the hill and began to run toward the boulders, letting gravity pull him, feeling the great expanse of nature all around.

"You're gonna dah-dah-dah and dah to the sky ..." He awkwardly sang what he could remember of the English words as he rounded the rocks and jumped into the cave entrance.

SMACK! His body flew backward and he landed flat on his back, winded by an unseen force. It was as though he'd run straight into the rock face and ricocheted backwards. But then he heard a laugh. A nasty, deep laugh.

"Da da-da da-da," laughed Hermann.

Peter lifted his head. Hermann's bulk filled the cave

entrance. Peter must have run right into him. He looked into the cave beyond and could just make out Kurt grinning crookedly. Otto and Gunter were behind, with long faces.

"He followed us, Peter," said Otto. "Before we knew what was happening, he was here in the cave and he sort of took over. I'm really sorry."

Hermann laughed. "Yeah, he's really sorry he's so stupid. You guys leave a trail a mile wide. You couldn't do reconnaissance to save your lives. In fact, if you did reconnaissance, you'd lose lives!" Kurt made a sound like a short, sharp explosion. It was the closest he could get to a laugh.

"Well, what's it to you, Hermann? Why go to all of the trouble to track us?" Peter's head was throbbing from hitting the ground.

"Oh, it's no trouble at all. In fact, it's what the Party asks for. To make sure that everyone is doing his duty, that no one is slacking off. You," he said, pointing a thick finger at Peter, "you think you're so great, like you're above all this. Well, the Führer tells us it's not our job to think. It is our job to act. It is our job to stamp out weakness where we find it."

"Don't lecture me, Hermann," said Peter as he casually stood up, keeping Hermann in his peripheral vision. He reached to pick up his rucksack. "It's hard on your brain. It's difficult enough for you to string two words together, let alone a sentence." Otto and Gunter laughed.

"Shut up, pretty boy, and show some respect," growled Hermann. Peter could see him flexing his fists, but he walked calmly away from the cave and stood in the bright sunlight on the slope of the hill.

"Put up your shootin' irons, we've no desire to eat you," Peter said. It was a line he loved from *The Treasure of Nugget Mountain*. He'd always wanted to use it. He faced Hermann in his best imitation of a gun-slinging cowboy. Hermann's face was contorted with disgust. "I thought we'd settled this back in Hamburg," Peter said.

"You cheated in Hamburg! You took advantage of me. It was just luck. A puny, skinny, pretty boy like you is no match for the likes of me."

Hermann horked a big glob of spit at Peter's feet. "That's what I think of you and your games. Your little secrets. SFGBS, whatever stupid thing that is. Yeah, I've heard your secrets," Hermann snarled when Peter's face reacted. "That one," he said, gesturing to Gunter, "he's got a 'whisper' that carries for miles!" His face got serious. "It's time for a real match." Hermann's voice was low. "One on one," he added, narrowing his eyes.

"Peter!" Suddenly, Scholl's voice cut through the circle of tension that Hermann had created. Peter kept his eyes on Hermann but backed up several paces. In his peripheral vision he could see Scholl and the rest of the boys in their group, standing on the top of the rock face. He shot up his arm up in salute, keeping his eyes on Hermann in the cave entrance. He wasn't sure what Scholl's mood was, but he knew that the salute would help. Peter realized that from where Scholl was, all he could see was Peter, saluting a pile of rocks. He probably thought Peter had lost his mind.

"You had no permission to leave the group," Scholl shouted angrily. "Where are Otto and Gunter?"

Hermann stepped deftly out of the cave, followed by Kurt, Otto, and Gunter, taking Scholl by surprise. Hermann's hand shot up in a salute. "I have them here. I saw Peter, Otto, and Gunter leave the group and I tracked them. Peter is their leader and, by his actions, he has displayed disrespect to the Führer." Hermann looked at Peter with a malicious grin. "I hereby challenge him to a duel."

Peter opened his mouth to protest. It was absurd. Hermann was making up something that sounded official but was just an excuse for a fight. Scholl liked proof of loyalty to the Führer, and Hermann was using Peter as a way to impress Scholl.

He really didn't want to fight Hermann again. He suspected that Hermann was right—the last time had been a fluke. He had been angry and the adrenalin had made him strong. This time it was Hermann who was angry. He'd been carrying that anger for months now. He'd use it to his advantage.

On the other hand, if Peter didn't fight him now, Hermann would make sure to find him later, when Peter wasn't prepared. At least here, with a proper duel, there would be witnesses to his final moments.

"A duel is serious business," said Scholl slowly. Peter could see a small smile at the corner of Scholl's mouth. Apparently, Scholl was looking forward to a bit of afternoon entertainment. "But a charge of disrespect to the Fuehrer must be answered."

He's been listening to too many speeches on the radio. He sounds like he's addressing a crowd of thousands, thought Peter.

By now, all of the boys in the group had joined Scholl and come down from the top of the rock. They assembled on the flat clearing. Peter could see their eyes glinting with the thrill of a blood sport. He knew that he could not back down. At the least, it would mean that it would be a proper duel, with rules, rather than a messy no-holds-barred brawl. He decided to answer Scholl in the formal tone that had been set, and answered the charges in rapid fire.

"I maintain that I showed no disrespect to the Führer. However, I will admit to the charge that I did not show any respect to Hermann. Hermann is not my superior, nor is he, in and of himself, owed any respect when he himself has behaved in a sanctimonious and officious manner, exceeding his standing within this group. His behavior must be answered for. Heil Hitler!"

Peter clicked his feet together and saluted briskly. He knew that Hermann wouldn't have understood half of what he said, and he would be seething at the use of words beyond his vocabulary. He saw Scholl's eyes go wide.

"Heil Hitler!" Scholl answered back.

"Heil Hitler!" echoed Hermann.

"Heil Hitler!" answered all of the other boys.

For a moment, Peter saw the ridiculousness of the scene. Fifteen boys standing in the middle of the countryside, in the middle of nowhere, saluting their Führer. He and Hermann were about to engage in a formal fight to prove that they were loyal citizens. *How can we expect to win a war if we are fighting each other?* he wondered.

"Here are the rules," began Scholl, clearly making it up

as he went along. "You may only use your fists. There is to be no biting, no use of sticks, stones, or other weapons. You will remove your uniforms and fight in your underpants. You will fight until one of you concedes, one of you is knocked out, or until I stop the fight and declare a winner. You must fight within the circle."

Already the boys were forming a wide circle around Peter and Hermann. Peter could feel waves of rage emanating from Hermann. *He is stoking his anger*, Peter thought, *to keep himself strong. I have to go the opposite way. I have to stay calm and focused. Fight smart. Outwit him.*

He removed his tie and began to slowly unbutton his shirt. Gunter suddenly appeared before him to take his things. "He has a blind spot on the left," he whispered.

"What?" Peter asked below his breath.

"I sit beside him in class. His peripheral vision is awful, particularly on the left. I've tested it out by drawing dirty pictures and moving them around my desk. If they are in the middle of the desk, he notices them right away. But if they are just a little bit down and further out, he can't see them at all. Surprise him on his left." Gunter carefully folded Peter's shirt as he took it off.

Peter slowly removed his short pants. He was glad that Scholl hadn't insisted that they fight in the nude, like classical wrestlers. He handed his trousers to Gunter and removed his shoes and socks. He turned around to see Hermann at the other side of the circle, laughing.

"This is the future of Germany?" Hermann laughed scornfully, looking Peter up and down and playing to the audience. "This skinny pretty boy?" He stood with his fists balled at his hips, his upper arms pushed back to maximum effect.

Hermann had put on more muscle since their fight in Hamburg. His upper body was large, his biceps well-defined and firm. He had anger, weight, *and* strength on his side.

Peter was wiry and fast. If Hermann was a raging bull, Peter was a cheetah. His one hope was to tire him out, to make him spend his rage uselessly.

Scholl walked to the center of the circle. Peter and Hermann took positions on either side of him. He grabbed both of their right fists and pushed them together. "For the Fatherland," he shouted as he jumped back toward the circle of boys.

Peter immediately sprang to his left, startling Hermann who seemed to expect him to just stand still and be hit. Peter began to move around the circle clockwise, keeping to the edge of Hermann's right side. Peter was forcing Hermann to spin in a tight circle.

"It's not a dance," growled Hermann as he crossed the circle in two quick strides, anticipating Peter's movement and pushing his fist forward.

But Peter saw this move as though it was a game of chess. He had already leapt the opposite way, to his right, steps away from Hermann's left side. Hermann's swing pushed through the empty air, throwing him off balance and propelling him counterclockwise, where he tripped over Peter's outstretched right foot. The dust of the dry earth flew up, as Hermann dug his feet into the ground to avoid falling.

Peter knew that his best hope was in staying just outside of Hermann's range, to keep moving and force Hermann to keep moving. That meant not trying to land any blows. Not just yet, anyway. He moved backward to keep his distance as Hermann corrected his fall and twisted around to face Peter again.

"You cheating moron!" Hermann yelled as he barreled toward Peter. Again Peter leapt to his left, out of the way of Hermann's forward movement.

But Hermann suddenly smashed sideways with his fist. Not as powerful as a punch, but still a strong backhand hit, narrowly missing Peter's head but landing full force on his neck. It threw Peter off balance and temporarily winded him, sending him careening to his left. Hermann spun around to face Peter full on and smashed his fist into Peter's left cheek.

The shock was immediate. The hit of adrenalin was like fire in his veins. Peter had been trying to buy time, but he had no time now.

The punch had sent him spinning to his right. Rather than correct the spin, he let himself use that momentum, coming around in a full circle, leading with his fist, and smashing sideways into Hermann's lower rib. He felt a crack, heard Hermann's scream of pain and rage. Hermann spun, countered the movement, and pushed back toward Peter.

But Peter was now on Hermann's left side and saw his advantage immediately. His anger and his sense of self-preservation were instinctive and he plunged his fist into Hermann's face, right into Hermann's nose.

Peter knew that Hermann hadn't seen the punch coming.

Hermann was shocked, and the surprise gave Peter the opening he'd been looking for. He planted himself squarely in front of Hermann and hit him again, this time driving his knuckles into Hermann's cheek.

Peter felt as though time had slowed down. He could see everything clearly now. There was blood pouring from Hermann's nose. He watched as Hermann righted himself after the last punch, and waited until just before he had his balance back to hit him with his left fist, jabbing upward into Hermann's stomach, aiming just below his abdominal muscles and cutting upward into the soft cavity.

Hermann was off balance, surprised by the ferocity of Peter's punches and the quickness of his response. He surged forward, pushing off his back foot to come back at Peter. But Peter had moved in close, too close for Hermann to connect, and he swung his fist into Hermann's blind spot, hitting in exactly the same place on Hermann's cheek, sending him spinning in a circle. Peter followed him as he started to spin downward, and he punched with both fists, on his head, his back, his stomach—wherever he could connect. His blows were precise and fierce. He felt invincible. Even when Hermann was falling, Peter was hitting him. Even when Hermann wasn't fighting back, Peter was hitting him. He felt alive. There was nothing, no one, except him and the mass at his feet. The sound of his breathing, the sound of his punches.

Suddenly he felt fingernails biting into his scalp. His hair was grabbed and he was pulled backward. He lost his balance and fell and a boot pushed down on his chest.

"Stop! Now!"

Scholl was glaring into his face. For a moment, time froze.

Slowly, Peter felt the anger in his body begin to dissipate. He lay there panting, with Scholl's boot planted on him, his lungs heaving.

"It's over. Didn't you hear me? I've been trying to get you to stop. What the hell were you trying to do, kill him?" There was a look of horror and panic in Scholl's eyes.

The rest of the world began to come back into focus and Peter was aware of an unearthly quiet. He turned his head. He could see the other boys all silently staring at him. To his right, he saw Hermann curled on the ground. Still.

"Is he okay?" Peter asked.

"I'm going to check. Don't move." Scholl released the pressure of his foot. Peter watched as he went over to Hermann. Pain was beginning to seep into his hands and face.

Scholl gently shook Hermann's back. Hermann coughed and groaned.

"Hermann. Hermann, can you get up? It's over," said Scholl.

Peter watched as Hermann slowly began to uncurl. There was blood, sweat, and dirt drying in splotches on his face. A purple swelling rose beside his nose. He held his side, and spat a globule of blood into the dirt as he started to get up.

"A fair fight," said Scholl formally. Peter heard a slight tremble in his voice. "You've got to shake, both of you. You have to accept the results of the duel and move on." Clearly, Scholl was trying to establish some kind of order in the chaos that had overtaken the afternoon. He looked over his shoulder at Peter. "Are you ready to get up now?" he asked.

Peter nodded silently. He was shocked by what had happened, shocked by the ferocity of his anger and the immediacy of his violence. He was shaking as he got to his feet. This wasn't like the last time. When he'd won the fight during Capture the Flag, it had felt like it was part of the game. This time it was real.

He stood quietly, waiting for Scholl and Hermann to approach, looking down at the ground.

"You've got to look each other in the eye and shake hands," said Scholl. He sounded scared.

Peter slowly raised his head. Hermann's puffy face looked nothing like the boy who had challenged him. It was devoid of emotion, drained. Hermann dully held out his hand. Peter shook it with the lightest of pressure. His hands were throbbing horribly now.

"We're all going to go to the river to have a swim and a wash before we head back. It was a fair duel, and now it is over. Heil Hitler!" Scholl clicked his heels together. The boys in the circle responded. "Heil, Hitler!" Peter and Hermann raised their arms weakly. "Heil, Hitler."

Word of the fight spread quickly through the school. The bruises on Peter's cheek went from blue to black to a sickly yellow. His lip had split open, and he had to eat out of the side of his mouth.

But what was more noticeable to Peter was the subtle shift in people's attitude toward him. Since the fight, the boys treated him differently. Even Gunter and Otto left a space around him. They checked to see what he decided before making up their own minds. Even Scholl asked his opinion and deferred to his judgment. He found himself alone more often. *This is what power feels like*, he thought.

He drew into his solitude. His violence had shocked him. He knew that he should enjoy his new position, but a part of him was horrified and disgusted with himself. Late at night, images of the fight flashed into his mind. He relived the sensation of his fist smashing into Hermann's nose, and the dreadful crunching noise it made. He heard the gasp that Hermann made as he'd punched upward into his gut, and the gurgling noise that Hermann made as he lay on the ground. He wanted to cry and beg Hermann's forgiveness. But he knew that there would be no absolution. He had to live with his victory and work to find a way to forgive himself.

As each bruise faded, he became increasingly disconnected to everything around him. At Christmas, they had a dress-up party and Peter made himself a large mask out of *papier mâché*. He painted it bright white and said he was the Man in the Moon. The wanderer, carrying a heavy pack. Banished.

Chapter Twelve

Neumarkt,
March 1941

... I'm standing at the top of the Rathaus. Crows take off from the ledge. Their wings spread out. They are nuns in the courtyard below me. The class is walking away. I want to be with them but they don't turn around. Eugene looks up. "Why don't you just jump?" I start to fall ...

Peter jerks awake. His heart races, then slows, and his mind goes blank ...

"You need to see more of the Reich, to understand the Party and what we are fighting for." Herr Birkmann's voice jolted Peter out of a daydream.

"Tomorrow we're going to Nuremberg, the city of the Reichsparteitagsgelände," continued Herr Birkmann, "the Reich Party Congress grounds dedicated to the annual National Socialist Party rallies."

"Are we going to a rally?" Gunter blurted out.

"No, Gunter," replied Herr Birkmann condescendingly.

"The last rally was in 1938. They will begin again once the war is over."

The teacher allowed himself a rare smile. "I was born in Nuremberg and lived there until I was sent to teach in Hamburg. I haven't been back since the war started. That was one of the reasons why I requested the assignment to teach you here in Neumarkt, where we are just an hour from Nuremberg."

Peter had never thought of his teacher as being from anywhere other than Hamburg. To be truthful, he'd never really thought of Herr Birkmann as having a family or of doing anything other than teaching. His teacher seemed to soften in front of his eyes, but then the moment passed and Herr Birkmann was once again standing crisply and efficiently before them.

"Needless to say, your uniforms must be immaculate. Many of you have been getting lax in your attention, and I have seen you returning from hikes with mud on your trousers and scuff marks on your shoes. These things can be overlooked in the country, but not in the city. Tomorrow, you will wear your winter uniforms, which have been reserved for special occasions. Group leaders—ensure that your group spends time this afternoon making preparations for the trip."

Peter was glad to get out of his short trousers. His skinny knees were always blue from the cold. And he had to admit that his uniform was looking a bit the worse for wear. One of the sisters had remarked on a tear in the leg. She'd fixed it, but he'd had to put up with a lecture about discipline and duty. He spent the afternoon happily shining his buttons, insignia, and belt buckle. He polished his winter boots, and carefully brushed stray dust from his hat.

As they boarded the train to Nuremberg the next morning, Peter remembered how excited he had been when they'd traveled to Neumarkt. But he'd been here for four months and any sense of adventure was long gone. Throughout the bleak winter, he'd felt restless and bored with this small town. They received little news of the outside world. Herr Birkmann told them that England was close to surrender. Places he'd never heard of before—Coventry, Plymouth, Southampton— were being destroyed. The German army was now in Africa. But here in Neumarkt, life was quiet. Real life was happening everywhere else. He was glad to get out. He had his camera with him and was looking forward to taking photos of the Congress grounds.

He stepped briskly onto the train, enjoying the feeling of his boots clicking on the steps. He straightened his spine and took his seat by the window. He felt so much older than when he'd arrived. In two months he'd be twelve.

As he looked out the window, he saw Hermann getting on the train. In the months since their fight, Peter had grown. His uniform was tight everywhere. Hermann seemed to have shrunk. His wrinkled winter uniform hung off him awkwardly. His cap sat at an odd angle. He was alone as he stepped into a car further down the train. Peter knew that he too would end up sitting by himself for the trip. The fight had isolated them both. He felt a whisper of loneliness and almost felt sorry for Hermann. Almost.

The sky was overcast and threatened rain. Peter was glad

for the thick wool of his winter uniform. He let his mind wander as the train moved slowly from the sparsely populated countryside to the city. Red slate roofs began to fill the landscape. A castle sat on top of a hill, poetically silhouetted against the gray sky. Then he saw another, and another. Three castles guarding the town, the fortifications spreading downward and enclosing the city within their walls.

Neumarkt has made my mind dull, he thought. *It's time to wake up.*

At the station in Nuremberg, he could hear excitement bubbling out of the group. He stepped off the train and made his way down the platform. Gunter fell into formation beside him as they started their march into town.

"Otto's spent the whole trip talking about the artist, Albrecht Dürer. Apparently he lived here," Gunter said. Peter was aware that Gunter kept trying to bridge the gulf that had grown between them. "I've never heard of him, but Otto says he was a great engraver in the sixteenth century. Anyway, he's hoping we're going to visit Dürer's house. He bugged Herr Birkmann about it all the way here."

Peter had seen some of Dürer's drawings in a book at the library. They were amazingly detailed, full of strange images. He could remember one with a skull and a lion. The drawings were dark and depressing. "Well, that's just like Otto to get all excited about some drawings," he said offhandedly.

Gunter fell silent. Peter decided he didn't care. He was content to wrap himself in his mood. He wanted to be alone with his thoughts.

Two other groups joined them, forty boys in all, walking

double file from the train station, through the entrance archway to the city. The narrow streets of the medieval town opened out to a wide bridge, crossing a spacious canal. Painted houses dipped to the water's edge and small boat docks sat bobbing on the surface.

Peter had a momentary ache as the canals in Hamburg leapt into his mind. They weren't picturesque like this canal, but they were his, and he knew every square inch of them. He forced his attention back to Nuremberg's red roofs, dotted with tiny windows. Some had circular windows with tall spikes jutting toward the sky. Perfect spaces to have a private desk, to read or write, thought Peter. How long had it been since he'd been alone, really alone, to read whatever he wanted. He imagined himself high in an attic space, looking down on his group as they marched. He saw it vividly in his mind, like a black and white photograph, and he looked up at the window, almost sure he'd see himself looking down.

A tall rectangular spire rose above all the other buildings. Peter's group turned a corner and stopped in a large open square in front of a church. He had a strange sense of déjà vu, as though he'd seen it before. The church was built in the same kind of triangular shape as the Rathaus in Neumarkt, but it was much bigger, more dramatic. The roof was ornamented with spikes going up each side, and the central tower had a huge blue clock surrounded by a number of small carved figurines. Why did it look so familiar?

"The Frauenkirche, built six hundred years ago by the Holy Roman Emperor Charles IV," said Herr Birkmann. "I used to come here as a boy," he continued, spreading his arms wide and taking in the whole square. "There was a big market, the Chriskindlesmarkt, every Christmas in this square. There were wooden toys and the smell of Lebkuchen everywhere."

Even Peter had heard of Lebkuchen gingerbread, although he'd never tasted it. He tried to imagine Herr Birkmann as a boy. He tried to imagine the market through Herr Birkmann's eyes.

"Good King Wenceslas was baptized here," continued Herr Birkmann, pointing at the church. "Wenceslas was Emperor Charles's son. The clock at the top commemorates the Emperor's Golden Bull, which was a law that changed the way kings and emperors were chosen. And the Golden Bull is one of the reasons why Nuremberg is so important to the Führer. You are standing in the very heart of the National Socialist Party."

Peter lifted his camera and looked down at the view finder. He turned the lens to focus on the church. Otto's thin voice buzzed into Peter's ear, cutting through his thoughts. "I feel like I've seen this church before," he whispered, "but I've never been to Nuremberg. Is there a church like it in Hamburg? I can't think of one, but it seems so familiar."

Peter's finger clicked the shot. "I was just thinking the same thing," he mumbled. "Herr Birkmann," he called out, lowering the camera. The teacher wheeled his head around to face Peter. *Even the teachers treat me differently since the fight*, thought Peter. "I feel like I've seen this church—well, actually, this whole square—before. But I've never been to Nuremberg." Several of the boys nodded in agreement.

"Very observant. You are right, you have seen it before.

In fact much of what you see today will look familiar," replied Herr Birkmann with a slight smile.

"Two years ago, when you first started Gymnasium, your class was taken to a movie theater in Hamburg. Do you remember? You watched *Triumph of the Will*, made by the great film director Leni Riefenstahl. The movie showed the glorious Nazi Party Congress of 1934, attended by 700,000 party members. I was living in Nuremberg then, and the city opened its arms to them all. Toward the end of the movie, our Führer inspected troops from his podium right over there." Herr Birkmann pointed to a spot in front to the church. "There were seats for special guests, visiting dignitaries, all through here. And down there, where the street comes through the square, hundreds of thousands paraded through the town. The workmen, the SA, the Hitler Youth—thousands upon thousands of people marching to drums, trumpets, and flutes. I was there." He pointed to a window two stories above the square. "My mother, my sister, and I all watched from the window. It was a day I will never forget."

Herr Birkmann seemed to be shimmering as he stood where the Führer had stood. Peter remembered sitting transfixed in the dark theater, the Führer's words making his heart swell.

"It is our wish and our will that this state, this Reich, should remain in existence in the coming millennia. We can be happy in the knowledge that this future will belong to us totally. When the older generations can barely walk any more, the youth will dedicate itself to continuing our work."

Hitler had held his hands crossed over his heart, and he'd

smiled as he talked about the youth, about himself, about all of them. Hitler was speaking directly to them, telling them that Germany, their home, was the greatest country on the planet. The movie had ended with the *Horst-Wessel-Song* and everyone in the movie theater had joined in. Peter had walked out of the theater with Gunter and Otto, singing.

"Comrades shot by the Red Front and the Reactionaries march in spirit together in our columns!"

Peter's attention was brought back to the square as bells from a distant church began to chime the hour of twelve o'clock.

"Ah. It is starting," said Herr Birkmann.

Peter followed the teacher's gaze to the sumptuous blue and gold clock face on the tower. A large seated figure sat regally below. As he watched, a silent band began to play. Two figurines on either side raised long thin trumpets. A drummer began to tap on a tiny drum and a flute player lifted a thin, silent flute.

Another figure sat in a small window, ringing a tiny bell. His bearded mouth opened and closed as though he were calling out in celebration. Another raised and lowered his hand. Peter couldn't quite see what he was doing—he looked like he was strumming a long-lost guitar.

Suddenly bells in the tower began to chime, and Peter looked up and saw two figures with mallets on the top, hitting a large bell. A door opened to the right of the seated figure— Peter assumed he must be Emperor Charles IV—and a line of richly decorated figurines swung out and circled around him, exiting through the door on the left. Charles IV raised and lowered his scepter as the figures moved past.

"The Princes-Elect," whispered Herr Birkmann. Peter looked over and saw his teacher's face filled with child-like joy.

The Princes-Elect circled around three times and then all the huge bells in the church began to ring. The sound was almost deafening. It was a sound that reminded Peter of the bells of St. Katharinen Kirche, a sound that was an essential part of his days in Hamburg. Unbidden memories of his home flooded into his body like an illness. He focused his attention on the clock.

Everyone stood rooted to the spot until the sound of the last chime died away. Then Otto started clapping, breaking the spell, and even Peter laughed.

Herr Birkmann clicked his heels and took a small bow, as though he had created the entertainment especially for them.

They left the square and began to march out of the old city center, crossing the canal again. A long thin lake opened out to their left, steely gray but beautiful and calm. Peter could imagine holiday people sitting under umbrellas in nice weather. He thought about the docks in Hamburg, and how they had always been busy with ships from all over the world. Since the war, the only ships he'd seen had been war ships.

He couldn't stop himself from thinking of his mother. He'd had no contact with her since he'd left. He felt a huge pang of regret and loss. Why had he been in such a hurry to leave? He hated thinking of her alone, cold and hungry.

"We are going to pay our respects at Ehrenhale, the Hall of Honor," said Herr Birkmann as they continued away from the city center. "It is the memorial to the 9,855 soldiers from Nuremberg who died in the Great War. My father was one who gave his life to his country. He died before I was born."

Peter thought of Otto's father dying of the yellow gas in the war. So many deaths. But this war would be the last. This war would finally bring peace.

Peter's winter boots pinched at the back of his heel, and he started to sweat under the woolen weight of his uniform. But he lifted his head and marched briskly with the group, as the road took them to the front of a large building with a series of columns and arches. They stopped on the cobbled terrace.

"When I was a child, I was brought here with my mother and sister to honor my father. Herr Hitler was here to commemorate the war dead, but also to honor the sixteen dead of the Hitlerputsch, the infamous Beer Hall Massacre of 1923. Fires burned on top of these pylons—I knew then that I would become a proud member of the Nazi party. Now turn around."

When Peter turned around, he couldn't help gasping. The arena was enormous, far bigger than any open area he had ever been in. It gave him a sick feeling in his stomach, a dizzy feeling, as though he was falling inside himself. He felt small, vulnerable, exposed, and his legs wobbled as the group began to march along the wide granite road to the grandstand beyond. He looked ahead and saw gold glinting on the parapet. As they got closer, he realized there were two enormous golden eagles on either side of a curved grandstand, each taller than a house. He remembered seeing them in the movie. The arena had been filled with hundreds of thousands of troops. Troops that were now fighting for his freedom.

"What you are seeing across the Luitpoldarena is the Ehrentribüne. And just past that, the building that you can see gleaming and shimmering? That is the Luitpold Hall, built for the grand Bavarian exhibition in 1906."

"Why is it shining like that?" asked Otto. "It looks as though it's polished."

"Shell limestone. It is coated in it. Shell limestone has a pearlescent quality. Inside is the largest pipe organ in Germany. It was here, in 1935, that the Party passed the Reich Citizenship Law and the Law to Protect German Blood and Honor. These laws now shape our country and define us as a nation. It is because of these Nuremberg laws that our country is becoming pure and whole."

Peter quickly aimed the camera and took several shots before the group moved on. They turned and an enormous road abruptly opened up before them. Peter felt all of the boys around him straighten up.

"The Great Road," said Herr Birkmann. "It was only finished two years ago. It is this road that we will use for the next rally. It is on this road that we will march."

Peter raised his eyes. They went into formation, four across, but the road could easily have held twenty across. Small manmade lakes sent off ripples of light in the breeze. Their boots rang as they passed the lakes and walked beside meadows that stretched into the distance. Peter imagined the road filled with troops and the parkland filled with spectators. The wind in his ears became the roar of the crowd.

He wondered if Herr Birkmann was right—would they march here with thousands after the war was over?

They passed a huge stadium under construction. "The Deutsche Stadium—it was started in 1937, for sporting events. It will be finished after the war and it will hold 400,000 spectators," said Herr Birkmann.

They continued marching toward the field at the end of the road. As they drew closer, he could see that it was surrounded by stone towers stretching up into the sky.

"The Märzfeld," said Herr Birkmann as they arrived at the entrance. "You could fit eighty football fields in here. There are only eleven towers now but, when it is finished, there will be forty, each twelve meters high. Märzfeld will be the greatest parade ground in the world. One hundred and sixty thousand people will come to pay tribute every year. Tribute to Mars, the god of war, and to March 1935, when the Führer became our leader."

They were marching again, back down the Great Road, but this time Herr Birkmann took a turn to the right, down another road.

"Over there," Herr Birkmann pointed to his right "is the Stadium of the Hitler Youth. I myself competed there in the fourth Deutsche Kampfspiele in 1934. It was the largest sporting event ever organized in Germany. I competed in shot-put and high jump."

Peter looked over at Herr Birkmann. In one day, his teacher had looked like a dull teacher, a little boy, and now a strong athlete. *Adults*, he thought, *are full of surprises.* He would never have suspected his teacher of so much history and inner life.

"When the war is over, you, too, will compete here for

your country. You will show the world what it means to be German."

As he looked ahead, the sun broke through the clouds, and he realized that he knew the final place that Herr Birkmann was taking them.

"The Zeppelin Field, where the great Ferdinand von Zeppelin landed one of his first machines," murmured Herr Birkmann reverently.

Three sides of the field were ringed with stands for spectators. There were towers jutting out, and flagpoles that should have had flags snapping in the wind lining the back. Everything faced the grandstand. It was so wide Peter couldn't hold it all in his line of vision. So wide it was impossible to try to capture it all with his camera. So vast it was impossible to imagine it filled with people.

Yet it had been filled. He had seen the movie.

There were pillars along the width of it, and he remembered that there had been long banners with swastikas between them. And then he saw the central rostrum that Hitler had spoken from, where he had waved and inspired the nation. He focused his camera on the podium.

"The war is almost over," Herr Birkmann announced with pride. "Next month we are going back to Hamburg. There is no more need to stay away. The enemy is being defeated. One day soon, you will come back here. You will come here to the rallies, to pledge your allegiance directly to our Führer, to pledge blood and soil. You will join hundreds of thousands, millions just like you, brought here by your loyalty."

Herr Birkmann's voice rose. "You must remember the

words of the Führer: Every hour, every day, think only of Germany—the people, the Reich, the German nation, and the German people!"

Peter felt pride swelling in his chest. He looked around at the rest of the class. Gunter and Otto were radiant. He realized they were mirroring his own smile, and he smiled back. The distance between them evaporated. He felt a burst of joy. Was this what it felt like to be drunk? It was a miracle. This was the work of gods, not of men. A divine right that was theirs. The war would be over and there would be celebrations and food for all. He was tiny, insignificant, but he was a part of the greatest country in the world.

Herr Birkmann turned to face the huge golden swastika that topped the grandstand high in the air above them. "Heil Hitler!" he shouted. "Heil Hitler!"

"Heil Hitler!" they all answered, arms raised. "Heil Hitler!"

Part Two

Chapter Thirteen

Hamburg.
June 1941

Peter was happy to be back in the city. He'd arrived home just before his twelfth birthday and his mother had made quite a fuss. Oma Ballin had managed to find a tiny bit of marzipan to make a small cake. Herr Ballin surprised them all with a bottle of beer and a toast. "To peace." It was a great homecoming.

There were fewer air raids and fewer nights spent in the shelter. Food was still scarce and it was hard to get in supplies. Shipbuilding had ground to a halt with the last bombing of the shipyards. But for the most part, people were going about their daily lives, using ration cards for the necessities and the black market for everything else.

Peter was startled, however, by his mother's new boyfriend. Hans Corm was tall with shiny blond hair. He was incredibly confident and clearly younger than his mother. He had a motorcycle. The first time Peter met him, he strode into the apartment in his helmet and jacket, sank into their one comfortable chair, crossed his long legs, and rested his feet on the table. His leather boots were so shiny you could see your face in them. He offered Peter a cigarette.

"Your mother says you were in Nuremberg! I was there for the rally in '34 when I wasn't much older than you. The Congress of Victory. You saw the movie? I was there! It changed my life. I took the pledge that day and I have been happy ever since." Hans beamed at him. "And now? Now I am SS. I live to serve the Führer and am grateful to be in his elite service." His voice dropped to a whisper. "And women are very excited by the uniform," he said with a grin and a wink at Peter.

It was partly because of Hans that Peter went back to Eutin for the summer. The apartment wasn't really big enough for the three of them. He worked for Tante Elsa, gardening, fixing the house, and preserving vegetables for winter. As the summer went on, more and more troops came marching right by the farm gate. Gerta rushed out to give them homemade bread and jam, apples, bits of cheese—whatever could be spared. In exchange they told her news. At first, all they talked about were the work camps that they were guarding. Boring and smelly work, they said. There was a big labor camp just on the outskirts of Hamburg, Neuengamme, where they had to watch the prisoners make bricks and dig canals.

Peter had heard about the work camps. They were the "economic engine of Germany," Herr Birkmann had said. Prisoners were sent to the camps to make the things Germany needed. He wasn't sure where all of the prisoners were coming from, though. He assumed most of them were prisoners of war, but he also knew that anyone who said anything against the Führer or the Reich was sent to work in a camp until he changed his mind. He thought of the Jehovah's Witness man. Hans Corm had said something about Jews being sent to the camps. Peter knew that Germany needed a lot of workers, and there certainly seemed to be a lot of guards walking past the farm.

But then the troops' talk was of the Soviet Union. The Non-Aggression Pact hadn't worked after all, and now Germany was at war with the Soviets. It was going to be a long march to get to Leningrad, but at least they weren't doing it in winter, they laughed. The war would be over before the winter, they said.

Because they were now at war with the Soviets, Peter had to bury his beautifully bound collection of Russian books. Not only was it forbidden to read them, but even owning them was illegal. He remembered his long days in the hospital, and wondered what had become of the Fraus and the rest of their libraries. He couldn't resist wrapping the books in an old blanket, like a shroud, before he lowered them into a hole behind the barn. *War and Peace* wasn't there, though. He must have left it back in Hamburg. *I'll have to remember to get rid of it when I get back*, he thought.

That autumn, when Peter went back to Hamburg, he was surprised to hear that Hans Corm had been deployed to Libya, in Africa. The war was stretching into countries he'd never even heard of. Then, just before Christmas, the Japanese bombed the Americans in a place called Pearl Harbor. At

Gymnasium, they scoured the maps to find the tiny island in the Pacific. The Americans declared war on Japan, and Germany declared war on the Americans. There didn't seem much to celebrate as 1942 began.

During the long winter nights, his mother listened to the radio broadcasts from the BBC in England. It was illegal to listen to foreign radio. He should have reported her to Scholl. But of course he would never do that. He tried to pretend he wasn't hearing it but, when the radio was on, he couldn't stop himself from listening. He knew it was wrong. The British said that *they* were winning the war, and they encouraged Germans to overthrow Hitler. They said they didn't want to bomb German cities, but that Hitler was forcing them to do so by his aggression against England.

Peter knew the British were lying. But the broadcasts gave him this odd sense of huge events taking place somewhere else, things he wasn't supposed to know about. He tried not to think about it.

Then one day Gunter came over with a pamphlet.

"I found it stuffed in my coat pocket," he explained. "I have no idea where it came from, or when it was put there. I know I should have reported it at once, but ... well, I don't know who wrote it."

The pamphlet was typed on red paper. A swastika was stamped on the front. Peter held it to the light.

German boys! Do you know the country without freedom, the country of terror and tyranny? Yes, you know it well but are afraid to talk about it. They have intimidated you to such an extent that you don't dare talk for fear of reprisals. Yes, you are right; it is Germany—Hitler Germany! Through their unscrupulous terror tactics against young and old, men and women, they have succeeded in making you spineless puppets to do their bidding ...

Peter stopped reading. He looked up at Gunter. "We have to burn it," he said. "We both have to forget that we have ever read it."

A tense silence filled the room. Writing such a thing—even reading such a thing—could put you in jail for life. Or worse.

"Who do you think wrote it?" Peter lowered his voice to a whisper. He thought about Gunter's father. Could he go that far? Would they have to report him?

"I don't know," said Gunter. "I don't want to show it to my father. I don't know what he'd say ..." Gunter let the words hang in the air. "You're the only person I could come to."

"I haven't read it. I have no intention of reading it," Peter said sharply. He opened the grate of the coal fire and shoved the pamphlet in. They both watched in silence as the paper curled and blackened. Peter stirred the ashes. He tried to make his mind a blank sheet, where the forbidden words didn't exist.

Peter forgot about the pamphlet until February, when his mother told him about a sixteen-year-old Hamburg boy named Helmuth Hübener who'd been arrested for writing anti-Nazi propaganda.

"It was in the newspaper," she said, her face grim. "He wrote about the things that the British say are happening here in Germany. Rumors. Lies. What he wrote was treason and he'll be executed."

Peter kept his face very still.

"You didn't know him, did you?" his mother asked anxiously.

"No," said Peter. "I've never heard of him."

"He passed out pamphlets to boys in the Hitlerjugend. He put things in people's coat pockets when they weren't looking. You've never seen any letters, have you?"

"No, of course not," he said.

"It says in the paper that a boy named Gerhard was arrested for just reading the letters and not reporting them." She searched Peter's face.

"I told you, I didn't read any letters," Peter snapped at her. "I don't know what you are talking about." He made his mind and his face a blank. He did not think about Gunter and Gunter's father.

Chapter Fourteen

Hamburg,
July 1943

... and I'm in a chair. Hans Corm is standing in front of me. He slaps me hard across the face and I start crying. I'm sobbing like a baby. I'm begging him for something. "You're a useless, fatherless bastard," he laughs. His face becomes Hermann's. "And your friend is a Jew." Suddenly I hear the sound of English voices laughing. And I'm in a hole, buried up to my neck, and Hermann is stacking books on my head. A page of *War and Peace* sticks to my face. It covers my mouth and nose and I can't breathe. "Traitor!" Hans mashes the books into the hole, suffocating me. I try to twist and struggle to get my hands free, but I'm pinned in the hole and I can't breathe, I can't scream, I can't ...

The sound of a siren jerks Peter to semi-consciousness. The dream fades, but a feeling of fear remains. He stumbles up, avoiding the mirror as he gathers his papers to go to the shelter. He's afraid the reflection might not be his.

Early in 1943, the Americans started bombing Germany. Their first target was Wilhelmshaven, which was only about

150 kilometers from Hamburg. Now that the Americans had joined with the British, there were twice as many bombers flying over the city. There were air raids every night, but few bombs actually fell on Hamburg. The planes were usually just passing over on their way to other cities.

Night after night of interrupted sleep took its toll. Peter stumbled through his work at Gymnasium. Sometimes he wasn't sure if he was awake or asleep. His fourteenth birthday went by in a haze.

But then in the spring, things quieted down. There were fewer air raids and little news. The summer of 1943 arrived with an unnatural stillness. All of Hamburg seemed to be on edge, waiting.

Peter walked along the edge of the Zoll Canal, searching through the rubble of the previous night's raid as he did most days. A flash of metal caught his eye and he pulled a silver key out from under some plaster. He dusted it off and was putting it in his pocket when a movement in the air made him look up. Paper was floating down from the sky. There were thousands of pieces of paper falling through the air, like yellow leaves falling from the birch trees in autumn. He stared as they twirled and danced on the breeze.

"Don't touch them!" a familiar voice behind him shouted. "They're poisoned. The enemy has poisoned the paper. Touch them and you will die!"

Peter turned and saw a uniformed Franz, his eyes wide, staring at the floating papers. In the two-and-a-half years since he'd seen him last, Franz had filled out. Peter had heard that Franz had gone for training in France. He wore the uniform of a senior Hitlerjugend cadet. Although he was short for eighteen, he was clearly muscular. His neck and upper body were thick. His eyes flicked nervously back and forth.

Peter instinctively put his hands behind his back, afraid that they might move on their own and grab a corner of the poisoned paper. But as the leaflets littered the ground, he leaned over to try and read them.

People of Hamburg, one began. It was written in bad German. He turned to see if anyone was watching him, but Franz had moved along the canal and was warning others not to touch the papers. He carefully turned a paper over with his foot. He could only read a portion.

Hamburg will be destroyed. You must leave the city immediately. We do not want to kill you. The Dictator Adolf Hitler must be stopped.

"Propaganda!" Peter wheeled around. Franz had returned. "They are trying to frighten us. DO NOT READ THEM! IT IS ILLEGAL TO READ THEM!"

Peter quickly turned away and rushed home, taking his front steps two at a time. He burst through the door and ran straight into Herr Ballin.

"There are papers floating from the sky," he panted breathlessly. "They say Hamburg will be destroyed," Peter gasped.

Herr Ballin pulled Peter into his apartment. He yanked open a drawer in his cabinet and thrust a small brochure into Peter's hands. "They're trying to frighten us. To intimidate us. To terrorize us. This Churchill is a madman!"

Peter turned the booklet over in his hands. *The Attack on*

Köln. "Last spring they unleashed all of their might on Köln," continued Herr Ballin. "They destroyed Köln's treasures, art that defined European culture. The greatest cathedral on the continent, a cathedral that took six and a half centuries to build, a cathedral considered sacrosanct by the entire civilized world—all of it they destroyed in mere minutes! But they did not destroy the will of the people. German people are stronger than Churchill's terror!" Herr Ballin's voice rose to a fevered pitch.

"Köln was destroyed?" Peter asked incredulously.

"Feel proud, Peter. It is because of the Hitlerjugend and the Nazi Party that losses were minimized. Civilians were cared for, fires were put out, and the city triumphed!"

"But I've read about Köln. It's supposed to be a beautiful city." Peter was stunned. How could he not know something this important?

"The city triumphed!" Herr Ballin repeated. He grabbed Peter by the shoulders and looked directly into his eyes. "We will not run. You, Peter, will be one of our heroes. We will show this madman, this terrorist, what German people are made of! And we will win this war!"

Later that night, Peter sat with his mother. Her reaction to the leaflets was different. "I do not think the same way as Herr Ballin," she whispered. "I'm not convinced that we are winning the war."

Peter opened his mouth to speak. He didn't want to hear his mother talking this way. But she held up her hand to stop him. "Our army has failed in Leningrad and Stalingrad." She lowered her voice to a whisper. "There are rumors that the

British bombed Düsseldorf last month. They say thousands died, and that the bombing caused a storm of fires, everything burning, people becoming living torches, trying to outrun the flames and becoming stuck in the melting asphalt."

"That's impossible," said Peter, trying to shake the horrific images from his mind.

She reached across to Peter's hands and held them. "It may be just a rumor. There's no way to know for sure. But if Hamburg is going be next, I don't want us to be here. I want us to survive this war."

"But we're safe here,' cried Peter. "We're protected. They've built that huge shelter in the park by the river and it's lined with FLAK towers that can knock out any bomber. Besides, Herr Ballin says the leaflets are just trying to frighten us."

"Maybe. Maybe," said his mother. "But Franz came this afternoon to tell us that your school and unit are being evacuated again. You are to report to the train station in the morning."

Peter let the weight of the words fill the room. He felt hugely conflicted. Hamburg had been relatively peaceful this spring, and he and his mother had established a good routine. But being evacuated meant travel, it meant adventure, it meant independence.

He carefully controlled his voice. "What about you?"

"I will go to Tante Elsa's," she said. "Just in case." He could see her struggle to relax the tension in her face and smile. "Don't worry. I'm sure it will be just a few weeks."

Peter kept his face a mask so as not to reveal his

excitement. He didn't want to hurt his mother, but he desperately wanted to be on his own again.

The next morning, he was on the train with the rest of the evacuees. They left on July 21. A lovely summer's day. Not a cloud in the sky. It felt unreal. It felt like a summer vacation. A summer vacation in Hungary.

Chapter Fifteen

July 1943

... Momma is running to me. Her dress is torn, the buttons undone. Her feet are bare, her face is covered in soot. Her hair is wild, flowing behind her. I'm in the canal, wet up to my neck. The sound of wind fills every space. My mouth won't work, I can't call her. Suddenly the edges of her hair spark and the fire catches her. It runs down her hair and jumps onto her dress. She is still running. She's almost at the canal. I reach to grab her but she stops and she's a pillar of flame. Flames shoot to the sky and become a column of smoke. The wind gusts through and the smoke is gone and there is nothing left. She is nowhere. There is only silence ...

Peter wakes with a start, gasping for breath. He is totally disoriented. There are sounds of other people breathing, gently snoring around him. A sense of gentle swaying. A far off mechanical sound. His heart is racing from his dream. What was it? Something about fire. He drifts back to sleep.

It took two days on the train to get to Donaueschingen at the mouth of the Danube. They'd been warned that this was the most dangerous part of the trip because the British were bombing all the train tracks. But they were on a secondary line, avoiding the large cities—Hannover, Frankfurt, Stuttgart—and chugging slowly through the countryside. Everywhere they stopped, women greeted the train with homemade breads, packets of cheese, bits of sausage. Peter felt pampered and cared for as they traveled the length of Germany and headed for the river.

In Donaueschingen, they walked the short distance from the train to the river. Rectangular fields planted with cabbages and flaxseed stretched out from the banks of the river. He was astonished by the quiet beauty of the Danube River. It was nothing like the turmoil of the huge ships on the Elbe. "The river of the future," Herr Hitler had called it.

A steamship with a large paddlewheel waited for them. Peter thought it looked like something out of a fairy tale, and was glad he'd brought his camera so he could take a photograph. Just like when he had arrived in Neumarkt three years ago, it was hard to believe that there was a war going on. But if it hadn't been for the war, he wouldn't have been evacuated. Not for the first time, he caught himself being grateful. The war was giving him a chance to travel and see the world. All he had to do was follow orders and train.

Peter stood on the deck. The steamboat moved slowly. As the river widened, Peter saw it fill with ships carrying cargo and supplies. Small Nazi boats buzzed on constant patrol, guarding them. He loved watching the busy activity on the river. It comforted him. Trade and commerce. It was a sign of things moving normally. The hot July sun sparkled and danced on the water. He hoped that his billets weren't going to be too strict. He was looking forward to whatever adventure he could find.

Chapter Sixteen

Bistriz, Hungary,
July 1943

"There are two girls," said Gunter.

"Girls?" repeated Peter.

Gunter nodded seriously.

"What kind of girls?" asked Peter.

"Girls, girls. Germans. Sisters. Fourteen and thirteen. Shy. They just stare at me all the time," said Gunter. "Who lives at your place?"

"Just the lawyer and his wife."

"I thought he was an officer," said Gunter

"He is. But not active. I think he's got something to do with the relocation. Wow! Quite the view!"

Peter and Gunter had climbed up to the cathedral on the hill to look out over their new home. Bistriz stretched out in front of them. Hundreds of low country houses with red tiled roofs were nestled together along tidy, tree-lined streets. Some of the streets were just dirt. No pavement, no cobblestones. In the distance were the soft purple peaks of the old mountain range. Very peaceful. Very rural. Foreign, yet German. A very different landscape from Neumarkt. Peter got out his camera and focused on the picturesque village.

"I think they might have had a boy," he continued as he clicked the picture. "But maybe he's dead. There's a photograph of a boy on the piano. I've pretty much got the place to myself."

"Sounds creepy," said Gunter. "But at least you don't have to share the bathroom with two staring girls."

"What are their names?"

"Olga and Marthe." They turned to head back into the town, toward the central square. "They're half Schwaben," Gunter said, his voice sounding unsure.

"The Schwaben are all right," said Peter. "They're German, after all."

"Oh, I know they are, but sometimes it's really hard to understand them," said Gunter. "I know they're speaking German, but their accents are so thick. I don't think they're very smart. I mean, how could they be, living out here?"

"Brains aren't everything," Peter said suggestively. "What do they look like?"

"Olga, the older one, is really pretty. Thick, dark brown braids. Soft, long eyelashes," said Gunter. "Just my type," he laughed.

"And she'd have to be pretty stupid to be interested in you," Peter joked. In the last year, he and Gunter had talked a lot about girls. It had brought them together again, although Peter still felt a slight sense of separation between himself and all his old friends. He assumed that was a natural way of growing up. None of them were children anymore.

They began to wind their way back toward the center of town.

"Scholl said that one of the reasons they sent us here for the evacuation is that the Führer wants to make sure there are more Germans all along the Danube," said Gunter. "There are plans to give houses and money to anyone who settles here, anyone who marries a Schwabe." He grinned at Peter slyly. "So maybe I could just do a bit of patriotic duty." He puffed out his chest. "In two years I'll be sixteen and in training as an officer. I'll need a sweetheart to think about when I'm at the front!"

"I think you'll have other things to think about when they send you to the front," laughed Peter. "Besides," he added, "in two years the war will be over for sure. Then you can come back here and while away your life as a country bumpkin, raise a pack of Schwaben kids, and learn how to talk good. You'll fit in real well."

Gunter smacked him on the head and Peter raced down the hill. They came out on a boulevard, where a couple sat at a café table sipping coffee in the shade. Peter was aware of the couple watching them as they ran along the street and turned into the archway of a colonnade. Just like in Neumarkt, he was an outsider, a stranger. But he had full rights to be here in Hungary. The Führer had sent him here as a member of HJ. He had a sudden flash of resentment. How dare they look at him that way? They were the foreigners, not him.

It was midday and the July heat was baking Bistriz's central square. Wagons waited idly. Horses drooped under the glare of the sun. Peter felt slightly nauseous as he watched flies crawling in the yellow goop in the corner of a horse's eye. They turned to walk in the shade of the arches of the colonnade.

"They said I could invite you to dinner," said Gunter.

"Who did?"

"Frau Egeler. The mother."

"You sure you want me to meet your Schwabe girlfriend? Don't you think she'll want to run away with me once she's met me?"

"Well," said Gunter, "there are two of them. I really can't manage them both." Gunter affected a world-weary pose. "Frau Egeler said tomorrow night. If it's all right with your people."

Peter sniffed. He hated these rules. He resented having to check to see if it was all right. But Herr Birkmann had made it clear that they had to be polite to their billets.

"I'll ask tonight," Peter replied. "They're already setting the table for me three times a day. Not that I'm complaining about the food. But I feel like I'm their prisoner. And I don't know what they'll think about me hanging around with Schwaben. The way they talk, they must be German royalty."

They turned a corner and came into the central market square.

"Whoa!" said Gunter.

The square was packed. There was color and noise everywhere. It felt like a carnival. Peter felt his mood suddenly lighten. He hadn't seen a full market in years. In Hamburg you were lucky to find an old turnip rotting in the back of your cupboard. In Neumarkt, food only came to them through the nuns. When had buying and selling food become an unusual sight? When had a market become an extraordinary event? The colors, the smells, the noise were all a shock to Peter's system. He'd gotten used to a city perpetually drenched in sepia and gray.

Dark Gypsy women dressed in leather skirts were sitting on the ground beside woven cloths and bright fabrics. Village women were fingering the materials, testing the weave. There were stands all through the market square, covered with piles of onions, potatoes, carrots, and cabbages. Men dressed in heavy woolen coats—despite the heat— stood beside rows of straw hats. In one corner, he saw goats tethered to a wooden stake and rabbits crammed together in a wooden cage. A heavy smell of goulash reached his nostrils. His eyes searched until he saw a broad-faced Gypsy woman stirring a huge cauldron set out over an open fire.

"Grawwk!"

A sudden squawk beside him made him jump.

"Tell the future! Tell the future! Grawwk!" A bright orange parrot sat on top of a wooden stand under the shade of a large black umbrella. He stared at Peter with dark beads of eyes. Peter grabbed his camera out of his rucksack and snapped a picture.

"Who are you? Who are you?" squawked the parrot.

"Tell your fortune, young man?" A quiet crinkly voice rose from a bundle of dark clothes. Peter looked down to see the small face of an ancient, wizened woman. She was sitting on the ground below the parrot, staring at him intently.

"I ... I mean ... we ..." Peter stammered. He slid the

camera back into the pack, suddenly embarrassed about behaving like a tourist. The woman was so strange, so alien, but so intense. He couldn't take his eyes off her. He felt as though he was in the middle of some exotic legend. Could she know the future? His future?

"How much?" Gunter suddenly piped up. Peter had forgotten that he was standing beside him.

"Not you," said the voice. "You," she said, staring into Peter's eyes.

"But ... I don't have any money."

"Yes, you do. You have a pfennig. A pfennig for a tale."

Peter felt as though he were hypnotized. He stood outside of himself, watching himself reach into his pocket and pull out a pfennig. He didn't know how it had gotten there. He watched himself hold it out to the old woman and saw her gnarled fingers take it, her eyes never leaving his. She lifted the coin to her mouth and bit it. Satisfied, her hand went to her lap and searched until it found a pocket in the folds of her skirt. Peter saw this, his eyes still held by hers. His ears were filled with the sound of his blood pumping and a thick silence. It was like being underwater.

"You will make a promise, a pact, with yourself. You will travel across the ocean to live in forests."

The heat haze pressed in on Peter. There was no sound. He felt suspended in time. For a brief moment, he wondered if he was going to faint. Or drown. But still her eyes held his.

"You will know love, you will know death. You will walk, but you will never find peace. You will forget, and you will live. And one day you will remember and tell the story."

"Grwaak! Tell the future! Tell the future!" The parrot suddenly jolted Peter out of his trance. The woman looked away. She seemed to shrink into herself and go to sleep. Clearly, the fortune-telling was over.

"Well, that was a waste of a good pfennig," said Gunter as they walked away. "What about the usual—you will be rich, marry a beautiful girl, and have eight Schwaben children?"

Peter felt as though he were emerging from a deep sleep, trying to recall a dream on the edge of his memory. As he grasped at it, it shredded like bits of gauze. He turned to Gunter.

"Do you remember anything she said?"

"Some mumbo jumbo about a promise and walking and forgetting. Oh, yeah, and something about living in a forest. Look, if you've got any more money to throw away, do you think we could buy some of that goulash? I'm starving!"

Peter turned back to look at the old Gypsy woman. From a distance, she looked like nothing more than a pile of old rags, topped with a bright headscarf. The parrot sat motionless under the umbrella. What had she said? A promise? Forests. You will live.

Could knowing the future change the course of events?

A sound broke into his thoughts. The sound of ... he looked to his left and saw one of the Gypsy women squatting in the dirt, lifting her leather skirt, and relieving herself. She caught his eye and laughed wickedly as he looked away.

A waste of money. He suddenly hated this place, and he hated that his life was on hold. How could he have a future when he didn't even have a present?

Chapter Seventeen

Bistriz, Hungary,
July 1943

As it turned out, Herr Schnauble did not allow Peter to have his first Sunday dinner with Gunter. "Perhaps another night, Peter," he said gruffly. "You are here as our guest and as a part of our family. We will have Sunday dinner together." And so Peter sat down to his first formal Sunday meal in Bistriz.

He had spent the day indoors, reading. Although it was a beautiful hot summer's day, Frau Schnauble had insisted that he stay in the house. "Our habits may be different from yours, but it is important for you to fit in for the time you are with us."

Truth be told, Peter was actually grateful for the time alone. He'd had days on the train, followed by days on the boat, and had not had a moment to himself. The fortune-teller had unnerved him and he felt tired.

The Schnaubles' house was clean and sparse. Peter found it hard to get comfortable. There were so many rules. Take off your shoes when you come in and leave them by the door. Don't put your feet up on the sofa. Never leave a glass on a table, except at meals. Hang up your clothes. Fold your underwear and put it in the dresser drawer.

However, he had a room to himself for the first time in his life. Frau Schnauble had made it clear that she would always knock before coming in, but that she expected him to keep the room tidy. When he arrived, he'd changed out of his travel clothes and, without thinking, left his socks lying on the floor. She patiently showed him where to put his "soiled clothes" so that they could be washed.

So although Peter stretched out on his bed to read for the day, he was wary. He wasn't sure if it was all right to put his feet on the bed while wearing his socks.

Had it really come to this?

But he knew he needed to try. It had more to do with the rules of the Hitlerjugend than anything else. He must be a model of the Party, exemplary in character. Here, in the middle of Hungary, there were not many Party members. The Hungarian government had taken over the area from the Romanians in 1940, so the people were still quite backward in their thinking. It was part of the job of the HJ to inspire the Schwaben Volk and other pure Germans so that they could work with the Hungarians and take their rightful place as rulers of the country. From what he could see, they were sorely needed. The place was backward and primitive.

He could hear Frau Schnauble moving quietly in the other room, starting her long, careful preparation of the afternoon meal. "Tick. Tock. Tick. Tock." The grandfather clock slowly marked the passing day. He opened the new book they were reading in German class. *Faust*, by Johann von Goethe. His eyes took in the richly textured illustrations, the seductive, evil eyes.

Tick. Tock. The smell of stew wafted into Peter's room.

Let us sate the fervors of passion
in depths of sensuality!
May your magic be ready at any time
to show me miracles whose veil cannot be lifted!

Tick. Tock. The heat of the day made the room airless.

... Gunter's face is close. I can smell his breath. It makes me think of strawberries. He puts his hand on my cheek. I don't want it there. I move my face away; my mouth is on his lips, and I know I should move away but I can't, and he's kissing me and Hermann is laughing. 'He's mine!' and his eyes are glowing with hate and he is a dog; he's growling and ...

Peter's moan wakes him. The book is heavy on his chest. The heat of the room makes him feel sick.

Dinner was stew. It was mostly potatoes, but there was a brown gravy, a few carrots, and small bits of meat. Frau Schnauble made a dark heavy bread to go with it. Peter scooped up a huge spoonful. He hadn't realized how hungry he was. He couldn't remember the last time he'd had a stew like this. His actions were fast and noisy, so it took him a moment to realize that the Schnaubles hadn't yet begun. They were both quietly watching him with their hands in their laps. He stopped with his spoon in mid-air, not entirely sure what he'd done wrong. But he put the spoon down and swallowed his mouthful.

"We grew up saying grace and we've never really gotten out of the habit," explained Herr Schnauble.

"Not that we are religious," Frau Schnauble hastened to add. "We just take a moment before we eat, a moment to be grateful for the food. With the war, we are very grateful to have anything."

"Sorry," Peter muttered, looking at his half-finished bowl.

The Schnaubles bowed their heads and closed their eyes for just a moment. They seemed to take a breath together. Then Frau Schnauble looked up at Peter with a smile on her face. She picked up her fork.

"We realize that you must be very hungry—a big growing boy like you—and this must all seem so strange and new," she said. "But we are glad to have you with us. It is something else we are grateful for. Now, please, eat." She delicately took a bit of potato from her bowl, blew on it, and placed it in her mouth.

"It's very good," mumbled Peter.

"Thank you, Peter. You are very kind," said Frau Schnauble.

I may go mad here, thought Peter.

The next day was the first day of school. Frau Schnauble insisted that he have a piece of toast and a small bit of cheese before heading out the door. "I hope your day goes well," she said as he left. "I will look forward to hearing all about it tonight."

Peter headed down the dusty street and met up with Otto and Gunter coming from their billets.

"The woman I'm staying with has got me doing chores already," complained Otto. "I spent the weekend digging a hole for a new outside privy." He spread his hands to show wet and weeping blisters. "Her husband's in the army and she's got three little kids. She says she's happy to have the free labor."

"Too bad you couldn't come to my place for dinner last night," Gunter said playfully. "Olga and Marthe were showing off their Schwaben costumes. They told me there's a special festival coming up—St. Bartholomew's Day—at the end of August. They showed me the dresses they'll wear. There'll be dances and lots of great food."

"Remember the Christmas festival in front of the Rathaus when we were little?" said Otto. "There was always something good to eat."

Peter smiled with the memory.

"Their costumes are kind of strange," Gunter continued. "They've got these big puffy white sleeves," he said, gesturing and describing with his hands. "The skirts go all the way to the ground, and they've got flowers and hearts and things running around the bottom. But the really funny part is these little hats that sit on the top of their heads. They're sort of a tube, just kind of perched there, with long ribbons streaming off them."

"You sound like a dressmaker," Otto said jokingly.

Gunter started parading down the street, swinging his hips and holding his hands above his head in a circle. "Oh, yes, I'm a fancy Schwabe on holiday," he laughed.

"Hey, cut it out." Peter was suddenly irritable.

"What?"

"Don't make fun of them."

"I'm not! Geesh, what's the matter with you this morning?"

"Nothing. I just don't think we should make fun of them. They're Germans and they've got different traditions. That's all."

Peter had noticed a man up the street, eyeing them as Gunter did his little performance.

"I wasn't making fun of them. I was just showing Otto what they looked like."

The man was walking straight toward them. He was wearing a yellow star. He was on a direct course to them. There wouldn't be enough room on the sidewalk for all of them. The man's eyes flickered to meet his. Suddenly he pulled a gun out and aimed it right at Peter.

"Wha—" Gunter froze mid-sentence. The man was still walking toward them. Without thinking, Peter took two steps back off the sidewalk and stood in the street to give the man room to pass. He walked straight past, his jaw stiff, his eyes staring straight ahead.

The three of them stood stock still until he'd rounded the corner and moved out of sight. Otto let out a deep breath.

"What the hell was that all about?"

"Guess he just wanted to walk on the sidewalk," said Peter warily.

"Wasn't a real gun, you know," said Gunter.

"What?" said Otto.

"It was a starter pistol. We use them all the time in the races. Besides, a Jew wouldn't be able to have a gun. He was

just some crazy creep. Didn't scare me at all. School time!"
Gunter bounded in the door of a long, low building.

Peter shook off the image of the man and the gun. So
much in Bistriz was foreign. School, at least, was familiar.
He was looking forward to the normalcy, to being surrounded
by all of his friends and classmates. Strangely, he was even
looking forward to seeing Hermann.

"I hope you have settled in well with your billets," said Herr
Birkmann. "I realize things are a bit different from your
homes in Hamburg. But here in Bistriz we'll be able to
continue your training, and you will be able to show the local
people what the youth of Germany are made of.

"Your studies will continue where we left off in June.
Geography, mathematics, science—these will be your focus
at school. But even more important will be your training as a
Hitlerjugend member. Now that you have graduated from
Jungvolk, you will have more track and field events, boxing,
archery, and swimming. You will take Physical Education
tests at the end of the month. Anyone failing these tests will
be expelled from the school."

Boxing! Ever since the fight with Hermann in Neumarkt,
Peter had wanted to get better. He'd scared himself with his
violence. He thought that if he could control a fight through
skill, he would be less brutal but more effective.

"This is Karl, your new group leader," Herr Birkmann
continued. "You'll start with him today, right now, out in the
field behind the school. It is far too nice a day to be inside."

Peter's heart leapt at the idea of spending the day

outdoors. He filed out with the others, following Karl's broad back. Karl's light brown hair gleamed in the sunlight. It was carefully trimmed, every hair in place. Peter could tell that it had been recently cut—Karl had a dark bronze tan, but there was a pale streak around his hairline.

Behind the school was a huge grassy field, bordered by low wooden fences that blocked off the neighborhood houses. Peter had never seen such a large field in the middle of a town. The short stubbly grass was dry from a summer of little rain.

"Formation!" shouted Karl. Peter easily fell into his old school habits. "Strip down to your undershorts." He quickly pulled off his shirt, tie, and short pants. The air was dry on his skin. "Fifty push-ups. Go!"

Peter felt joy as his muscles strained, the sun warmed his back, and sticky sweat tickled around his ears. He wanted to be the best that he could be.

After an hour of push-ups, sit-ups, squat jumps, and runs, Peter's muscles were wobbly and his body was glistening with sweat. He lay down on the stubby grass and looked up at the clear blue sky. All around him he could hear the voices of the other boys, laughing and happy.

"I see your billets are fattening you up already."

Hermann stood looking down at him. Over the last two years, Peter and Hermann had entered into a truce. Peter knew that Hermann liked to goad him, but it was all empty words. Time had brought, if not friendship, then at least a familiarity where they both recognized that they were on the same side. They were all working together as a team. The future belonged to them collectively, not as individuals.

"It's the least they can do for the Fatherland," Peter joked back. "I hope your billets have got lots of soap and hot water— I can smell your push-ups from over here."

"Ha!" snorted Hermann. "They've got an endless supply of Jewish soap. It's the least *they* can do for the Fatherland!"

Peter frowned up at Hermann. He wasn't sure he understood the comment, but before he could ask, Karl interrupted.

"Okay. Break's over. Hike time. Get those uniforms back on and let's show this town what you're made of."

Peter thought it was funny to be "showing off" for this backward little medieval village in the middle of nowhere. But he knew that he was representing the future of Germany, the future of Europe. The town had been under Romanian and Hungarian rule for centuries and was filled with Gypsies, Hungarians, Transylvanians, and Jews. As far as he could tell, the Germans—the Schwaben—were in the minority. But now that the Hungarian government had made a pact with Germany, more Germans would come to live here after the war. That's why it was so important to set a good example.

Peter felt momentarily chilled as his sweat started to dry. But he was happy to march on such a day. They headed out of the field and onto one of the streets that led away from the town.

It was midday. The sun was high and the streets were quiet and still. Peter wasn't sure where everyone was. Ever since the market on Saturday, the town had seemed pretty deserted. How could they show off their strength if there was no one around? They rounded a corner and, as they passed a large white temple, he heard glass crunching under his boots. He looked down and saw glass everywhere on the sidewalk and on the road. He looked up at the building—all the windows were broken. Karl stopped and the group stared.

"It was a synagogue," Otto said quietly.

"That's one of the reasons they sent us here," said Hermann behind them. "These people had a big school connected to their church. As if they had anything to teach!" He snorted.

"Where'd you hear that?" asked Peter.

"My billets told me last night." Hermann spoke authoritatively. Peter suddenly remembered Otto's secret. He didn't dare look at him. "Jewish schools have been illegal for years, but no one bothered to stop it. They're stopped now. My billets told me that the Schwaben got together, went into the synagogue, pulled everything into the middle, and lit a fire. They burned the books and anything they could find. The fire was so big it blew out the windows," Hermann continued. "I wish I could have been here. It would have been quite a sight!"

Peter thought about the man with the star and the gun. He wondered if he'd been part of the school.

"They said those Jews'll be back at work now," Hermann continued. "There's a camp close by. They'll be there doing the work they should be doing."

"Forward," called Karl. They fell in line, marching behind him, and turned a corner. A beautiful river flowed along the edge of the town. The road became a bridge and they crossed to the other side and into the cool of a forest. Large pine trees shaded them and a sharp, sweet smell rose from sticky pine needles underfoot. The town vanished from sight. The road wound through the woods, occasionally opening to a clearing that revealed small log cottages. Peter felt a deep happiness.

"Forward, Forward, The Fanfares sound!" Karl began singing at the top of his lungs, his voice filling the woods.

"Forward, Forward, We know not danger!" They were all singing, singing as they marched through the woods. Peter felt the skin on his face taut from smiling.

"Germany, you will stand shining, Even if we perish."

It was a glorious moment out of time. Peter wasn't thinking of the future. He wasn't thinking of the past. He was just here, in this moment of sunshine in the woods, marching and singing.

The trees cleared and he could see that the road led across a short dam. On one side was a deep reservoir, on the other a long lake.

"Forward! Forward!"

And suddenly he was running. They were all running, unknotting ties, ripping off their uniforms, jumping on one foot, pulling off sweaty socks and underwear, and leaping into the air with great whoops and cries, hitting the gloriously cool water, surfacing with splashes and laughter.

He'd never felt so alive.

The first weeks of school were filled with days of exercise, marching, and swimming. As the days became shorter and the sun less intense, they began to spend more time indoors. A boxing ring was set up inside the auditorium. Peter felt his new muscles press against the fabric of his uniform. He was aware of being taller. His hair and his skin were golden. When he spoke carefully, his voice was deep. Frau Schnauble always gave him the choicest bits of meat for dinner. She somehow managed to get butter for his bread, and cheese and sausage for breakfast.

"Now you look like a god," she said, her voice tinged with pride. "A Teutonic god. You will do us proud!"

In class they focused on geography and history. Every day, it seemed, there was new information about the changing borders of the Reich. The empire, his empire, was stretching throughout Europe.

When he finally met the Egeler family, he was welcomed with open arms. Aside from Olga and Marthe, there was little Bruno and baby Tomas. It was a big, noisy household, filled with laughter—the opposite of his own billets, who were so quiet Peter thought he might explode. He joked and played with Bruno and told stories about his life in Hamburg to Olga and Marthe. Soon he was a regular fixture at their house. The thought of being with the Egelers made it possible for him to get through the week at the Schnaubles.

And Olga. Gunter was right—she was beautiful. Her long brown braids framed a kind, round face. It hadn't taken long for Peter to make her laugh and for her to overcome her shyness. She seemed interested in everything he said, everything he thought. He spent his days thinking of stories to tell her, stories about Hamburg and his past life, stories that would impress her, delight her.

"Peter?" Frau Egeler was clearing his plate from the table.

"Yes, Frau Egeler?"

"Would you like to come with us to our cabin this Friday night? Do you think that the Schnaubles can spare you? We'd be back on Sunday morning in good time for your Sunday meal."

"Thank you, Frau Egeler. I would like that very much. I will ask Frau Schnauble tonight."

And so it was done. Frau Schnauble hesitated but she couldn't complain. The Schnaubles knew the Egelers, of course, and were polite about them. But Peter could tell that they didn't really approve. Frau Schnauble's list of instructions about personal cleanliness and hygiene were re-doubled whenever he went to the Egelers.

Peter had endeared himself to the Egelers by his love for their horse Beau. Beau was a beautiful, rich brown bay, with a glossy black mane and tail, and a large white blaze running down his face. He was healthier, stronger, and younger than Willy, Gerd's horse, but he reminded Peter of his time on the docks. It seemed a hundred years ago.

Peter arrived on Friday afternoon with an apple core in his pocket, which he held out to Beau as Herr Egeler harnessed him to their old-fashioned wagon.

"I know we should get a truck," Herr Egeler said, "but with the price of petrol these days ... well, it just makes sense to keep on using this old wagon as long as we can."

Just what Gerd said, thought Peter. He wondered what had happened to Gerd and Willy. Horsemeat was pretty valuable in Hamburg. He buried his fingers in Beau's mane and inhaled the warm smell of the horse.

Herr and Frau Egeler sat up in the front of the wagon with baby Tomas, while he, Gunter, Olga, Marthe, and Bruno crowded into the back. Marthe got in and sat against the back of the wagon, facing forward. "I feel sick if I have to face backwards."

"That's all right," said Olga," I'm happy to sit up here," she said, taking her place with her back against the bench seat.

Gunter sat along one side. "I guess that puts me over here, facing your ugly mug," teased Peter as he sat down opposite his friend.

"I get to sit beside Peter!" squealed Bruno. Bruno had quickly become Peter's sidekick, following him everywhere. "And you can tell me the rest of the story about Franz and the broken bike and the jazz records. What's a jazz record, anyway?" He wiggled down beside Peter, squirming his legs onto everyone else's in the middle of the wagon.

"Here, spread this over you. The sun is beginning to go down and it will start to get cool," said Frau Egeler, passing them a scratchy orange and brown plaid blanket. It had bits of straw stuck to it.

The wagon jerked as Beau stepped forward and, under the blanket, Peter's hand brushed against Olga's. He froze. His heart began to pound. He felt her hand slowly move closer and, without thinking, he was holding it. He didn't dare look at her face. He kept talking to Bruno, telling him about his life on the docks, but all he could think about was Olga's hand.

The cabin was like something out of a storybook. There was an allotment for growing potatoes, carrots, and cabbages. There was a small barn where the Egelers kept chickens. Oma Egeler, Olga and Marthe's grandmother, met them at the door. The smell of freshly baked bread and chicken dumpling stew enveloped them.

After supper, they sat at the table playing *Schwarzer Peter*. The losing card was a picture of the clown *Schwarzer Peter* falling off a ladder, and it seemed to always end up in Peter's hand. But he didn't mind getting stuck with his namesake card and losing. Bruno drew a picture of Peter as a clown falling over, and he laughed and laughed. Peter looked over at Olga. Her eyes were shining brightly, as though they were polished stones.

The cabin had only two bedrooms, so all the children bunked down on the floor for the night. Bruno squeezed in on one side of Peter. Gunter plunked himself down on the other. Olga and Marthe stretched out on blankets under the table.

"Good night, Oma. Good night, Papa. Good night, Momma," Marthe and Olga called out in singsong voices.

"Good night, good night, good night," Bruno rattled off.

"Sleep well, everyone," said Frau Egeler, cradling baby Tomas in her arms as she left the room.

Peter lay quietly thinking. He'd never experienced this kind of fairy tale family. He'd lived in the country, but Tante Elsa's house was drenched in sadness. It was a house where people died. Here people lived, laughed, and loved.

Did people actually live like this? Could he live like this? He thought of his mother, of their small family of two. He wondered where she was now.

Peter's mind slowly became awake. It was very, very dark and very, very quiet. He listened to the sound of quiet breathing all around him. The cottage didn't have running water and he knew he had to leave his warm blankets and go outside to pee. He didn't want to wake anyone, so he moved slowly, carefully, as he had always known how to do. His feet stretched across the floor, his toes searching out the quietest places on the creaky wooden floor. He held his breath as he lifted the latch and let himself out into the night.

It was moonless, but the light from an infinity of stars was enough to see by. He walked away from the cabin to do his business behind the outhouse. As he peed, he stared up at the sky. Had there always been so many stars? Had pine trees always smelled so sweet? He listened to the deep silence around him and felt a slight shiver as the night chill began to cool him. He finished and began to make his way back to the cabin door when something brushed his arm. He jumped and almost screamed, but a soft hand covered his mouth and a quiet "shhhhh" filled his ear. He turned to see Olga standing in her nightdress, pale under the dark sky and so very, very beautiful. She backed up and he followed her to the far side of the barn, away from the cabin. The cold earth was hard beneath his feet, but he was holding her hand and she was leading him into the barn. His feet touched the scratchy straw. He heard the small snuffling sounds of chickens sleeping. It was darker here, out of the starlight, but his eyes adjusted and he could see her pale face shining against her dark hair. She leaned her back against the wall, still holding his hand and squeezing it softly.

And he was kissing her. There was nothing in this moment but him and her. And there was everything in this moment, this moment of kissing, of love, of stars, and of night.

And then she was gone. And his life was changed forever.

All through the autumn, Peter spent his weekends with the Egelers at their cabin. Gunter asked him once if there was something going on between him and Olga. Peter had just taken a secret photograph of Olga outside the barn, her hair blowing softly in the breeze. His mind was filled with the image, but he'd laughed and shrugged and said, "Of course not. Don't be jealous." He felt guilty because he knew Gunter didn't believe him and was hurt. He knew he should tell him, but he wanted to keep it private, a secret. He felt as though he and Olga were playing a game, a game where they pretended not to notice each other. But his mind was filled only with her. School became impossible. All he could think of was Friday night, the cabin, the barn. The ache for her was terrible.

Once, when their kissing was getting very exciting, she suddenly stopped and whispered, "This is only kissing. No more." She looked deeply into his eyes and he realized he was pressed hard against her, his whole body rigid. The force of his need was overwhelming, blinding. He felt a flash of anger. Then he looked at her and saw fear. Her fear jolted him. He tried to slow his breath and kiss her gently, while his body screamed.

With November came the rains. The short days were dark and dreary. There were no trips to the reservoir, no trips to the cabin. The school building was cold and damp, the Schnaubles' house was cold and damp. The only time Peter was comfortable was when he was at the Egelers'. The large family made their tiny house feel warm.

He'd been in Hungary almost three months.

It was Friday night. He had just come back from school, had dumped his books in his bedroom, and was about to head over to the Egelers' when Herr Schnauble stopped him.

"Peter. We need to have a talk."

Peter looked at his host. His mind raced, trying to think of what he had done wrong, how he might have offended Herr Schnauble. All he could think of was Olga. Had Herr Schnauble found out what was on Peter's mind night and day?

"There's something I have to tell you," Herr Schnauble said. "Please. Come sit." He guided Peter toward the table.

The way Herr Schnauble spoke made Peter go very still inside. This wasn't about Olga. Peter moved across the room and sat down.

"It's bad news." Herr Schnauble paused. His eyes drilled into Peter's face. "Hamburg was bombed, just after you left."

Is that all? thought Peter. *Hamburg was bombed all the time while I was there.*

Herr Schnauble swallowed. The sound seemed to fill the room. "This was not a regular bombing," he said, in response to the question that hadn't been asked.

Peter took a moment for the words to sink in. "What do you mean?"

"Just after you left the city, the British, Canadians, and Americans dropped many thousands of bombs on Hamburg. The British and Canadians bombed all night. The Americans bombed all day. For two days and two nights. The bombing set off fires, what is called a firestorm. In those two days, the city became an inferno. Huge sections of the city were incinerated."

Hamburg will be destroyed. You must leave the city.

A vein in Peter's temple began to throb. "Like Köln? Düsseldorf?" he asked.

"Worse."

Peter's mind began to race. "But what about the huge shelter? What about the FLAK towers? The gunners were supposed to protect the city." His voice began to rise. "What went wrong?!"

"Apparently the English dropped metal strips from their planes," said Herr Schnauble. "The strips threw off the radar. The gunners couldn't find the bombers in the rain of metal strips." Herr Schnauble looked down at his hands. He swallowed. He looked up at Peter. "They think there may have been forty thousand people who died in the fires."

The words sat between them.

"Hamburg is gone," said Herr Schnauble quietly.

Peter could hear his blood pulsing in his ears. *Hamburg is gone.* Three years ago his mother had said, "Opa is gone." Opa was one sad little man. Hamburg was a city. Forty thousand people?

The leaflets had tried to warn them.

"When?"

"July. July 23 and 24."

He had left on July 21. Had his mother left, as she said she would? Did she get out that day? The next day?

Peter's chest felt tight. His throat constricted. All this time he had been picturing his mother in their apartment, or with Tante Elsa in Eutin. "*Just a few weeks,*" she had said.

Anger jerked his head to face Herr Schnauble.

"Why are you telling me this now? Months later?"

"We were just told. Communications were down. It took a long time for the information to reach us here." Herr Schnauble took a deep breath. "I'm sorry."

Herr Ballin, and Oma Ballin. Gunter's father.

"All of the billets have been instructed to tell you children today," said Herr Schnauble. Peter noticed his use of the word "children." *Is that what I am? A child? An orphan child?*

"You are a refugee now." Herr Schnauble's mouth was pursed with tension. "You will continue to stay with us until the spring, at the least, until Hamburg is habitable again."

Suddenly Peter was up. His chair clattered to the floor. In three strides he was out the door and on the move.

His feet pounded the ground. His fury drove him. He wanted to get as far away from Herr Schnauble as possible.

He wasn't an orphan. He wasn't a refugee. He was someone whose home had been destroyed.

I should have been there.

He ran.

I should have been there. I should have died with Momma, with Oma Ballin, with my city—not exiled in this stupid foreign country in the middle of nowhere.

His mind swirled with pictures. Burned trees. Crumbled buildings.

I have to get back. I'll jump on trains. I'll hitch rides with passing cars.

I'll ... what? Swim the Danube River?

He was in the forest, his feet pounding on the hard ground. Home.

The docks. The warehouses. Little side streets he knew so well. His mother. *Where was she?!*

He was gulping at the cold air.

These last three months had been a lie.

I've been sitting here getting conceited and self-centered, smug and fat. Falling in love. I've been tricked, tricked by them all, tricked into coming here, tricked into falling in love. It's a lie. All of it. A goddamned lie.

Tick Tock. In his brain the Schnaubles' grandfather clock, again and again. Tick. Tock.

He ran and ran.

Then he was at the reservoir, screaming across the water, trying to empty himself of words, of thoughts. He screamed until his throat was raw and his stomach was twisted into a cramp. He screamed as he smashed his fists into a tree, smashing until blood splattered from his hands. Smashing and screaming across the miles and the months.

And when he was finally finished, when there was nothing left in him, he was overcome by an emptiness as vast as the sky. He was startled to look up and see stars. In Hamburg, he'd never noticed the stars because the city was always so bright at night. But the same stars twinkled above Hamburg, mocking his city, as though it was a place. As though it had been important.

His mind was numb as he stripped off his clothes and plunged into the icy water. He welcomed the shock that took away his breath. He went under to wash off the pain in his hands, to wash off the past.

He pulled himself out, shook off as best he could, and began to dress.

And then he walked. Back toward Bistriz but not into the town. Around, following the walled battlements. Not touching the town. Not yet. He walked as the darkness deepened. Not seeing. Not hearing. The entire circumference of the town and then around again. Until at last the sky began to lighten. Had he heard church bells ringing the hour? Distant sounds of movement, people starting their Saturday morning.

Home was gone forever.

As the dull sun came up, exhaustion overtook him. He wandered through the Sugalete, weaving aimlessly through the passageways from the castle walls. Under the shadow of the tall stone church tower, his mind flashed to St. Nikolai Kirche. For as long as he could remember, the cathedral marked his way home. Home to his mother.

All of his landmarks were gone.

Mechanically, his feet reached the Schnaubles' house, dark and still with its tick, tock, and he crawled into bed with his clothes on, not even caring about his mud-covered boots between Frau Schnauble's clean sheets.

Chapter Eighteen

Bistriz, Hungary,
Winter 1944

It was two weeks before Peter could speak, a month before
his voice was back to normal. But he didn't care. He had
nothing he wanted to say. There were no words. He felt locked
away inside himself. He had no interest in anything or
anybody.

For a while he continued to go to the Egelers' for Friday
dinner, if only to get away from the Schnaubles' oppressive
concern. The Egelers seemed to respect his silence. Gunter
had tried to talk to him. He knew that Gunter was scared for
his family, but he couldn't make himself care. He didn't want
to share his emptiness. He no longer sought out Olga's eyes.

Eventually the tension at the Egelers' became so uncomfortable that Peter told them he had too much homework and
couldn't come over. He spent his Friday nights sitting silently,
eating at the Schnaubles' table, blocking out the sound of the
clock and the Schnaubles' doleful looks. He spent all weekend
reading in his room.

At Christmas, Frau Schnauble made a special roast goose with chestnut stuffing. Peter had never had anything like it before, not even before the war. Frau Schnauble's gift to him was a used copy of *The Magic Mountain*, by the German, Thomas Mann.

"I know that we are not supposed to read his books now, but I have had this copy for a very long time. I thought you might like it," Frau Schnauble said shyly.

Peter managed a weak smile, for their sakes. As soon as he could, he retreated to his room.

The Magic Mountain began in Hamburg. At first he was furious. He didn't want to be reminded. But the story drew him in, and soon it was a comfort to go back in time and live in his city again. He stepped into the world of Hans, empathizing with his being an only child and an orphan. He secretly imagined *he* was Hans, leaving his home to learn about politics, culture, and love. In his mind, he played out the final scene on the battlefield again and again. It was easy for him to feel he was part of the book. He could almost believe Hamburg was still there.

That winter was hard. Apparently Regent Horthy, who ran Hungary, had disagreed with the Führer about how to run the country. The Schnaubles argued at dinner about the number of Jews that should be deported. Of course they sided with the Führer. Peter couldn't understand why anyone would bother to disagree with the Führer. But mostly, he couldn't see why any of it mattered. All winter, Peter went through the motions, as though nothing had happened. He assumed that's what everyone was doing. He was numb.

If he thought about it at all, he heard Herr Ballin's voice in his ear, talking about Köln. "The city has triumphed."

Then in March, when Germany officially took over Hungary, Peter could definitely feel the difference. The Hungarians in Bistriz who had been pleasant and welcoming were now distant and cold. Where they used to exchange pleasantries in broken German, they now crossed the street to avoid him.

There was little discussion of Hamburg at school. Herr Birkmann had said he didn't have much information. "I don't know the facts," he'd said, "and until I do, I don't want to comment." As a group, they were cut adrift, floating in this place, waiting, imagining.

And then in April, just as suddenly as they had left Hamburg, they were to leave Hungary. It was a beautiful spring day, the kind that used to make Peter's heart light. The plum trees were in bloom, and their blossoms made a canopy above his head as he walked to school.

"As you all know, there have been many changes in Hamburg," Herr Birkmann began. "Apparently, the city is now safe to live in, but many parts are still without running water and electricity. The Party has decided that your help is needed in rebuilding. Our time in Hungary is finished. We will be leaving Bistriz tomorrow."

Peter partially emerged from his fog. There was a dull thud in his chest, a flop in his stomach. Olga flitted across his mind before he could stop her.

"You will pack and be ready at the train station by 7:00 tomorrow morning. Remember to thank your hosts. I am sure they have all been very kind in what has been a difficult time."

Gunter caught up with him as he left the school. "Are you going to come over to say goodbye?" The question was pointed. He and Gunter hadn't spoken in weeks.

"Yes. Of course."

They walked together in silence. A part of him hated being so cold and cut off, but he didn't know how to break out of his isolation. He was watching himself, frozen, like something made of stone. He couldn't reach through to the outside world.

"What do you think it's going to be like?" Gunter asked.

He heard himself respond automatically. "I don't know. I can't imagine it." It was a partial truth. He hadn't wanted to imagine it. He worked hard to shove imagined images from his mind.

"The Egelers told me that the east side of the city was hardest hit. Barmbek, Elbek, Borgfelde, and Hamm. The Altstadt might still be all right," Gunter added hopefully.

Suddenly Peter's anger flared. He was furious at Gunter's optimism. "*The Altstadt might be all right?*" Peter mocked. "Our city is gone!"

Gunter stopped. "You don't know. They wouldn't send us back if everything was gone. My father is alive. I know he is. I'd feel it if he wasn't." His voice was rising in anger, too.

"You'd 'feel' it?! Did you 'feel' that the city had been destroyed? Did you 'feel' the forty thousand who burned up?" Months of pent-up fury exploded on Gunter.

"You're not the only one who is scared!" Gunter yelled back at him. "You aren't the only one who misses home. All this winter you've been such a prick. Do you know what it has been like, seeing Olga's hopeful face every Friday afternoon and her sad face every Friday night? And now we're leaving and it's too late."

Peter kept on walking.

"We're going home to death and chaos, and we're leaving good people who cared for us, and all you can do is think of yourself."

He didn't care what Gunter thought. Ice filled his veins.

The Schnaubles were waiting for him. Frau Schnauble stood up when he walked into the house and gestured for him to sit in her chair. As he sat, he caught a glimpse of her face. He could see she'd been crying. But it meant nothing to him.

Herr Schnauble looked at him formally from his chair. "We thought it might be nice to celebrate the time you have spent with us," he said. "Will you join me in a small beer? I have a bottle that I have been saving since the war began."

Frau Schnauble waited expectantly. Peter felt the enormous weight of their attention. All he really wanted to do was escape, to be on his own, to make his mind blank. But he nodded. Through a tight jaw he made himself say, "That would be nice. Thank you, Herr Schnauble."

Frau Schnauble went to the kitchen and came back with a dark bottle and two glasses. Herr Schnauble carefully filled the glasses, tipping each one so as not to create too much foam on top. The beer was a deep amber color. A strong malt smell filled the room.

"Peter," began Herr Schnauble, handing him a glass, "we realize that it hasn't always been easy to live here, away from your familiar life. We know that you have missed your mother and are worried about her. We pray that you will find her alive and well when you return."

Peter looked down at his feet. He really didn't want to have this conversation with the Schnaubles. But he knew that he owed them this much. He owed it to them to try and be nice. He took a swallow of the beer and pushed his irritation down with it.

"We have liked having you here very much," continued Herr Schnauble. "We hope you have been comfortable. Perhaps when the war is over, when you are a young man, you will come back to our village to visit." Herr Schnauble cleared his throat. "You will always have a home here with us," he said.

Peter listened to the clock. Tick. Tock. He let the bitter taste of the beer warm his throat. "Thank you, Herr Schnauble," he said. He cleared his throat. "I will always remember your kindness to me," he said formally. He forced himself to smile and look at Frau Schnauble. "I will always remember your delicious Sauerbraten."

She smiled back, with tears in her eyes. "When you first came here, you were just a skinny boy. Now look at you. Now you are a man. You are ready to do the work of the Reich. Ready to help the Führer in his mission. Here," she said, handing him a book, "we have a small gift for you."

Peter took a slim volume from her hands. *The Small Rose Garden*, by Hermann Löns. Poetry.

"He is a favorite poet of the Reich. He loved nature, just like you. They call him the 'Poet of the Heath.' It is not new, but I thought you might like to have it. To help you remember your time in the country."

He opened the front cover. *For Peter. Bistriz, April 1944. Best wishes, Freja and Gerhardt Schnauble.* His thumb rubbed against the page. He'd never known their first names.

"Thank you, Frau Schnauble, Herr Schnauble. I will treasure it always. It will help me to remember the important things in this life."

Peter looked from one to the other. Their faces were strained, but kind. *They have only meant the best for me and I have repaid them with anger and impatience,* he thought.

He put down his empty beer glass. "Would it be all right, Herr Schnauble, if I went over to the Egelers' house to say goodbye before supper? They have been very good to me."

"Certainly. I am sure your friends will all miss you very much," said Herr Schnauble. Peter thought he saw a look pass between the Schnaubles as he left the room.

It had been many weeks since he'd been at the Egelers' house. He tried not to think of how he'd behaved to them over the winter. He'd wrapped himself in grief and fury. There had been no room for Olga, no room for the Egelers' kindness. A slow dawning realization of the extent of his cruelty began to seep into his mind. It was hard to know how he would be received.

"I'm so glad you have come," said Frau Egeler as she opened the door. She had baby Tomas perched on her hip. The warm smell of freshly baked bread enveloped him. "I've made you a loaf to take with you on your journey."

The family was crowded around the small dining table, the pack of *Schwarzer Peter* cards distributed among them. They all looked up as Peter entered.

"Peter!" squealed Bruno, jumping up to drag him to the table. "You've got to play with us. I keep getting the *Schwarzer Peter* card and losing. But if you play, you'll get it and I can win again!"

"Oh, all right," he said forcing a small smile. "But you never know—I might have been secretly practicing all this time. I might just beat you!"

"Here, you take my place," Gunter said icily. He stood up and handed Peter his cards. "I should go pack."

"This is a terrible hand," said Peter, trying to make a joke as Gunter left the room.

"Beggars can't be choosers," said Marthe, laughing.

"It seems I have very little control over my fate," he said, looking down at his cards. He began to feel the wound from Gunter's words. *All you can do is think of yourself.* He did not look at Olga, sitting across from him.

"Are you going away, too?" asked Bruno.

"Yes, Bruno."

"Why haven't you visited us? Olga kept asking Gunter but he said he didn't know. Ouch! Marthe, stop that."

"Bruno," said Herr Egeler, "you mustn't pester Peter. He's had a lot on his mind."

"All I said was—"

"Enough," said Herr Egeler.

Peter kept staring at his cards. He didn't trust himself to

say anything. He was afraid that if he let himself feel any part of what was happening around him, he would shatter into a thousand pieces. He swallowed. "I will miss your family, Herr Egeler," he said formally. The weight in the room was oppressive.

"And we will miss you, too, Peter," said Frau Egeler.

"Play the game!" said Bruno.

And so Peter played. He deliberately played badly and Bruno won hand after hand. For a time, this had felt normal. Sitting with a family, laughing, smelling supper cooking. Now he was going back to his "familiar" life, where nothing would ever be normal again. He felt brittle and tired, deeply tired.

"Will you stay for supper?" asked Frau Egeler as he lost yet another round.

Peter looked up. He hadn't realized it was so late. He was seized by a frantic desire to stay, to stay forever, to cry and laugh and be a part of this family and never have to go back to the home that didn't exist anymore. But he coated his mind and stood up. He knew that this was the last time he'd see them.

"No, I'm afraid I really must go." He stood up. He held out his hand to Herr Egeler. "Thank you, sir, for all your kindness. Please say goodbye to Oma Egeler for me."

"Goodbye, Peter. And good luck."

"You'll need luck to beat me at *Schwarzer Peter*!" said Bruno. "When I get bigger, I'll go to Hamburg and challenge you to a *Schwarzer Peter* duel!"

"It's a deal," said Peter. He reached out and shook Bruno's hand. He cleared his throat. "Goodbye, Marthe," he said with

a small formal bow. He felt his voice catch. "Goodbye, Olga."
He still had not looked at her.

It took a huge effort to cross the room. "I'll see you in the morning, Gunter," he called over his shoulder.

Frau Egeler opened the door for him. Suddenly she gave him a hug. She wrapped her soft arms around his stiff body. His arms remained pinned to his sides. "Take care of yourself, Peter."

He turned and walked out into the dusty street. He heard the door click shut behind him. Twilight was falling and the first stars were starting to twinkle. His mind was blank as he put one foot in front of the other.

He was startled by the sound of running feet. "Peter," Olga called softly as she caught up with him. "Mother forgot to give you this loaf of bread," she said, "for your journey."

He turned around. She was standing straight and tall and still, her pale round face looking up at him. She handed him the bread. His hands touched hers, warm from the bread. His body was trembling from the effort of not looking at her. Against his will, his eyes found her face. Her eyes were filled with understanding. His were filled with tears. She kissed him softly, and then she was gone.

Chapter Nineteen

Kingdom of Hungary,
May 1944

... and Olga's fingers are on my face. "I'm coming with you," she whispers. She kisses me, her tongue pushing into my mouth, startling me, tasting salty; there is water pouring out of her mouth, flooding into mine. I'm afraid I'll drown but I don't want to leave her lips. "I'm coming too!" says Bruno. He's tugging at my leg. "I want to be a soldier!" Bruno is tugging and Olga is kissing and behind me I hear the sound of the chickens in the barn. They're shrieking and I smell smoke. The barn is burning behind me and I'm choking but Olga is pressing her face against me, hard now, and I'm drenched with water. "Give me your gun!" shouts Bruno. His face is Hermann's. Olga's fingernails rip across my back and my head bangs against the wall and—

He is in a train. The train begins to move out of the station. He is starting the journey home, where there is no home. He rubs his head where it hit the window. How long has he been asleep? There is a bit of wet drool at the corner of his mouth. He closes his eyes ...

Peter stared dully out the window as the train chugged slowly through the Hungarian countryside. He was glad they were traveling during the day. They stopped frequently to pick up passengers in small villages. There seemed to be a lot of people on the move. Nazi guards patrolled the platforms with sleek Dobermans pacing beside them. In Szamosujvar, Peter watched a Hungarian family present their identity cards to the train guards. A girl about Olga's age carried a young child on her hip. A mother held a baby in her arms. Two young boys carried woven baskets. Peter watched as the guards passed their papers back and forth. Eventually they gestured for the family to get on, into a carriage at the back.

Olga. What would she be doing now? What would she be thinking? Did it matter? Did any of it matter?

They pulled into the town of Koloszvár. Peter's empty eyes took in the tall church spire surrounded by tidy red-roofed houses. *The station house has certainly seen better days*, he registered blankly. White paint was peeling from the plaster and many red bricks lay in pieces on the ground. One of the beams holding the awning shelter was listing to the side. *The Reich will repair that soon*, he thought.

The platform was filled with ragged Jewish families, wearing their yellow stars. Women, children, old people. The children carried small suitcases. Peter saw a young boy that reminded him of Bruno, holding a small teddy bear in one hand and his mother's hand in the other. He looked away. *They look so dirty*. He was glad they weren't coming onto his train. They were boarding a different train, the kind that usually held cattle.

So many Jews were being taken to work in labor camps. These ones were probably going to the copper mines in Yugoslavia. They'd talked about the copper mines in geography class. You need a lot of copper to win a war. So he assumed you needed a lot of workers to mine it.

He wasn't sure why they had to take their children with them. *But I guess you can't leave children on their own*, he thought. Besides, the children would soon grow up to be good workers, replacing some of those old Jews.

His eyes drifted to look out the window again. Nazi guards were checking the Jews' papers. He watched a girl Marthe's age helping an old woman climb up into the high open doors.

Stop thinking about them! Peter shouted inside his head.

He shut his eyes, put his head back, and rested it on the comfortable leather cushion of his train seat. He listened to the quiet in the carriage.

He tried to see his mother's face in his mind. He thought of her laughing as he told her about the Schnaubles, about the slow tick tock, and saying grace. But he couldn't find a place to tell her. He wanted to think of her in their apartment. But …

All day and into the night the train swayed slowly through the countryside. The scene at Koloszvár was repeated in Szolnok, and then again in Monor. More Jews, more cattle cars. The train stopped in every little town. Occasionally other people got on their train. No one got off.

It was afternoon as they came into the outskirts of Budapest. Peter had dozed fitfully. He was looking forward to stretching his legs on the walk to the docks.

"We're going through the city in formation," announced Karl. "Otto—get that tie on straight. Gunter, your boots are covered in mud—spit on them and get them clean. Peter." Karl looked him up and down, slowly shaking his head. "When was the last time you brushed your hair? Do you think this is any way to represent the Reich?"

Peter thought about both questions. The last time he'd brushed his hair was probably two days ago, the day before they were told they were leaving. And a small voice inside him said, *I don't give a damn about representing the Reich.* He immediately dislodged the thought by pulling his brushes out of his kit bag and smoothing his hair into place. He straightened his tie, checked to make sure his shirt was properly tucked and that his boots were clean. He squared his shoulders and readied himself to set an example to the citizens of Budapest.

The city was newly occupied by German forces. Tanks were parked along the streets, and troops were stationed along every major thoroughfare. Guards with dogs patrolled the market and shops. Everything was calm and orderly.

Peter marched as he had been taught, chest out, shoulders down, head high. He remembered how happy he had been when they marched in Nuremburg. He'd felt a part of something great and good and important.

"Sieg Heil!" Their unit stopped, clicked their heels with precision, and saluted. An open personnel car carrying several important dignitaries drove past, Nazi flags on the front of the car snapping in the breeze. The dignitaries smiled and saluted as they passed.

"March on," shouted Karl, and they continued through the city on the main street, heading to the docks.

There had been none of this marching in Bistriz. After the first week, they had just settled into living with their hosts—their families. He felt like he was playing a part in a movie of someone else's life. He was supposed to be going back to a familiar world, going back into his real life, except that nothing was the same, and nothing would be familiar.

It was getting harder to make his mind a blank.

They reached the dock on the south shore of the Danube. The Hungarian parliament buildings glistened directly opposite. Had their marching been impressive enough? Had he done his job well?

As Peter stepped onto the steamboat he'd stepped out of nine months before, he put the last piece of Frau Egeler's bread in his mouth. He let it sit on his tongue and he slowly inhaled to savor the rich molasses scent.

Enough, he railed at himself.

It took almost a week to get to the outskirts of Hamburg. Their steamer chugged slowly as patrol boats whizzed up and down the Danube. Their train stopped frequently and the stations were filled with Jews getting on or off other trains. So many people on the move.

Finally, at the outskirts of the city, they slowed and stopped at a crossing.

"This is as far as we go," said Karl. "The tracks into the city have not been repaired. We'll have to go the rest of the way on foot."

Herr Birkmann gathered them together outside the train. "You may find it difficult to locate your homes. Landmarks have been destroyed and many of the streets are still blocked with rubble. Travel together, those of you who live near each other. If your house is not there, you must ask around to see if your family has left word for you."

Gunter and Otto both caught Peter's eye. He knew they expected to work together, just like old times. He gave a small nod. He owed them that much. Everything was familiar. Nothing was familiar.

"Your job as HJ is to help people rebuild. Your muscles are needed to carry bricks and lay mortar, to shovel what is left of the broken buildings, and to help make Hamburg whole again. Much has been done already, but people are tired and will be grateful for your help.

"School classes are suspended until the end of August, but you are expected to report for HJ training weekly."

It was a sunny day and they all set off down the train tracks. Peter tried to force his mood to lift. Hungary had been an adventure, a beautiful one, but, as they'd traveled, it had begun to fade into a place where it didn't exist. It was a fiction. Peter took a deep breath and inhaled the familiar sour, salty smell of the sea. A buzz of city noise reassured him.

But suddenly the train tracks came to a stop. There was a huge jumble of track and bulldozed buildings. A dead end.

"Let's try this way," said Herr Birkmann, gesturing for them to follow. He led them around a fence and a hedge to walk up a hill and get their bearings. They scrambled up, losing their footing amidst broken glass, rusted metal, and bits of lath. Peter hesitated at the bottom. He looked up at the group picking their way to the top.

If I stay here, I won't have to know, Peter thought. *My future is on the other side of that ridge. Here, on this side, everything is just the same as when I left. But once I see it, everything will be changed forever.*

Peter watched as, one by one, the members of his unit reached the top of the hill and stared into the distance. He wanted to stay on this side forever. He had a wild thought that he could get back on a train, get down to the Danube, take the steamboat, get on the train in Budapest, and get back to Bistriz, back to the Egelers, back to Olga and a world outside the war. It was the same impulse that kept him reading *The Magic Mountain*—he could live in a world that didn't exist. But he knew that in reality the war was already catching up with Bistriz—he'd seen it from the windows of the train. He knew he couldn't go back. He knew he had to go to the crest of the hill.

When he got to the top, he thought there had been a mistake. They'd gotten off the train too soon. He'd tried to prepare himself, but there was no way to make sense of what he was seeing.

He could see the river, so he knew he was looking north. He could see some ships on the river, where the docks should have been. But between them and the river, all he could see were clusters of partial buildings, followed by miles and miles of rubble, punctuated by the occasional wall.

Ever since he was a child, he'd oriented himself by the steeple of St. Katharinen Kirche, just down the street from his house. Where was it? Where was St. Katharinen Kirche?

"Look," said Otto, pointing. "There's St. K. It's still there."

Peter felt as though scales were lifting from his eyes. A spire rose from the rubble and he began to see the outlines of the city.

"That section, there," Herr Birkmann said, pointing to the right, "that must be what's left of St. Petri Kirche. That must be the Domplatz. The Gymnasium used to be on Schopenstehl, across from the park. We'll make our way there."

Rubble was piled up in neat rows. The streets had been swept clean. The apartment buildings were little more than walls with holes for windows. There were no roofs, no doors. Many were open on one side—they looked like oversized dollhouses.

As they walked down the wide boulevard toward the Domplatz, Peter could see a tent city set up in the park. A woman was hanging her laundry from a tree. *How had people managed all winter?* he wondered. *If this is what the city looks like now, what had it been like in the cold of January?*

On the other side of the boulevard stood silent buildings. He tried to make sense of the vacant lots. He walked on high alert, trying to get his mind to recognize something, anything that would tell him where he was.

An instinct deeper than thought moved his feet and took him away from the group. Before he knew what he was doing, he had slipped invisibly away on his own, disappearing between the shells of two buildings. His mind was blank as he picked his way across empty lots piled with rubble. He turned onto a narrow side street. And he stopped in front of a staircase.

It was the dip in the first stone step that convinced him. That dip, that worn indentation, had threatened to trip him many a time as he'd raced up and down those steps.

Beside the staircase was a large bomb.

He stood there staring, trying to put the pieces together. It was like a jigsaw puzzle using a familiar picture to make a nightmare.

Up there was where he and Herr Ballin had watched the first night of bombing. But there were no windows, no walls, no attic for Oma Ballin.

The bomb sat there silent, undetonated. He walked gingerly up the steps. There was no door to open, but he could see the outline of the hall that led to his apartment. He took another step up. He could see through to the back of the building, to the room where his mother had listened to the radio, where he had heard Herr Hitler tell him that this war was for him, for his future. He took another step up, and began to slowly walk down the hall that he knew so well.

A thick layer of dust covered everything. He walked into the kitchen. Someone had been here recently. The table had been wiped clean. He opened a cupboard. Familiar plates, with patterns of delicate roses around the edges, were stacked ready for use. He felt suspended in time.

Suddenly, movement in the hall caught his eye and he froze. His heart pounded with adrenalin and he looked around to find something he could use as a weapon. Just in case. And in that moment, the figure came into the room.

"Welcome home."

Chapter Twenty

Hamburg.
May 1944

This isn't real, Peter thought. *I'm asleep and dreaming.*

His mother stood in the doorway, smiling. A flock of starlings flew overhead, dipping into the space that used to be a ceiling. Peter heard the sound of their wings as they wheeled through the sky.

If I stay very still, I won't wake up.

"Peter?" she said tentatively.

Sunshine slanted through the walls, creating a pattern of light and shadow. She moved in and out of the beams as she came toward him, her feet making prints as she walked through the plaster dust on the floor.

Maybe I'm dead. He wasn't breathing. He was sure of that. *I don't remember being shot. I don't remember an explosion. But they say you don't. It just happens and you don't know a thing.*

His mother stood in front of him. He looked down into her eyes. She reached up to his face and cupped her hand around his cheek. "You've grown," she said. Two fat tears welled up and rolled down his cheeks. Still, he didn't move, didn't breathe. "It's all right," she said, wiping the tears with her hands. "You're home." And with that, he broke.

His mother held him. A floodgate opened and he had no way to control it.

If she was shocked, she didn't show it. She just held him as tenderly as if he were a baby. She sat on the floor with him, rocking.

He cried for his mother who was here and alive and not burned in the firestorm. He cried for Eugene, for Jakob with the lines on his face, for the man with the starter pistol, for his neighbor the Jehovah's Witness, for the mother dog with no pups, for Hamburg. He cried for Olga, for Hungary. He cried until there were no more tears in the world.

A lifetime later, he whispered, "Were you here?"

"No. I got to Tante Elsa's just in time. The bombs started the next day." Peter remembered their last day together. She'd promised him she would leave, and she had. They had both survived.

"After the bombing, no one was allowed to come back. The roads were filled with the refugees. At Tante Elsa's we took in as many as we could. Three families in the house, others in the barn, others sleeping in the field. A winter of soup made from grass. A winter of burying bodies.

"Then we were ordered to come back to the city. To show the enemy that we would not be defeated. There was talk that Herr Hitler would come to see us, to see our suffering. But he never came."

Peter thought he heard a note of anger in her voice. Just a momentary flash. But then it was gone.

"We are still finding bodies. Charred remains in basements. No one bothers to identify them anymore. People are either here, or they are not here. You are here," she said with a smile, "and I am here. I knew you'd come to the apartment first. I knew this was where I should wait. I've come every day for a month. I knew what time the trains arrived. I knew you'd be on one. One day."

She rocked him and he let himself be comforted.

... I hear sounds. Birds calling. A moment of falling. Then nothing ...

He wakes from a deep sleep to the sound of his mother's voice softly calling. "Peter. Peter. It's time to go." Part of a dream. He stretches and his foot hits something. He is disoriented and confused.

Did he just hear his mother's voice?

"It's getting dark. We need to go."

Peter opened his eyes. His mother was kneeling beside him. He looked up and saw the underside of a table.

It all flooded back. He was home, in Hamburg. His mother was here; she'd made him a bed of blankets.

"I have an apartment on Neuer Rahm, beside Zoll Canal. It's not far. And believe it or not, I have a job."

Of course, they couldn't stay here. There were no walls, and only patchy bits of ceiling. And there was that unexploded bomb out front.

"Bring the blankets with you. I've been carrying things over a bit at a time. You'll like it. It's a room above a cigar shop. I work next door developing photographs."

"Photographs?" Peter was still feeling dazed.

"It's good work. The photographer works for the Gestapo, so he gets paid regularly. They take a lot of official pictures. We're always busy."

Peter slowly gathered up the blankets. He shook out the dust—there was greasy dust everywhere—and folded them over his arm. He picked up his rucksack. A photography shop. His mother's resourcefulness never ceased to amaze him. He didn't know that she knew anything about developing photos.

As if reading his mind, she said, "I lied a bit to get the job." He followed her as she picked her way carefully down the staircase and onto the street. "When I heard about the job, I went to Herr Weber—you remember, Franz's father? He likes cameras almost as much as he likes jazz records. He gave me that one for you, the one I gave you when you left that first time. Do you still have it?"

Peter nodded slowly. He had lost so much, it was strange to think that he still had the camera. He had a roll of undeveloped film. He'd finished it at the Egelers' farm, a thousand years ago.

"Herr Weber took some cameras apart and showed me how they worked. He taught me enough of the words that I could sound like I knew what I was talking about in my interview."

Herr Weber's shop. It was four years ago when Peter and Gunter had gone there to get the bike. He wondered what had happened to Franz. The last time he'd seen him had been the day before he'd left. Had Franz been here during the firestorm?

"I told Herr Girmann—my boss—that I'd done photographic work before the war. I said I'd had a job with a Jew, that he'd taught me all of the skills. I knew he couldn't check up on it, because all the Jews are gone. Anyway, he gave me the job and I moved into an apartment in the building beside the shop."

They walked down the middle of the road. The city was quiet. As his eyes started to adjust, he became aware of his surroundings. Ahead, he saw a man pulling a wagon. A woman was pushing from behind. The wagon was piled with clothes, pots, bedding, suitcases. They struggled down the street, maneuvering around holes in the road. He saw a young boy on top of a pile of rubble, picking up bricks and stacking them on what used to be the sidewalk. A toddler was sitting beside the stack, sucking a dirty thumb. A young girl picked something up—he couldn't see what—and put it in the basket she was carrying. Everyone was moving slowly, methodically. Along the narrow street they walked, catching the occasional smell of onions cooking. He followed his mother down the road as the shadows lengthened.

Peter tried to recognize something, to place himself in the city, but nothing looked familiar. But as they turned a corner onto the high street, he was suddenly jolted. There was Lindstrüm's shop.

In a flash of memory, he remembered buying a pickle. He could see Herr Lindstrüm taking up a pair of silver tongs and reaching into a deep barrel. The grocer had turned his broad smiling face to Peter and handed him a big fat garlic pickle. Peter must have been about five years old. The pickle was all he could afford, but it was delicious. Better than any candy. Herr Lindström had always stood under the archway—that archway—laughing and gossiping.

The shop was empty now, the windows gone and the inside blackened. By contrast, the rubble outside looked pristine and gleaming white. There was no sign of Herr Lindström. No indication that the building had ever held a shop.

And there was St. Katharinen Kirche. The top of the tall brown church spire was gone, but the clock and the base were still there. There were large jagged burn marks all along what was left of the roof. He saw a flash of blue and yellow as a small bird streaked into the church.

The front wall had been blasted off. He could see right inside. Starlings and blue tits were perched along the backs of the pews. When he was a child, he'd sat in those pews on rainy Sundays. The huge organ—the biggest in all of Europe, he'd been told—made a sound so deep that everything vibrated. He used to go just for the sheer pleasure of feeling that sound. He'd loved watching the organist pumping with his feet, his hands flying from the keys to the stops, controlling this enormous music. He'd liked the pieces by Bach best. His mother had told him that Bach himself had visited the church hundreds of years ago. He'd written music especially for the St. Katharinen Kirche organ.

Peter felt his eyes stinging, pricking with fresh tears.

This was his city, his home. All that was left was a shell. He swallowed hard. He would not cry. It *was* his city. What was left of it. That was something to hold on to.

Chapter Twenty-One

Hamburg,
Summer 1944

His mother's apartment was just a large room. She tied a string from one side to the other and hung a blanket so he could have some privacy. They shared a bathroom down the hall with five other families. They cooked on an electric hotplate in their room.

In the days that followed, they established a routine. Every morning, his mother got up early to go to work. Somehow she always managed to look clean and tidy. Peter felt as though he'd been grubby for months. The last time he'd felt really clean was after swimming in the reservoir in Bistriz. But he wasn't going to think about that. Bistriz didn't exist.

While his mother was at work, Peter spent his days scrounging. He knew he was supposed to check in with his HJ group, but he didn't bother. He took off his uniform and joined the thousands of people who were going through the piles of rubble looking for cans of food, clothing, anything that could be used, sold, or traded.

Slowly, landmarks started to emerge. Faces of new neighbors became recognizable, although there was little conversation. A smile, a nod. Occasionally the offer of a trade. Peter was often asked to help as people dug out their homes. He'd lift a chunk of stone, or shore up a bit of wall, or carry some planks of wood to a new building site. In return, he'd be given part of a dry loaf of bread or a few potatoes.

One day, a tiny white-haired woman on Reimerstwiete asked him to help her get into a blocked apartment.

"My son lived here with his wife and children. I lived in Horst, near Maschen. We heard the explosions. We saw the fires. I could not come into the city until now. I have been searching for them," she said with a shaking voice. "I think they must have escaped. Perhaps they are in the countryside, yes? A farmer has taken them in?" She looked into Peter's face for reassurance. "I just want to see if there is anything left in the apartment. Something to remember them by," she said.

He spent the whole day clearing the entrance to the apartment. By afternoon, he'd stacked the rubble so that there was a bit of a tunnel into the building. Most of the roof had caved in, and every step seemed treacherous. He didn't think she should go in alone. He stooped low as she picked her way carefully through the ruins of the charred rooms.

The floor was littered with broken china, scraps of furniture, and rotting clothes. The woman picked up a metal picture frame, blackened by smoke. Peter watched her stare, trying to reconstruct the shadowy shapes in the damaged photo. Beneath a metal bedframe they found a porcelain doll's head. The hair was burned off, and the cloth body and clothes were in ashes. She held it and sat on the floor, rocking back and forth.

"Sleep, baby, sleep,
Your father guards the sheep,
Your mother shakes the little trees,
There falls down one little dream.
Sleep, baby, sleep ..."

She sang in a whisper, her old voice cracking.

"I have to go," Peter said. "It's late. I have to get back for my mother." He'd spent the whole day trying to help, but there was nothing for her here.

The woman turned her gray face toward him, reading his impatience. "Here," she said, "take this." She pulled a small brown bottle with a torn label out of her bag. "Schnapps," she said. "It is all I have." She held the doll and the picture frame and rocked. "It is all that I have," she repeated, as he walked away.

That night, Peter and his mother had boiled potatoes and schnapps for dinner. She poured it out in small glasses. "Prost!" she said, clinking glasses with him.

The schnapps was like liquid fire. It hit his tongue, then smashed into the back of his throat. He took a breath and began to cough as it burned down his chest and into his stomach. His eyes watered with the shock.

His mother laughed. The more he coughed, the more she laughed. He wanted to cough forever.

"The trick is not to breathe," she said. "Take it into your mouth. Let it sit there. Breathe in through your nose, then swallow. Like this." She demonstrated, swallowed, and licked her lips. "Oh, my God, that's good," she sighed. "Thank you. Thank you for helping that poor woman," she said as she filled their glasses.

Maybe it was the schnapps that made his mother bold. "Would you like to come to the shop in the morning? To see what I do? Herr Girmann is going to be away in the morning. A funeral. He's left me the keys. I can show you around."

Peter knew that Herr Girmann's work was confidential. He was working for the Gestapo, which meant that the photographs were classified information.

As if reading the question on his face, his mother said, "It's all right. He won't be there."

Peter thought of his camera and his roll of undeveloped film.

"Can I bring my film? Would you be able to show me how to develop it?" The photo was burned in his mind. Olga, at the cabin. Her hair blown across her face, a radiant smile.

"Yes, of course. Perhaps we can share some of this wonderful schnapps with Herr Girmann in exchange for the developing solution and the paper." She smiled because he smiled. "I just won't mention that you came into the studio with me," she said slyly.

Peter's head was thick the next morning as he walked down the stairs and out of their apartment. Three smartly dressed Gestapo officers were just coming out of the cigar shop, laughing. *People are starving but the Gestapo still buys cigars,* thought Peter, before he could stop himself. He avoided looking at them and tried to make himself invisible.

At the street, they turned right and walked up the stone steps to the photography shop. A metal folding screen protectively covered the front. His mother unlocked it and folded it back to reveal a window filled with portraits. There was one of a pretty blonde girl in a BDM Faith and Beauty uniform. There was a family portrait—mother, father, and two boys in Jungvolk uniforms, a tiny Schnauzer dog at their feet. There were several posed portraits of men in uniforms. His mother slipped a large round key into the keyhole of the heavy door and pushed it open. A strong smell of chemicals stung Peter's nose.

"You get used to it," his mother said, switching on the overhead light.

The front room was much like any shop in the district. A glass counter displayed a variety of cameras, flash attachments, tripods, and lenses. In the center of the display was a beautiful sleek black camera, with shiny brass fixtures and a gold embossed eagle of the Third Reich on it. Peter went behind the counter and picked it up. He turned it in his hands, admiring the weight.

"That's a Leica," said his mother as she counted the money in the till. "Best camera you can buy."

Peter put it down carefully and picked up one that looked the same but had Cyrillic lettering and a Russian star in place of the eagle. "Fed 1 Commander. Cheap Russian imitation," his mother said authoritatively.

Peter picked up a camera with a complicated-looking lens mounted on a black bellows. The word "Cameo" was printed on the track where the lens moved back and forth. He looked through the viewfinder and followed his mother as she walked through the room. "I'll make you a star!" he said in an affected voice. She laughed and struck a pose. "I was born to be a star, Herr Director Gruber!" she said, thrusting her shoulder forward and looking back at him flirtatiously.

Click. He took the photo in his mind. His mother smiling like a movie star. Happy. It was so unexpected.

"Come on and I'll show you where the real magic happens."

He followed her through a door and into the back room. She switched on a lightbulb that hung in the center of the room. An eerie red glow filled the space. "One crack of regular light can destroy a whole roll of film. We only work in red light, and we make sure to lock the door," she said, turning the lock.

There were strings, like clotheslines, strung up along the sides of the room. Photographs were pinned to the strings like rows of fresh laundry, and the shelves were piled high with photos.

"Have you brought your film?"

Suddenly Peter felt shy. He wasn't sure he wanted his mother to see the pictures he'd taken when he was away. But he handed the spool over to her.

"This is the only really tricky bit," she said, picking up a round canister about the size of a pudding bowl. She slid a metal clip onto the spool of film, and Peter watched as her fingers confidently separated the film from its paper backing. "You need to get the film off the paper but you can't let any light touch it. So you put it into this clip, slide the clip into the side here, and then gently pull the film into the canister. Then you attach it to this spool—see how it clicks into place? —and then you put the top on to seal it, so there's not a drop of light. You turn the spool slowly to wind the film into the canister, separating it completely from the paper backing."

Peter looked at her face, shining in concentration. She was beaming, proud of her skill. All during the years Peter was growing up, his mother had been a cleaning lady. She'd arrived home late, tired, her back hurting. She hadn't smiled much. He knew that before she'd moved to Hamburg, before she'd had him, she'd been at school in Lübeck. He wondered what her life might have been like if she hadn't had him, hadn't moved, if his father hadn't left ...

Too many ifs.

She handed him a long sheet of paper. "That was on the back of the film. See the numbers on it? That's what you saw in the red window at the back of your camera, so you could know how many you'd taken."

Peter remembered when he'd reached number 10. In Bistriz. At the farm. The last picture on the roll. He looked at the 10 on the paper in his hand.

"Now we pour the developing solution into the top of the canister, carefully so that we don't make any bubbles, gently moving it to make sure the film gets completely coated. Now, count to sixty."

Peter's voice sounded thin in the small room. He watched his mother slowly rotating the canister in her hands. He could understand why she liked the job so much. There was a peaceful feeling in being here, away from the outside world, separate. He thought of all of the memories in the room.

"Sixty," he said. His mother carefully unscrewed the lid of the canister and lifted out the large spool, dripping from its bath. She unwound the film and carried it over to a small dish.

"We have to rinse it, to seal the images," she said, dipping the film into the liquid in the dish. She lifted with one hand and dipped with the other, going back and forth in a smooth see-saw movement.

Peter's eyes were glued to his mother. She looked like she was performing a magic trick. It *was* a kind of magic. On that little piece of film were moments that would now last forever.

Finally she held the film in the air and dangled it in front of him.

"It needs to hang to dry overnight. Tomorrow, we can make prints."

"Can I see?" he asked, reaching toward the dripping brown strip.

"Make sure you hold it by the edge, here, where the holes are. Don't touch the pictures."

She passed the strip over to him and he held it cautiously between his fingers. He frowned as he tried to make sense of what he was seeing. His mother laughed gently.

"It's reversed. What was white shows up as black on the negative, and vice versa. That's because the light is actually burning itself onto the film. When we make a print, it gets reversed again."

He looked at the tiny images on the film. Memories flooded back. He'd forgotten about taking a photograph on the boat, but he remembered how warm it had been, sitting in the sunshine as the steamboat headed down the Danube. There was the Gypsy parrot in Bistriz. His eyes flicked to the last frame. Olga. Backwards, her soft white face was black, her shiny dark hair white.

His memory filled in the red of Olga's lips.

"Hang it over here, out of the way, to dry." His mother directed him to one of the strings. Peter carefully pinned the top of the film onto the line. He pulled his eyes away from the images.

"Come, I need you to help me take down the prints I did yesterday. They're dry now. Someone will be coming to pick them up later today." She gestured to photographs hanging from another line. Peter went over and began to unpin them. He looked at the first one in his hand. He'd expected it to be a portrait, like the ones in the front window of the shop. It took him a moment to make sense of what he was seeing.

Three men in German army uniforms were hanging from the limbs of a huge tree. Their heads were flopped over. One was turned away from the camera and Peter could see that his hands were tied behind his back. The men's feet dangled about six inches from the ground. A German officer stood formally beside the bodies, looking directly at the camera.

"Deserters." His mother had come over to stand beside him. "The photo is taken as proof, and to set an example."

His eyes slid up to the next picture on the line.

He saw a group of prisoners in striped uniforms, each with a yellow star like the one he'd seen on the man in Bistriz. Like the stars he'd seen on the Jews boarding the trains. In the picture, their heads were shaved and they wore little boxed caps. Their cheeks were hollow. Their eyes stared blankly at the camera. They looked impossibly thin.

"I think that is from Neuengamme," his mother said stiffly. "It's a work detail." Peter slowly unpinned it from the string. He was mesmerized by the image. "Come, put it over here," said his mother, "and start on the other string. We need to take all the dry ones down to make room for today's film."

Peter put the photo down on the pile and walked over to unpin the other row of photographs. They were a mixture of images. There were photographs of smiling officers, clinking beer steins—sitting in a café. There were snapshots, tourist pictures like his, in front of the Eiffel Tower in Paris and the Colosseum in Rome.

His hand had unpinned the next photo before his mind understood what he was seeing.

A pile of bodies. Naked skeletons, with only the thinnest covering of skin. Men. Women. Children. Arms stuck out at odd angles. No hair. He froze.

"Yes," his mother said as she gently took it from him. "I have seen a lot of these recently. I'm not sure where they are from. I think some are from Neuengamme, but there are others that I think are from a work camp in Poland called Auschwitz." She spoke dispassionately. "I can't think about it," she said, answering the question he hadn't asked. "It is a part of my work. I don't think about it."

Peter watched her put it with some others from the same order, presumably the same photographer. He reached over and looked at another in the pile. There was a gate with an iron sign. *Work Makes You Free.* Suddenly Hermann's voice was in his head.

"They've got an endless supply of Jewish soap. It's the least they can do for the Fatherland!"

What did he mean? Peter's mind snapped shut. He put the photo back on the pile.

"I need to open the store," said his mother. "New orders usually come in on Friday and everyone wants them for Monday morning." She steered him back into the front room where an unusual stream of sunshine magnified the dusty counter. Peter's mind was numb. He felt disoriented.

"I'll go to the lake to see if I can catch anything," he said distractedly, gathering up his bag. "There aren't many fish around but it's worth a try."

"Good luck," his mother said, opening the door for him. "We'll develop your photos tomorrow and you can show me your trip."

The morning sun was hot when he stepped outside, but his body was rigid with cold. The red-tinted darkroom had seeped into his bones. He turned left and walked back up to their room. He wondered if there was enough schnapps in the world to warm him up.

It was late afternoon when Peter finally made his way to the lake with an improvised fishing line. His mind was thick from drinking and sleeping. He stared down into the water, empty of thought.

"Peter!"

The surprise made him jerk the line into the air. There

was Gunter running up the path toward him, waving with all his might.

Peter stared, almost not recognizing him. It had been spring when they had arrived together in the city. Now it was late summer, and Peter realized that he hadn't even thought of Gunter, or Otto, or anyone from the Gymnasium. He'd walked out of one life and into another.

Peter looked down at the line in his hand. The worm he'd dug up in the park still wriggled on the end of the safety pin hook. He dropped it back into the water.

Gunter came panting up. "Where have you been? We've looked all over for you. One minute you were walking with us, and then suddenly you were gone. And then you never checked in with HJ. We thought ... well, we thought something had happened."

Something *had* happened, Peter thought. Until that moment, he hadn't realized the enormous shift that he'd undergone in these couple of months. Gunter belonged to another life, a life that he now knew he didn't want any part of.

"We went to your old apartment. Pretty rough," Gunter said. "My building is in good shape. My sisters are still in the country, but we've got some neighbors living with us. Everyone is pooling their ration cards."

Peter stared silently into the water.

Gunter hadn't mentioned his father. Herr Schmidt had been more like a father to Peter than anyone he had known.

Except for Herr Egeler, a voice inside quietly reminded him.

"Your father ...?" he asked abruptly, to silence the voice.

Gunter hesitated for a moment before he answered. "He's

alive. He was here during it all. Our section didn't burn. It was afterward that was hard, I think. When the fires were finally out. He helped bury corpses. He won't talk about it. He doesn't talk much about anything."

Peter thought about Herr Schmidt's confident laugh and how he'd reassured his mother that day when the shelter was bombed. How many lifetimes ago was that?

"The HJ has been meeting regularly. We've been keeping up our calisthenics to try and stay strong. Look at this ..." Gunter pulled up his sleeve and flexed a bicep. "Not bad, eh? Or at least it's a lot better," he said when Peter remained silent.

"Anyway, Herr Birkmann says that once we're in Bamberg we'll really put a push on. Lots of marching and practice manoeuvers. Probably even target practice."

"Bamberg?"

"Yeah, the next evacuation center is Bamberg. It's on the way to Neumarkt—I think we might have even gone through it last time. Apparently there are seven hills, just like in Rome, and castles and things sitting on them. There's even a part of town they call little Venice, along the river, with little boats and everything. Birkmann says it's very 'picturesque.'" Gunter's optimism filled Peter's silence.

"We started trying to clean up the Gymnasium. Did you see it?" he continued. "What a mess! The tables are smashed up and the windows are blown out. The blackboards are shattered. Anyway, the HJ is supposed to move out because the bombs are still falling. They want to make sure we keep up our training so we'll be ready."

Gymnasium. HJ. They seemed like foreign words. Peter

couldn't imagine why anyone would go to school. What on earth was the point?

"Everyone is going to be so glad I've found you! Hermann's been such a pain—I guess you know he's been back on the black market scene—and he's charging double what anything is worth. Have you got anything on the go?"

Peter looked down at his line in the water. It all seemed so remote. "No," he said. His black market dealings were private now. Neighbor to neighbor trades. Just survival.

"Well, we won't need it much longer, anyway. Once we get to Bamberg, we'll be in the countryside again with lots to eat. Hermann said there's supposed to be great local beer, and there'll be a big beer drinking festival when we get there. And maybe some country girls will take pity on us!"

Gunter's laugh died as Peter looked up at him. "I'm not going," he said, slowly.

"What do you mean?"

"I mean, I'm not going. I'm staying in Hamburg."

"But you have to go," said Gunter. "Everyone in Gymnasium has to go. Everyone in the HJ has to go. Everyone has to go."

"I'm done with Gymnasium," said Peter. "I'm done with school."

"But you can't! What about your education?"

"I'm fifteen and that means I can work as an apprentice." Peter said the words before he thought them. And as he heard himself say the words, he knew they were right.

"But you were going to be a teacher. You were going to travel the world." Gunter sounded mystified.

Peter shrugged. "What the hell does an education mean now? Look, Gunter, we're going to lose this damn war, and then it will be just like the last time, only worse. They'll take away our land; they'll take away our food. And this time, we'll deserve it. We'll deserve to be punished."

Gunter was staring at him, his eyes large. He quickly looked around to see if anyone was listening. "Gymnasium and HJ make us strong," he said quietly. "You're right, we may lose the war, but we are going to need to be all the stronger to build our country again once it is over."

"I don't need Gymnasium and HJ to make me strong."

"You have to go to HJ. It's law," said Gunter.

"I can serve my country as an apprentice. I can get a trade and be useful. I can start my life."

"But trades are only for people who are too stupid to go to Gymnasium!" Gunter blurted out.

Peter felt his anger rising but it didn't reach his face. He looked out across the water. "I'm not going to run away and play silly war games in the woods. I'm not going to have polite suppers with peasants while the rest of the country is burning." He looked at Gunter. "I was never really that smart. Not like you. You'll go far." He didn't bother to keep the sarcasm out of his voice.

He turned his eyes back to the canal. He didn't want Gunter in his life anymore. Gunter was part of his childhood. It was time to leave that behind.

Gunter's eye followed Peter's to the water.

"I think you lost your worm," he said at long last as he turned and walked away.

Part Three

Vor der Katharinenkirche . 18.6.44

Chapter Twenty-Two

It was Hans Corm who persuaded Peter's mother that it was all right for him to drop out of Gymnasium. He thought an apprenticeship was a great idea.

"Yes! You should get a trade," he said. "Be useful. There's no learning in books. You'll still be in HJ and then, when you turn eighteen, you can be in full training."

Hans had come back from Libya where he'd been hit in the leg by shrapnel. He clomped around the apartment with a strong limp. "They've taken me off active service. They're going to make me a guard at one of the camps. Cushy job. But I'd go back to the front in a flash."

Peter knew he had to report to the Hitlerjugend office and register. He didn't want to be classified as a deserter.

"You should have registered the minute you got back from Hungary," the HJ manager scowled at him.

"I got separated from my team, sir. I spent the summer helping in the re-building."

The manager sniffed. "If you were a year older, I'd put you on a FLAK team. But you'll have to wait for that privilege." Peter wasn't sure if the manager was being sarcastic or not. The huge FLAK guns that surrounded Hamburg were designed to shoot enemy aircraft out of the sky. Trouble was, the minute you shot one, the enemy knew exactly where you were. He'd heard that the FLAK teams didn't last long. And they certainly hadn't been able to stop the thousands of bombers last July.

"We need good workers in Klockner," the manager said. "You'll learn drafting, mechanics, and engineering. Your duty to your country will be served as you help to make the best airplane engines in the world—the Messerschmitts."

The Klockner factory was south of the city, in Harburg. It took about an hour to get there by tram. He left in the morning before it was even light. But Peter quickly found that he liked the work—he enjoyed the precision of drafting and prided himself on his accuracy. There was no marching, no war games, no choices to be made. There was just the work and the need to do it well.

Because he was doing war work, he could eat at the cafeteria in the factory. It was the first time since leaving Hungary that he'd had proper meals. Not a lot of food, but there was some meat, potatoes, and bread almost every day. Steaming chicory coffee was given to him by a pretty girl who pushed a trolley around the factory floor.

There were about two hundred apprentices working at Klockner. Most started on the factory floor, cleaning up after the more skilled workers. They eventually graduated to building the engines. But because he'd been in Gymnasium, he was given an advanced position, starting as a draftsman. "We don't get many from Gymnasium," his supervisor, Lutz, told him.

"This is Fredrik," said Lutz, gesturing to a young man with thin blond hair and pale skin, sitting at a drafting table. His ears were pink from a recent sunburn. He was a few years older than Peter.

"He'll be your work partner. You'll share some tools. If you've got questions, ask Fredrik. What he doesn't know about engines isn't worth knowing."

Fredrik looked up at Peter, gave a slight nod, and went back to his work. Peter had a sudden pang, thinking of Gunter's friendly smile. He pushed it away and sat down at his drafting table.

"Not so fast," said Lutz. "I want you to see how the factory works. Max," he called across the room as Peter stood up. "I want you to show Peter around the floor."

A huge apprentice about Peter's age lumbered over. He gave a half-smile and Peter followed him on a silent tour. Walking behind him, Peter thought of Hermann's broad back. Max would dwarf him.

"Max," said Peter, tapping him on the shoulder, "who are they?"

Peter pointed to the other side of the factory, where about a hundred men in dirty uniforms were working machinery.

Max turned to him with the same half-smile. "Russian prisoners of war," he said in a surprisingly soft, light voice. "They live here full-time, in bunkers under the factory. They help to build the engines. They're also responsible for the fire extinguishers. If we get attacked, their job is to go to the bunkers, get the extinguishers, and put out the fires."

Peter quickly fell into the routine of the factory. Each morning when he stepped off the tram in Harburg, he was enveloped by the smell of the pine trees. It was quiet and calm as people went to their work stations. Peter was the youngest there, but he did his work quickly and efficiently and fit in well. There weren't any of the jealousies and in-fighting of his old HJ group. But then, there weren't any real friendships, either.

At lunch he chatted with the Russians. He felt an affinity with them because of Tolstoy and Dostoyevsky, and they seemed to have an endless supply of cigarettes to trade. They loved teaching him Russian words. *Sigareta* was easy. Cigarette. *Peevo.* Beer. *Wodka.* Vodka. "*Peevo n wodka pozhaluysta n spaseebo*," they said to the girl with the trolley. Beer and vodka, please and thank you. They all laughed over that.

At the end of each day, he returned home on the tram, carrying bits of leftover lunch. He soon built up quite a warehouse of food and cigarettes under his bed. The room was heavy with the smell of bread, chunks of cheese, and sausage. But he had to be careful who he bartered with—it was considered treason against your fellow citizens to buy and sell on the black market. You could never tell who might report you. Peter was determined not to get into trouble. He was going to survive and help rebuild when it was all over.

There were bombing raids almost every night. Apparently it was the same all over the country. No one talked about it, but Peter was sure they were losing the war. There was so much they couldn't talk about but, somehow, everyone knew they were losing. They'd already lost in Russia and France.

Would the factory keep him on after the war, after he'd finished his apprenticeship? What would they be building? Certainly not airplane engines.

"You wanted to be a teacher. You wanted to travel."

None of it mattered anymore.

"Damn," Fredrik swore under his breath. Peter looked over at him. "I've drawn the wrong scale. Point five centimeters to the meter, not one to one," he said. "A whole morning's work ruined. I guess that's what comes from lack of sleep," he muttered.

There had been two raids last night. Exhaustion was a way of life for everyone.

"Maybe I could re-do it," Peter offered cautiously. Fredrik was a perfectionist, and Peter knew how much it bothered him to make a mistake. He wasn't sure how he'd respond to the suggestion. "Copying your work in a smaller size would be a good way for me to learn."

Fredrik stared at the page in front of him. He sniffed. "Not a bad idea," he said. He stood up. His tall, lanky body looked like it might snap at any moment as he unclipped the paper from his table. Fredrik's paleness contrasted sharply with Peter's deep tan. Even though Peter was no longer doing the physical training of HJ, his muscles were a natural part of his build. Fredrik, on the other hand, looked like he'd never done a day's physical labor in his life. He looked at Peter through his thick glasses.

"Myopic," he said, answering the question that hadn't

been asked. "That's why I came here to serve. Instead of a regular Hitlerjugend." He passed the paper over to Peter. "Point five centimeters to the meter. And watch this corner here," he said, pointing to a drawing of a mass of wires. "You've got to pay close attention to what links where and—"

Just then an air raid siren cut through the room.

Peter froze for a moment, unsure of where to go. There had been no discussion of a shelter. There was a pause between siren blasts and he heard the bombers.

"Run for the bridge!" shouted Lutz. Peter dropped his tools and ran out the nearest door. As he left the building, he risked a glance up at the clear blue sky above him. Not a cloud. Not a shadow. Nothing between him and the planes he could see racing toward the factory.

The concrete bridge across the river was about three hundred meters away. The sound of the bombers was deafeningly close.

Workers were pouring out of the building, everyone running, looking for safe cover.

"Faster!" Lutz shouted behind them.

Peter's legs pressed into the dry earth, his feet flinging him forward toward the bridge. He heard the whine of a bomb as it began to fall to earth. Two hundred meters. He could see Fredrik just paces ahead of him, his long legs hardly touching the ground. One hundred meters.

Suddenly Peter was up in the air. The force of the explosion behind him threw him off his feet. He hit the ground, stumbled, and then was up again. Running. Fifty meters. He dove under the bridge and hugged the riverbank. He squeezed in with about fifty others and turned to look back.

Half of the factory was flattened. The half where he had been sitting moments before. His drafting table was crushed beneath the rubble.

He saw some of the apprentices crouched behind a boulder on the other side of the factory. He saw some bodies lying on the ground, just outside the factory doors.

Then he saw Max stumble up from the ground and start running as fast as his legs would carry his bulk. He held his breath as he heard the whine of another bomb falling. He saw Max reach the boulder.

The blast obliterated the other half of the factory.

BOOM!

An explosion inside. Instantly the whole building was engulfed in flames.

It was then that Peter remembered the Russian prisoners.

"If they hear sirens they have to go down to the bunkers, get the extinguishers, and put out any fires ..."

They'd be under the factory now. In their bunkers. With the fire raging above them.

A cold sweat broke out over Peter's face. He could taste bile at the back of his throat. The factory was an obvious target, but there had been no plan for the workers in case of attack. There were no shelters. But for the Russian POWs, there was a "plan." A plan of incineration.

Chapter Twenty-Three

Hamburg,
October 1944

... there's a weight pressing. I try to move my arms, to push it off, but everything is in slow motion. A hand falls beside my face, brushing my cheek. Just a hand. I know it's Eugene's. It's swollen and fat. Waterlogged. "Sieg Heil!" the hand says. It explodes in a blaze like a firework. I shield my eyes. How can it be on fire when it is so wet? "When are you coming back?" Olga's voice in my ear is crying. I turn to look at her but she's a skeleton. Her eyes are round, huge, empty. She's staring at me as flames begin at her feet. I'm screaming, looking for water to put out the fires, and she's just standing there as the fire leaps to her clothes, her hair, until she's a column of flame, just her eyes staring at me, a black pillar, and I scream—

"Peter. Peter, wake up." His eyes see his mother sitting beside him in the half-light of the early morning.

"You were shouting. You were having a nightmare."

He lies in the gloom trying to remember, trying to forget.

"Would you like a cup of coffee?"

He nodded slowly. His body felt sore, bruised. Memories of the day before started to form in his mind. Flying through the air. Bombs in the daytime. Fire.

His mother brought him a mug of steaming coffee with hot milk. It was sweet and strong and tasted incredibly good. "Is this real?" he asked her.

She smiled. "Yes. From Hans. And a bit of extra sugar. He's been very good to me."

He sat in bed, savoring every mouthful. He wanted to make this moment last forever so that he wouldn't have to go back to Klockner, so that he wouldn't have to face the bunker of incinerated Russians. But no moment lasts.

The gray damp reflected Peter's mood. *If only it had been overcast yesterday*, he thought. *They wouldn't have bombed during the day if it had been overcast. The Russians would still be alive.*

But he knew that this kind of thinking could split him apart. He knew that his job, his duty, was to report to work and help with the cleanup. He made his mind blank. Again.

He got off the tram and walked across the bridge. Such a short distance from the factory to the bridge. From life to death.

When they had sorted and stacked pieces of the building, they laid out the charred bodies from the underground bunkers in rows. *Wouldn't there be lists of names somewhere?* Peter thought. *Isn't there someone far away who should know that their son/boyfriend/ brother died a hero's death?*

They dug a large pit, threw the bodies in, and covered them up.

"The enemy cannot defeat our spirit. We will spend the winter re-building Klockner. Once again, we'll be the best airplane engine manufacturing plant in the world," Lutz intoned.

Why? Peter wondered. *Why bother? The war will be over soon. Everyone knows that. And once the war is over, we won't be building airplanes anymore.*

He couldn't bear the idea of such meaningless work. He couldn't bear the idea of wasting time rebuilding a factory that was going to be useless. He couldn't bear the idea of walking over that pit every day.

But the next morning Lutz gathered them all together.

"A change of orders has come through. Hitlerjugend apprentices will not be rebuilding Klockner. The Reich has determined that because of your bravery, you are ready to receive your further training ahead of schedule." He gestured to a weedy-looking man with a thin brown mustache. "This is Herr Jürgen from the Ministry's Education office. Herr Jürgen will tell you how you will best serve the Reich at this time."

Herr Jürgen stretched his neck out of his tight collar, as though he were trying to make himself look taller than he was.

"The time has come for you to serve your country with vigor and commitment. It is for your future that we fight, and it is time for you to embrace that future."

Oh, my God, they're recruiting us to be officers, thought Peter. *At fifteen.*

"You will be sent to a training camp where you will train as men. You can choose a camp in Poland, Bavaria, or Denmark. You will be well-fed and looked after. And in six short weeks, you will take your oath and serve the Führer. You will show our enemies what Germany is made of! Heil Hitler!"

Maybe it was the autumn gloom. Maybe it was the endless pots of turnip soup. Maybe it was the smell of burnt flesh that clung to his skin. He'd vowed to stay in Hamburg with his mother, but suddenly he wanted nothing more than to leave. He wanted to get out. He wanted to eat until his stomach stretched.

Poland, Bavaria, or Denmark. He thought of the sad photos Janusz had shown him of Poland, so long ago. He'd heard that all they ate in Poland was potatoes. Neumarkt was on the edge of Bavaria. He thought of the nuns' gray soup. Then he suddenly remembered eating Kopenhagener pastry with Oma Ballin before the war. Pastry from Copenhagen. Little nuggets of marzipan melting on his tongue. His mouth began to water. Denmark tasted exotic.

That night he discussed the offer with his mother and Hans. Hans was impressed. "Definitely," he said. "You should go. Smart young man like you—you'll be a captain in no time. And think of those pretty Danish girls," he added in a lascivious whisper.

Peter looked at his mother. "It's all right. I can manage," she said. "And six weeks is not a long time. You'll be back long before your sixteenth birthday. I'll make you a cake!"

She looked at them both and burst out laughing at the

idea that she might have some egg, a bit of butter, and flour for a cake. But it was a nice thought. A future to hold onto.

And so it was settled. He reported to the recruitment office and got his papers to travel to the training camp in Denmark.

Chapter Twenty-Four

Denmark,
November 1944

... I'm running. Faster. It's getting hard to breathe. But Fredrik sprints past me. "You're going the wrong way," he calls as he vanishes into the distance. I stop. Frau Cressman is forcing a pastry into my mouth. I try to push her away but she's shoving it in. It's choking me. "You are my darlink. You will always be my darlink!" She laughs and her teeth start to fall out of her mouth. Her face is cadaverous. I try to scream, but my mouth is still full of sticky pastry. She smells like death. I start to gag and—

Peter is moaning in his sleep, ignored by everyone else on the train. His eyes half open and register the blackness of the train as it sways through the countryside. Traveling at night, always in the dark. Trying to be invisible.

Denmark looked even more cold, gray, and damp than Hamburg. But there was a thrill to the sharp air of the North Sea. The train stopped at Sønderborg and, when Peter got out, the salty air slapped his face. He looked out over the steel gray water and felt the heavy stench of death in Hamburg begin to recede.

He walked from the train with other new recruits, across the King Christian Bridge and onto the island of Alsen. Then they boarded a small ferry that took them around to the other side of the island. As they pulled into the dock at the tiny town of Fynshav, Peter saw clusters of women, bundled in layers of sweaters and carrying baskets of every size, waiting to board the ferry for its return journey to Sønderborg. He heard the strange lilting sound of Danish. A row of low tidy buildings curved along the face of the harbor. A small brown church with a dark brown spire punctuated the end of the street. The town was brown on brown, gray on gray.

This landscape fitted him and suited his melancholia. Didn't they call Hamlet the "moody Dane?"

The recruits marched through the town, past a wood, and arrived at a large open field. High wire fences enclosed a series of low buildings that circled a central parade ground. Guards with automatic rifles monitored them from tall towers on either side of a forbidding gate.

Peter suddenly understood that this was not school. There would be no freedom here. He realized with a shudder that the remote location was probably to ensure that no one escaped.

He was trapped.

"Name?" A joyless guard stood at the entrance to register each boy as he arrived.

"Peter Gruber."

"Barrack eight. Name?"

Peter moved on to find barrack eight. He reminded himself that there hadn't really been a choice. All of the training camps would be the same. If he hadn't volunteered to train as an officer, he would have been sent to the front as a soldier. Or put on FLAK duty in Hamburg, as the HJ manager had threatened, and be dead in two weeks.

The barrack was bare and cold. He was sent to a room with three sets of bunk beds and three chests of drawers. One grimy window overlooked the parade ground. An officer's room was across the hall. Peter started to empty his pack.

"Peter?"

He turned. Deep brown eyes stared out from a chiseled face. A lock of light brown hair swept over a furrowed brow.

"Franz?" Beneath the exterior of the intense man in front of him, Peter could just recognize Franz's humorless face. He thought of the last time he'd seen him, when the papers had fallen from the sky, papers that had warned of Hamburg's destruction, papers that had tried to save them.

Franz colored and his spine stiffened, as if he could see the memory in Peter's expression. Peter's eyes flicked to the badges on Franz's uniform. Franz was already ranked as a junior SS officer. "You've done well for yourself," Peter said.

"I have worked hard."

There was a pause. So much had happened.

"Are you bunking here?" Peter asked, trying to capture a moment of camaraderie.

Franz snorted. "I am in charge of this unit. My private room is across the hall." He smiled officiously. "One of the privileges of rank."

The comment irritated Peter. They were from the same city; they'd known each other for years.

"I hear that your father still has the business," Peter said conversationally. "He helped my mother learn about cameras. He taught her enough so that she could get a good job. She was very grateful."

"My father ..." Franz paused, looking unsure for a fraction of a moment, and then his eyes hardened with resolve. "My father was not a loyal member of the party. And he was a cripple. He is being re-educated."

Peter tried to keep his face still. He knew that "re-educated" meant being in a camp for political prisoners.

"He was kind to us," Peter said quietly.

"His ideas were dangerous to the Reich." He saw Franz appraising him. "You're out of shape. You'll have to work hard. I am determined our team will win the contests."

Just then, another recruit arrived to claim a bunk. A familiar head of dark curly hair emerged from under a cap.

"Gunter?" Gunter started when he heard Peter's voice. They looked at each other in silence for a moment. There were so many questions. Peter felt the weight of their last exchange hanging in the air. "I'm glad to see you," said Peter tentatively.

"I'm glad to see you, too," said Gunter, looking Peter directly in the eye. His expression was filled with a warmth that filled Peter with shame. Gunter turned to Franz. "And Franz, too! It's like old home week," he said good-naturedly. "Remember the last time we were all together? '*Summertime, and the livin' is easy*,'" Gunter sang lustily in English. His voice had settled into a deep baritone. Peter remembered how high and squeaky their voices had sounded at Franz's apartment.

"That song is banned. You are forbidden to sing it," Franz said sharply.

Gunter opened his mouth in surprise. His eyes took in Franz's rank. "Whoa ... you've come up in the world," he said slowly.

"I have worked hard," he repeated.

"Guess the livin' won't be very easy around here!" Gunter mumbled as he started to unpack his bag. There was an awkward silence. Franz was staring at Gunter with cold eyes.

"Heil Hitler!" he said, clicking his heels and saluting.

Gunter straightened and turned to face him.

"Heil Hitler," both Gunter and Peter responded. They watched as Franz turned on his heel and left the room.

"I expect we'll all be good Nazis by the time they finish with us here," said Gunter.

Peter felt a stab of regret as he realized how much he had missed Gunter's friendship. "You were shipped from Bamberg?" he asked. He desperately wanted to bridge the gulf that the last year had made.

Gunter nodded. "How did the apprenticeship work out?"

"I learned a few things until they blew us up," Peter smiled good-naturedly. "Is Otto here, too?" He was filled with nostalgia for the days of the SFGBS.

Gunter's face fell. "Didn't you hear?" he asked seriously.

Peter went cold. "What?" he said.

Gunter took a deep breath. He slowly let it out. "Last

year, when we got back to Hamburg after Bistriz, his family was gone."

"The fires?"

"No."

The room was very still. Peter searched Gunter's face.

"No," Gunter continued. "While we were in Hungary, they found out about Otto's father being a Jew."

You can't prove anything about a person by their physical characteristics.

"But his mother wasn't Jewish," Peter said. "It's passed through the mother."

"She married a Jew. It's against the law."

"But she married him before it was against the law!" Peter's voice rose. Gunter waved his hand for Peter to lower his voice.

"She was sent to Neuengamme to work," Gunter said. His voice was flat.

To work. Photos from the shop were projected in Peter's mind.

"What about Otto?"

Gunter looked at him for a long moment. "The SS were waiting for him when we got back. I was there. We'd gone to his apartment together. They said he was impersonating an Aryan ..."

"What? But he is half Aryan and ..." Peter tried to interrupt. He didn't want to hear what was coming next.

"... and that he wasn't wearing a star and that the penalties were harsh for a Jew who didn't wear his star." Gunter's jaw was set. "They took him."

Peter was silent.

"There was nothing I could do," Gunter continued. "When I began to speak, they turned on me and said that there were penalties for harboring a Jew. That if I knew what was good for me, I would stay out of it. That was it. That was the last I saw of him."

"Remember the Christmas festival in front of the Rathaus when we were little? There was always something good to eat."

"Did you know?" Peter asked Gunter.

"Yeah, he told me that first year we were in Gymnasium. He said that you knew and he thought you might tell me, so he wanted to tell me first. But we never talked about it. And you never did tell me."

"No," said Peter sadly. "I just didn't think it was that important."

Silence hung heavily in the room. Gunter looked at Peter, then turned and began to put his things away. "Mind if I take the bottom bunk?" he asked.

Just then a strangely familiar voice hit Peter's ears. "Godforsaken little fishing village, that's what it is. The food had better be good, that's all I can say."

"Old home week," Gunter repeated with a quiet laugh as Hermann turned around. Hermann crossed his arms and leaned against the doorframe. In the last two years his body had become taut. Peter could see the heavy shadow of a beard on his face. Hermann loosened the tie of his uniform to reveal a mass of chest hair.

"Oh, God, that's all I need to make this perfect. The idiot and the pretty boy."

"Don't you think it's time we buried this hatchet?" asked Peter.

"Yeah, bury it in your skull," Hermann laughed, looking at the small redheaded boy beside him. The boy snorted. The sound was vaguely familiar. "Where've you been, anyway? You didn't come to Bamberg." Hermann said.

"I stayed in Hamburg. Worked at the Klockner factory. As an apprentice," Peter answered briefly.

"You quit Gymnasium?"

"I thought I could serve my country better as a draftsman," Peter said, hoping to keep the irony out of his voice.

"So what happened?" Hermann asked.

This is the longest conversation we've ever had without him hitting me, thought Peter. "The factory blew up. I figured they were going to draft me soon, so I decided to go for better training."

"And better food," Hermann laughed. His sidekick laughed. "Yeah, well, since we're in the same barracks and on the same team, I guess I'll wait until after the war to kick your ass again," Hermann said, as he turned to put his pack on a top bunk.

Peter looked at Hermann's back. For one moment he thought about reminding Hermann that it was he who had kicked Hermann's ass. *Let it go*, he thought. *Pick your battles*, as his mother would have said.

"You remember Kurt," Hermann said casually over his shoulder. Kurt gave Peter and Gunter a nervous sneer. Peter hadn't remembered him until Hermann had said his name. Kurt was not a memorable person. But his name immediately brought back the image Peter had of him as a weasel.

"He's gonna sleep in the bottom bunk," Hermann said authoritatively. "Who else is on the team? Please tell me we've got some strength, not just you two losers."

"Franz Weber," said Gunter. Hermann started to groan. "You better watch it. He's head of the team. He's taken the oath. He's an SS cadet already."

"That pansy? The one whose father turned their house into a junk heap? They listened to illegal records all the time. What's he doing as SS? How'd he get ranked already?"

"Hard work." A steely voice spat out the words. Franz eyed Hermann from the doorway.

Peter couldn't help but enjoy the moment. Franz in his crisp uniform, pulling rank on rumpled and unkempt Hermann. Up until then, he hadn't noticed that Franz wore a gun. He saw Hermann's eyes flick to the holster.

Franz's cold blue eyes took in Kurt for the first time. "You're not the wrestler," he said dismissively.

"No, I'm Kurt," Kurt laughed nervously.

"I guess that would be me." A familiar light voice spoke up behind Franz.

"Hey, Max!" said Peter happily. He hadn't seen Max since the cleanup of the Russian bodies at Klockner.

"Hey, Peter," said Max. "You chose Danish pastries, too."

Franz, Gunter, Hermann, and Kurt stared up at Max. His bulk filled the doorway, his uniform barely stretching around his forearms.

"You'll do," said Franz, clearing his throat and finding his voice. They watched as Max unpacked his things onto the last remaining bed. *Thank God it's a lower bunk*, thought Peter. He couldn't imagine Max hauling his massive size onto an upper bed.

"You're all due out on parade in five minutes," Franz broke the silence, snapping out the words. "Sieg Heil!" he saluted.

"Sieg Heil!" they returned. Franz turned smartly and left the room.

For the first time in a very long time, Peter felt a frisson of excitement. He felt as though he was waking up after a long winter's sleep. So this was to be their unit for the next six weeks. What were the odds? He'd signed up for training on a remote island in Denmark and wound up on a team with boys he'd grown up with. Men. Gunter and Hermann made him remember a part of himself he'd lost. Competition and friendship. It startled him to realize how much he needed them.

He was fifteen and a half, in an elite SS training camp in Denmark, fighting for his country. He was alive. Maybe it wouldn't be so bad.

Chapter Twenty-Five

Denmark.
Winter 1944–1945

The camp was nothing like the Hitlerjugend.

"You are here to train," barked Kommandant Trautmann. "You are not here to make friends; you are not here to play at war games. You are here to learn how to fight for the Führer and to prove that you are worthy."

There were over two hundred young men. They were berated constantly by the guards, camp leaders, and group leaders. Everyone enjoyed pulling rank on everyone else. The competition was fierce and nasty. This was the army, grueling and joyless. Night and day, guards patrolled with large sleek dogs.

Whenever they were given a few moments of free time, which wasn't often, Peter found solace in the woods. He loved the crunch of the icy moss underfoot and the way the trees creaked. He thought about Hamburg and wondered about his mother, and whether Hans had been called up as a guard.

He worked hard at not thinking about Hungary. He

knew that the country was a battleground between the Hungarians and Germans on one side, and the Russians and Romanians on the other. He'd deliberately left Olga's photo back in Hamburg. He didn't want to remember her. He'd lost all interest in taking photos, and he'd given the camera to his mother to sell at the shop. He knew she could use the money.

Peter had arrived at the camp with several cartons of cigarettes, a bottle of schnapps, two large rounds of garlic sausage, and three tins of canned peaches. He knew from his previous experiences what valuable trades these would be, and he wasn't disappointed.

Deiderik was the guard in charge of their group. Large, with a smooth round face, Deiderik had seen active service at the beginning of the war but, like Hans Corm, he'd been hit with shrapnel. In his case, he'd been hit in the face and lost most of the sight in his left eye, which meant he couldn't man the guard tower but he could be responsible for the recruits. The long white scars stretching down the left side of his face made him look older than his years. He wasn't very bright, but he was kind-hearted and seemed to take a liking to Peter. He found Peter's cigarettes on the first day and confiscated them. "But if you want some, just let me know. I'll sell you as many as you want," he said with a laugh.

Peter let him have the cigarettes without making a fuss. He knew that Deiderik would have taken them anyway, but he figured that keeping on Deiderik's good side was the best trade he could have made anyway. Each time he bought a cigarette, he had a chance to get news of the outside world.

Peter was keenly aware of their isolation. He wanted to know what was going on, and Deiderik was his lifeline to the news. Details were sketchy, but Deiderik told him what he heard on the state radio.

Deiderik was also useful in helping Peter trade with other guards. He acted as a middleman, "just taking a bit off the top," he said to Peter. He made sure Peter got enough money so that Peter could continue to buy back his cigarettes.

The bottle of schnapps was a big prize. Deiderik could have just confiscated it, but he surprised Peter by giving him an old Luger in exchange. Peter hefted the gun from one hand to another.

"Nothing we use here, you understand," Deiderik said. "And it's only got a few bullets. But you never know when it might come in handy. Keep it well hidden."

Peter fell into the routine at the camp fairly easily. Ironically, the food was the worst part. It made his stomach turn. It was greasy and there was smoked herring at every meal. He was sure his sweat smelled like fish.

Every day there were early morning marches, followed by calisthenics, obstacle races, and target practice. They were taught how to clean, load, and shoot a pistol, a rifle, and an anti-tank gun. At his first target practice, the backward jolt from the anti-tank gun smashed Peter so hard, he flew over backwards. Hermann laughed long and hard, until he shot and did the same thing. But Peter's aim was good, and he won Franz's grudging respect when their team came in first in the shooting competition.

Franz was determined to be first in every competition. They stood outside in a cold December rain while Franz outlined a new task.

"You are to carry your anti-tank gun as you go through the obstacle course. Do not drop or put the gun down, or the team will be disqualified. As usual, we'll be competing against the other teams at the end of the week.

"This one will put us out in front. We will practice and practice until you feel nothing. Remember, you are doing this for the Fatherland!"

Peter looked at the massive anti-tank gun in front of him. A meter and a half long, nine centimeters in diameter. His shoulder was still mottled in a yellow, purple, and blue bruise from last week's encounter.

Rain slid from Peter's hat onto his cheekbones, wound down his face, and landed under his collar. He hoisted the mammoth gun onto his shoulder. *Christ*, he thought, *the thing must weigh thirty kilos*. His boots sank deeper in the mud under the weight.

"On your mark," yelled Franz. "Get set. Go!"

Peter pushed off, trudging through the sodden earth, toward the first obstacle—a series of tires to run through, hopping from one foot to the other.

"Move! Move!" He was aware of Hermann beside him, pulling ahead. Franz was keeping pace with them, holding the stopwatch, running and yelling.

Gunter and Kurt were behind him, with Max bringing up the rear. Max was strong as an ox, and he could get them into first place on anything that required brute strength.

But nimble he wasn't. *He's not going to be able to negotiate these tires*, thought Peter.

"Focus! Move!" Franz was right; Peter was letting his mind drift. He was heading toward the second obstacle, a steep artificial hill, worn and pitted, with treacherous boulders sticking out to make an incredibly uneven surface. He hit the hill running, but his foot slid on the slippery rocks and he went down, smashing his knee. Still, he kept the gun held high.

"Jackass! Watch where you're going! Run, run!"

Hermann crested the hill ahead of him. Peter had to catch up to him or he'd never hear the end of it. He dug his boots into the mucky earth and pushed himself forward. He was soaked to the skin, but he wasn't sure if it was sweat or rain. He looked over the top of the hill just in time to see Hermann trip and roll. Going down was just as hard as going up, Peter realized. Hermann came out of his roll, covered in mud but carrying his gun aloft. Peter slowed down a bit, just to be more careful so he wouldn't fall.

"Don't slow down!" yelled Franz beside him.

He picked up his speed again and was alert to each footfall. He made it to the bottom of the hill and sprinted across the flat to the next obstacle. His heart sank. It was a small, dank, icy pond. He could see Hermann ahead of him, running into the water. Deeper and deeper he went, until his head was bent back to allow his nose to just skim the surface of the water.

Peter was a good four inches shorter than Hermann, probably a foot shorter than Max. He'd have to hold his breath and move through as quickly as he could. He heard the others crashing over the hill behind him.

"Don't stop! Keep moving! Run!" Franz yelled. Peter took off straight into the water, lifting his knees high as the water splashed up at him. He was so cold and wet already that he didn't feel any difference.

His arms screamed with exhaustion, but he pressed forward. He was walking on his tiptoes. He took a deep breath and, holding the gun above the surface, pushed forward under the water. He tried to kick his legs but, suddenly, he lost track of direction.

He panicked. Terror derailed him. He was flailing, thrashing, trying not to breathe, but the water was everywhere. He wasn't sure which way was up.

Just then, a strong arm grabbed him under the armpits and swung his head out of the water. He was being moved forward, propelled through the water, his gun still in the air, his eyes temporarily blinded, coughing, yet moving forward, his legs kicking air.

And then he was down, his feet on solid ground, Franz yelling, "Don't stop! Go! Go," and he made his feet move. In front of him he saw Max, Max who had effortlessly carried him and his gun in one arm, while keeping his own gun high with the other. Max continued jogging forward in his plodding way.

They headed to the last section, a forested area where they wove in and out of the trees. The home stretch. He could see Hermann and the others collapsed in the mud at the end of the woods. Max ran heavily but evenly to the end and towered above them all.

Peter came in last. He doubled over, spitting and coughing. He turned to Max. "Thank you," he said between coughs.

"You would have done the same for me," was all Max said. Peter tried to imagine hoisting up the gargantuan Max. *Everyone on the team does what he can*, he thought.

"Thirteen minutes," said Franz. "Pathetic. We've got to get it down to ten."

Peter was afraid he might throw up.

But by the end of the week, they did have it down to ten minutes, and by the time they went into the competition, they managed to get 9.75, handily beating the team from Bremen. Peter developed a technique for getting through the water, where he swam backwards, holding his gun up and kicking with his feet. If his head didn't go in, he could usually get through on his own. And since Max didn't have to help Peter, he could go faster. They won that week, and the next, and by the end of the six weeks of training, their team was the top ranked, much to Franz's delight.

Six weeks stretched to seven weeks and then eight. There was no talk of going home. Just more training. Peter was desperate for news of the outside world. He did whatever he could to cultivate his relationship with Deiderik.

"Deiderik, have you got a cigarette?" Peter asked innocently, making sure that no one was around to hear.

"Ah, Peter," Deiderik sighed, "I don't think I have one to spare. Sorry."

"I'll pay you five pfennig," Peter said.

Deiderik sniffed, his left eye staring straight ahead. But his crooked smile was reassuring.

"Seven," Peter said. "That's my last offer."

"If I wasn't so soft-hearted, I'd be rich," Deiderik muttered as he pulled out a cigarette and handed it to Peter. He bent to light Peter's cigarette, and Peter slid the money circumspectly into Deiderik's hand as he held the match.

"Any news?" Peter asked as he puffed to get the tobacco lit.

"Apparently the Polish resistance has finally surrendered to us. Warsaw's burned to the ground. Could have saved a lot of trouble if they'd just given in at the start."

Poland. Good thing he hadn't gone to the training camp there. It was the first he'd heard of a Polish resistance. What a futile effort.

"And our battleship *Tirpitz* was destroyed off the coast of Norway."

"Close to here?" Peter asked. He knew that Norway was just across the water.

"Not really. Up north of here. Up near the Arctic Circle. Ridiculous place to wage a war. A thousand sailors were killed," said Deiderik.

"Any news from Hamburg?" Peter asked.

"Nope. All quiet, I guess," was all Deiderik said. Peter wasn't entirely sure that he was telling the truth, but he didn't have any choice but to believe him.

Winter in Denmark was even colder and grayer than in Hamburg. On Christmas, Deiderik shared some of the schnapps with him. It was the only time Peter felt warm. Then two days later, a team from Schwerin tried to escape. Someone reported them missing (*Was it Franz*, thought Peter, *earning a special bonus?*). It turned out they'd been digging in the woods—just a little each day—and had managed to tunnel under the fence. The guards let loose the dogs and quickly found them up in the trees just beyond the camp. The unit was stripped, handcuffed, and made to stand outside all day and all night, naked in the freezing rain. Hermann laughed at their blue testicles. Whenever someone began to slump, a guard would fire a warning shot into the ground at their feet. The unit stood rigid for twenty-four hours.

It was after the failed escape that everyone in the camp was called together to take the oath.

"You are not children. You are not students. You are cadets, training to be officers in Hitler's army," said Kommandant Trautmann. "It is time that you pledged your allegiance to Chancellor Hitler. After you take the oath, disobeying orders or endangering the Reich is punishable by imprisonment or death."

And so it was that on a cold January day, Peter found himself, along with two hundred others, swearing a "holy oath by God, to obey the Führer of the German Reich and the people, Adolf Hitler, commander in chief of the Wehrmacht, unconditionally."

He was officially a soldier for the Fatherland.

Chapter Twenty-Six

Denmark,
April 1945

The days began to lengthen, and the weeks stretched into months. The camp was rife with rumors. Franz said that the British and Americans were retreating. "The American president has died," said Franz. "The new president will join with the Führer and defeat the English bastards."

Peter traded his last pfennig for a rare cigarette and some news from Deiderik. "The Soviets have taken Budapest," Deiderik told him. "The rest of Hungary won't be far behind." Russians in Hungary. Everyone said they were bloodthirsty and cruel. Especially to girls.

"And the Americans have crossed the Rhine at Remagen," Deiderik continued. His broad cheery face had become a pale pile of sagged skin. He took a long drag on his cigarette as they smoked together.

Remagen is just south of Köln, thought Peter. *Köln is only about five hundred kilometers from Hamburg. A week's march?*

"We're being squeezed," Deiderik continued sadly. "The

Soviets coming from the east, the Americans from the west, the British from the north." He exhaled a huge stream of smoke. "It won't be long."

Everyone in the camp was tense. Franz maintained a fierce energy, insisting that their team continue to train vigorously. "We must be ready to fight. Our Führer needs us!" he screamed at them. But with decreasing rations, their energies were flagging.

"It's purgatory, isn't it," said Gunter. "Neither in the war nor out of it. Like those moments before a thunderstorm when everything is calm but you feel kind of sick to your stomach."

The first of May dawned beautifully, leaving memories of the winter far behind. Peter got up early in the first light to walk through the woods before he had to be on parade. Soft tawny brown birds flitted in and out of the woods, making a high-pitched piping sound. The air was warm and gentle breezes carried the smell of the sea.

Suddenly he heard a gunshot. And screaming. It was coming from his barracks.

He headed back at a run. Now he could hear more voices yelling, but above them all, he heard hysterical screaming. He opened the door to pandemonium. He saw Max sitting on top of Franz, pinning his arms down on the floor. Franz was screaming but Peter couldn't make out what he was saying. Hermann was standing on Franz's right arm.

He was leaning down, trying to pry open Franz's hand, fighting to get hold of Franz's gun. Kurt stood frozen, staring down at Franz, his eyes wide and filled with panic.

Peter heard running and saw Gunter and Kurt charging down the hall, trailed by Deiderik.

"Mrraugh! Yrslell! Frmnspt!" Franz was thrashing under Max and Hermann. Deiderik went straight to him and slapped him on the face. Hard. Franz's head snapped to the side and he went slack. For a moment no one moved. And then Franz began to cry.

Peter was so astonished by the sound that he wasn't sure at first if it was actually coming from Franz. But it was Franz and he was weeping. *As though his heart is broken*, thought Peter.

Peter saw that Hermann now held the gun. He watched Hermann open it, take out the ammunition, and hand it to Deiderik.

Max slowly lifted himself off Franz. As he did so, Franz curled into a tight fetal ball and continued to weep softly. They all looked down at him.

Peter crossed the room to stand beside Gunter. "What happened?" he whispered.

"Don't know. He was in his room, listening to the radio like always. I was still asleep. Suddenly I heard him screaming at the top of his lungs. He came running in here with his pistol drawn. He fired once and hit the wall and, before he could fire again, Max had tackled him." Gunter's eyes were wild and his hair was sticking out at odd angles. He was still in his pajamas.

Deiderik clicked his heels together and walked into the corridor. Peter knew that the other boys in the barracks were frozen, waiting for an explanation. He saw Deiderick square his shoulders.

"All troops must report to the parade grounds for inspection. Immediately." With that, Deiderik turned on his heels, marched down the corridor and out of the building.

No one spoke a word. Franz slowly got to his feet and, with his head low, shuffled into his room and closed the door.

Peter's mind was racing. What on earth was going on? He filed out with the rest of the boys and took his place in the ranks. He stood as stiffly and quietly as possible, staring straight ahead as the others joined him on the parade ground. Franz filed in last. Peter could see out of the corner of his eye that he had straightened his uniform and brushed his hair.

Kommandant Trautmann strode in front of them. Guards positioned themselves in the corners. Peter felt a rising panic. Had they done something wrong? Had someone tried to escape again? Would they all be shot?

The Kommandant stopped formally at the front, in the center, to address them.

"Our Führer Adolf Hitler has fallen at his command post in the Reich's Chancellery."

There was a sharp intake of breath.

"His life was lived in service to Germany and he died a hero's death in the capital city of the German Reich. Before his death, he declared Gross Admiral Donitz his successor."

There was stunned silence throughout the ranks. Peter felt the terror roll through them like a fire.

Hitler dead? It was impossible. All his life he'd been taught that everything he did, he did for Hitler. It was as though an invisible rope that had held him to a mooring suddenly snapped. He'd grown up being told that Hitler was his Father.

He was Father to all of them. What happened when your father died? Did you carry on with your father's wishes, carry on with the war? *Or does this mean the war is over?* The thought flew into Peter's mind, unbidden. *Will the bombing stop? Can we go home?*

"Your training will continue. Group leaders, ensure that all endurance tests are completed as usual today."

Peter barely took in the words. He was numb. His body went through the motions. His mind went blank as he flew over hurdles, raced over tires, and nimbly shot bull's eye after bull's eye in the target range.

The next day passed in a haze of uncertainty. There was no discussion. Everyone continued on as though nothing had happened. But on the afternoon of the third day, Deiderik came into their room just as they were getting ready to go to lunch. He gently pushed Franz into the room ahead of him. He closed the door quietly.

"Things are starting to unravel," Deiderik said quietly. He paused. His face sagged, the long scars stretched white and vulnerable. He looked at Peter in silence for a long time. Not as a guard, more like a caring uncle.

"I'd like you to have a chance," he said at long last. Again, a long pause.

"Don't you see? It's over. You've got to get out. Get out while you can." He looked at their blank faces. "The British are in Denmark," he continued forcefully. "They have met up with the Danish Resistance. Do you have any idea what they do to enemy soldiers?"

"I know what the German army does to deserters," Peter

blurted out. The photo of the hanging men forced his voice out of his body. He had taken the oath. He was a junior SS officer. He was part of the machinery of war. If he left, he'd be a deserter.

"You're only a deserter if you're caught," said Deiderik quietly, his eyes boring into Peter.

"I thought we were going to be sent to the front," Hermann said plaintively.

"Do you know what is happening on the Russian front?" Deiderik's color rose as he turned on Hermann. He spat the words out. "Do you want to be cannon fodder? You're not even sixteen years old, for Christ's sake. I'm telling you, you've got a chance if you go."

Deiderik turned his back to them. "The leadership is having a meeting right after lunch," he said to the closed door. "All the guards will be there.

"It's not just about the war," he continued quietly as he slowly opened the door, his back still turned to them. Peter could barely hear his words. "They have found the work camps."

The pictures hit Peter's mind like a sledgehammer. The secrets that no one spoke. The horror. The British, the Americans—everyone would know the unspeakable.

With that, Deiderik turned the knob and walked out of the room, shutting the door behind him.

Peter looked at the others. Finally he broke the silence.

"We've got to get out. Back to Germany. We've got to get home."

"Are you crazy?" said Hermann. "Do you want a

Doberman's teeth in your ass? Do you want to be strung up as a deserter?"

"It'll take a while before they notice we're gone. You heard Deiderik, all the guards and the leadership will be at a meeting. If we're quick, we can get out." Peter's heart was thumping. He could see everything mapped out in front of him. The American and British soldiers invading. Finding the camps. The horror. The revenge.

"But where would we go? We're on a goddamn island in the middle of goddamn nowhere!" Hermann's voice rose and, with it, panic began to fill the room. Kurt's face was a mask of terror. He looked close to tears.

"We can do it if we work together," said Gunter. "We're smart and we're fast. The fastest in the camp." *Good old Gunter*, thought Peter, *always the optimist*.

"Strongest in the camp," said Max slowly, as though he was chewing over the idea.

"Smartest, fastest, and strongest," said Gunter with a smile.

They all turned at the same moment to look at Franz. Franz had sat quietly slumped in a chair the whole time Deiderik had spoken. There was no love lost between Deiderik and Franz, Peter knew that. Deiderik had singled them out because he liked Peter. He wouldn't have given Franz a chance on his own. But Franz was their group leader, and they couldn't try to escape without him knowing.

He could report us, Peter thought with a chill. The leadership would hang them right here, as an example to everyone else. He knew that everyone was thinking the same thought. How far would Franz go for his country?

Franz was looking at the floor.

Peter waited for Franz to snap and start ordering them around. But he just kept looking down, shrunken and defeated. Since the news of the Führer's death, Franz had collapsed. Peter looked at Franz's hunched body and realized that he wouldn't report them. More than any of them, Franz knew that all that he had fought for was over.

There was dead silence. Everyone seemed to be waiting to be told what to do. All the years of taking orders had left them with a terrifying inertia.

Peter looked around the room. The others were all looking at him expectantly. He realized he was the one who had to make this happen.

But can we make it? he wondered. *Can we escape from the camp, get off the island, get back to Hamburg with the British on our tail the whole way?*

"Okay," he said slowly. "After lunch, get on your civilian clothes, the ones you came here in. We'll change and just walk out and go into the town. As though it was perfectly normal." He took a breath. He straightened up. "I've got some Danish kroner. Anyone else have any money?"

"I've got a few Reichsmarks," said Hermann. "And half a bottle of schnapps."

"You've got schnapps?!" Gunter rounded on him. "You've had it all along and never thought to share?"

Hermann shrugged. "A man's got to have some secrets."

"I've got some chocolate," offered Kurt. Hermann turned to glare at him. "You're not the only one with secrets," Kurt said defensively.

"Great," said Peter. "Bring anything you can carry. We can use it to trade along the way. We'll head for the port and see if we can barter a ride to take us to the German coast."

Everyone seemed content to defer to him. The waiting was over. It was time for action. They were on the move.

It was terrifying to walk out of the camp. Peter expected to hear a "Halt!" behind them at any moment, followed by a gunshot and the snap and snarl of dogs. But they walked quietly out the front gate. There were no dogs, no guards, nothing. He hoped that the leaders' meeting would last all afternoon.

He remembered the Luger under his mattress when they were halfway down to the road.

He thought about going back for it. It might have been useful to have along. And if it were found, it would be incriminating. But he knew there was no turning back. They had to move quickly.

They walked down the road in silence, each trying to look more relaxed and confident than he felt. It was a stunningly beautiful spring afternoon, and a passerby might have thought them a group of close friends heading out for a day of adventure, a picnic, perhaps.

Peter's hearing was alert to every sound. But there was nothing but birdsong and the sound of their boots on the rough gravel.

"I think we should go through the woods," he said. "We're too exposed here." He was going on raw instinct, but he knew that he always felt safe in the woods.

Everyone followed as he headed off the road. He walked

quickly, determinedly, wanting to get deeply into the woods before they stopped to talk. Peter thought of the spring days in Neumarkt, exploring the woods and playing Capture the Flag. The adrenalin of his fear brushed aside his nostalgia.

"We've got to have a plan," said Gunter beside him. "We can't just walk into the woods and expect to come out in Hamburg. We all came here by ferry. We're going to have to leave that way."

Peter's mind was racing, trying to remember the steps they'd taken to get here six months ago.

"He's right," said Hermann. "This is madness. We don't even have a compass. We don't know where the hell we're going."

"HALT! WHO ARE YOU? WHERE ARE YOU GOING?"

Instantly they froze. The voice came from their left, a bit further on in the forest. Peter looked and saw that Kurt— vague, weasely Kurt—had wandered away, straight into the heart of a German patrol. The rest of them were camouflaged among the dense trees. The patrol hadn't seen them. Yet.

He saw Kurt turn to the patrol. He saw him gesticulating, answering questions. And then he saw Kurt point to where they were standing.

Peter went cold. *That stupid bastard*, he thought. *He couldn't have kept his mouth shut? Was this as far as they would make it? Caught in the woods a half-hour from the camp? Would they hang them here or take them back to the camp to string them up?*

"YOU MUST COME OUT. HOLD YOUR HANDS ABOVE YOUR HEADS. NO SUDDEN MOVEMENTS."

Peter saw guns aimed at them. He looked over at Gunter. They carefully began inching forward. The patrol leader gestured with his gun.

"Who are you and what are you doing out here? We can't get a word of sense out of this one," he said, shrugging back at Kurt.

Peter looked cautiously at the four-man patrol. They were wearing Kriegsmarine uniforms. The navy. The navy? They were carrying short pistols and looked nervous. They weren't from the camp.

"We're evacuees. Kinderlandverschickung," Peter answered, making it up as he went along. "From a boarding school." He wasn't sure there *was* a boarding school on the island, but he had to hope they didn't know that either.

"The Danish Resistance attacked and killed all of our teachers," added Gunter. Peter was impressed by how easily the lie came out of his mouth.

"We ran away," said Kurt, "And now we're lost." *In Kurt's case, that's the truth*, thought Peter. *He looks so naive and young. Like a scared kid.*

The patrol slowly lowered their guns. "You can't go through here," said the group leader. "The Resistance are everywhere. These woods are very dangerous."

"We're lost," repeated Max. He managed to sound like a little boy, even though he towered over all of them.

"You'd better come back to the ship with us."

Peter glanced around and saw a tacit agreement. What choice did they have? At least if they were at the dock, they might find a boat they could hire to get them off the island.

The patrol leader turned and began to lead them out of the woods. The other members of the patrol surrounded them on the sides and at the back. Were they protecting them or maintaining control?

They marched through the woods in silence. It hadn't even occurred to Peter to worry about the Danish Resistance. With every snapped twig, the patrol immediately stopped, crouched, and listened. *Great*, thought Peter, *if we aren't shot as deserters, we'll be shot by the Resistance.* Or taken captive by the enemy. Suddenly the decision to leave seemed madness. They had no plan and virtually no hope.

When they reached the edge of the woods, the patrol leader signaled them to lie flat against a little rise. A wide plain stretched out in front of them, leading to the back gardens of the town of Fynshav. Peter remembered the day of his arrival. It had seemed quaint and provincial. Now it was populated by people who wanted to kill him.

"We'll spread out to cross the field," said the leader. "Walk calmly, do not march. If you hear gunshots, run in a zigzag pattern. When you get to the streets of the town, walk straight to the docks."

Peter's legs felt rubbery as he began to cross the pasture. He listened harder than he had ever listened before. He tried to exude calm, as though he didn't have a care in the world. He thought about the way the late afternoon sun reflected off the roofs. It wouldn't set for hours yet. He made himself aware of the smell of the wet spring earth beneath his feet. He watched starlings swirl in groups in the sky. If he were to be shot in the back, he wanted these things to be the last things in his mind.

And before he knew it, they'd come to the outskirts of the town. The smell of sour fish soup reached Peter's nose. Housewives were out shopping, chatting in the late afternoon line-ups outside the stores. Mothers balanced babies on hips, while children played in yards. It was the picture of a normal day. But as soon as people caught sight of the group, they stopped talking. Every eye turned to watch them.

Peter kept his smile plastered on his face. He tried his best to look friendly. The townspeople stared coldly back. The patrol walked beside the boys, steering them down the main street of town and along to the docks. Peter didn't know what he was expecting to see. He hadn't thought about any of this beforehand. He looked around for the ferry, but it was nowhere. A few fishing boats were pulling away from the dock, heading out to sea, where presumably they would spend the night bringing in their catch. In the distance, he could see boats bobbing on the surface of the water.

But there, right in front of them, gleaming in the sunshine, was a U-boat. Painted on the side was the number 1102.

Crewmen stood on the deck, looking nervous. When they saw the boys with the patrol, they raised their guns.

"It's all right," said the leader. "They're just kids."

"Kids carry guns," said one of the crew.

"Not these ones," said the leader. "Their school was targeted. They're lost."

"Humph," snorted the crewman. "I'll take them to the commander and see what he wants to do with them. Follow me," he ordered.

One by one, they walked over a narrow gangplank,

climbed up onto the U-boat deck, and headed down the ladder into the control room. A strong smell of diesel gas enveloped them. Peter's eyes took a moment to adjust to the green gloom of the electric lights. What greeted him was a room with concave walls, barely the height of a man, filled with equipment. It was desolate and confining. There was a strange hollow throbbing sound. By the time all six of them had descended, there was hardly any space to move.

"Lieutenant Conrad reporting with 'guests,'" said the crewman, with a click of his heels.

Peter hadn't seen anyone else in the control room, so completely had the man blended into the drab gray surroundings. A tall officer stood up from a table covered in maps. He turned to face them. He was pale and gaunt, as though he hadn't seen the sun in years. *Perhaps he hasn't*, thought Peter. The officer looked at the boys, straightened his shoulders, and lifted his head.

"First Lieutenant Erwin Sell," he introduced himself, saluting the boys halfheartedly. His face was filled with such a depth of sorrow that Peter felt his heart tug.

"Sieg Heil," they all saluted back automatically. The commander raised an eyebrow.

"Sir," continued Lieutenant Conrad, "these boys said they were evacuated to a school on the island, but are now homeless. Apparently, their school was destroyed by Danish Resistance." The commander nodded his head as he eyed the boys.

"I didn't think it advisable to leave them on their own in the woods," continued the lieutenant.

Sell looked them over. He was quiet for a moment.

"Things are very unpredictable," he said at long last. "We are on high alert. The British have invaded the island."

At this, there was a sharp intake of breath from Franz.

"Can any of you fire a gun?"

The question caught Peter unawares. Without thinking, he said, "I've won many competitions, sir."

There was a slight pause as the commander and lieutenant processed this information. Peter held his breath. Had he just blown their story?

"Good to know that private schools value the art of marksmanship," Sell said. Peter listened hard to see if he detected a note of irony. But if they doubted the story, they didn't let on. Sell turned toward him.

"I want you to sit at the anti-aircraft gun tonight. We're not expecting anything from the sky, but I don't want to leave it unmanned," he said. "We lost the gunner last night to a Danish sniper."

Great, thought Peter. *Now I've got to add snipers to the list of things to worry about.*

"The rest of you are welcome to sleep in whatever bunks you can find. If you can fit," he said, eyeing Max. Then he turned away from them and sat down again, wearily poring over his maps.

They followed Lieutenant Conrad out of the control room and down a narrow corridor. Bunks were tucked into the curve of the walls. "Take your pick," he said. "The crew will sleep in their own boats tonight."

"Their own boats?" asked Gunter.

"One-man U-boats. We're the mother ship. Because we're on high alert, everyone needs to stay at his station. Ready to go." He gestured to Peter. "You, come with me."

The lieutenant led Peter back through the control room and up on deck. "The anti-aircraft gun is on the other side of the conning tower," he gestured. "There's a headset there that connects with the control room. If you see anything, call down. Only shoot in an emergency. If shooting starts, it could get ugly. But we have to protect the ship." Peter felt the tension in Lieutenant Conrad's voice.

"Yes, sir," he said as the lieutenant retreated back to the control room.

Peter was exhausted from the tension of the day. He found his seat behind the gun. It was similar to the anti-aircraft guns they'd been practicing with all winter. Except then, he'd been hitting stationary targets.

It's not a game …

It was late but the sun wasn't starting to set. Just weeks from the solstice, this far north it would be light for hours yet.

At least he'd be able to see something coming at him.

Chapter Twenty-Seven

Denmark, May 1945

... the sun slants down and shines on the ground. The ground seems to be glowing. It is glowing. It's on fire. There is fire at my feet. I turn around and see fire running all along the forest floor, licking the base of the trees. I start to run, but it's all around me and I don't know how to get out of the woods. I see Otto. "This way," he calls to me but I can't get to him. There are flames everywhere. My hands are burning. Otto is staring at me. His face is melting. His huge eyes stare as the flesh drips from his face. I try to run but my legs won't move. I move my hands to hold onto my face but it's not there. My face is gone and I try to scream ...

He wakes with a start. There is an orange glow in the distance. There is a hum from an engine. His body is rocking. His legs are numb. It takes a minute to remember that he is on a ship, sitting behind a gun turret.

The escape from the camp, running through the woods, the patrol, the town—yesterday's events flooded into Peter's mind. He was a deserter on a submarine, masquerading as an evacuee. He stretched out his legs and felt uncomfortable pins and needles as his circulation began to come back. How long had he been asleep? *The commander will have my head*, he thought. He wondered if he should make a run for it. Could he sneak through the town, cut across country and head for ... where? They were on an island. There was a bridge, he remembered that, but they'd come to the town by ferry. Was the ferry docked now? Could he sneak off the sub and stow away? He stretched his neck to look over the gun toward the town. It was then that he realized they weren't at the dock anymore.

The ship was moving. They were on the open sea.

He felt a moment of panic. He was trapped on a moving submarine, with no idea where he was going.

He tried to still his breathing. Think. The ship was moving slowly, steadily, across the water. Small waves slapped the metal. It was peaceful. But where were they going? It was a submarine. What if Commander Sell decided to submerge? Where was the hatch?

He stood up, steadying himself on the gun's casing. There was nothing between him and the water lapping close to his feet. He looked out over the sea. The orange glow was the early rising sun, sitting on the edge of the eastern horizon. Silhouetted against the light was a low black smudge of land.

Peter wondered if the commander had known from the start they'd be leaving Fynshav. He wondered if he knew they were deserters, escaped from the training camp. They had taken the oath. They had pledged allegiance to Hitler. They were supposed to be posted to the front. Now they were prisoners on a submarine heading God knows where.

He let his legs adjust to the gentle rocking of the ship and lowered himself down the ladder from his perch at the gun turret. Turning, he saw the hatch open, and was absurdly thankful as he realized he hadn't been forgotten after all. He grabbed the rail, swung his leg over, and lowered himself into the control room.

The hazy light made everything in the room look flat and two-dimensional. Commander Sell was moving purposefully around the room. Peter watched him pull out a large flat drawer, take out a map, roll it, and place it into a rucksack at his feet. Sell wasn't that old, he realized, probably not even thirty. But he looked like he had the weight of the world on his shoulders. His back was to Peter when he straightened and said, "Do you want some coffee?"

Without waiting for an answer, Sell walked over to a tin pot sitting on a small hotplate. He picked up a mug from the table, filled it, and handed it to Peter, looking at him for the first time.

"Thank you," Peter said, truly grateful for the hot mug in his hands.

The commander nodded and turned away, moving his rucksack to the far side of the room. Peter stood and quietly sipped the hot liquid. It was strong and bitter and made his mouth pucker. But it was comforting and reassuring. He watched in silence as the commander took various nautical instruments from the shelves and put them in his sack.

Finally, Peter couldn't stay quiet any longer. "Am I under arrest?" he asked nervously.

Sell turned his head. "Under arrest?" he repeated with a frown. "For what? Leaving your school? Wandering in the woods waiting to get shot by the Danish Resistance? We invited you on the ship, so you aren't exactly stowaways."

"But where are you taking us?"

"Where are we taking you?" Sell's frown deepened. He examined Peter's face closely. "You really don't know what is going on, do you?"

Peter shook his head slowly. He was being treated like a child. He was behaving like a child. But nothing made sense anymore.

"It's over. We are surrendering," said Sell.

"You're surrendering?"

The commander smirked. "*We* are surrendering. Germany is surrendering. We've lost. We're finished." He let the words sink in.

War had been the fabric of Peter's daily life for six years. It had been the structure for every decision, every action, since he was ten years old. He felt confused and anxious. There was too much uncertainty to feel relief. His body shook involuntarily.

"Sit," commanded Sell, gesturing to a chair. "Here," he held out a packet of cigarettes to Peter and thrust matches in his direction.

"I wasn't about to sit in Denmark and wait for the Resistance to take over the ship. The Danes are out for blood. I don't think they would have allowed us to surrender," he said with a smirk. "So we are heading home. I didn't think you'd mind being along for the ride, but I didn't want to tell you in case you did something stupid. That grim one is a hothead—I can see it in his eyes. He'd sell his grandmother to prove his loyalty. I didn't want to give him the chance to report us at the base in Denmark."

Peter thought about Franz reporting his own father. A deep sadness came over him with the thought that Franz's personality was so obvious. Were they all so easily recognized? He was glad of the cigarette. He let the smoke calm him.

"I'd keep an eye on him if I were you," said Sell.

Peter nodded. "So where *are* we going?" he asked again.

"The closest base is Kiel. We'll be there in a couple of hours."

Kiel! Peter's heart leapt. He had no idea they were so close. Kiel was near Eutin and Tante Elsa. Eutin was almost home. If the trains were running, he could be home in a day.

"Of course, we don't know what we'll find when we get there. The British are marching through Germany. With any luck, they won't be this far north and we can all find a way to disappear. If not, they'll take us as prisoners. All of us," he said pointedly. "I don't relish the idea of languishing in a prison camp."

"Is that why you're packing the maps and instruments? You're going to head across country?"

"We'll try ... if there is no welcoming committee," the commander said.

Then we'll all be fugitives, thought Peter. But was a deserter a deserter if the war was over? What were the rules when the game changed?

"Where are the others?"

"Your lot? Sleeping like babies in the bunks. All of my men are beside us, sailing their ships into the harbor."

"Can I take my coffee back up on deck?"

Sell reached over for the pot and topped up Peter's mug. "The ship is still mine for another hour at least. And while it is mine, you are my guest," he said with a wry grin. "I don't know where you've been, or where you are going, but I'm happy to have you along for the ride."

Peter juggled his coffee and cigarette back up the ladder. The sky had lightened since he'd been below and he could clearly see the headlands in front of them. He looked across the water and saw tiny submarines gliding silently in the water beside them. He felt a great sense of calm as he stood holding the rail, smoking and sipping his coffee. For a moment, he was safe. And he was going home on a submarine.

Chapter Twenty-Eight

Germany,
May 1945

"Stay here in the control room until we know what is happening on shore." Commander Sell eyed them seriously.

Peter had woken the others as the ship entered the harbor. He'd told them the situation as quickly as possible. Max was staring sleepily at the floor, while Hermann and Gunter looked impatient to be on their way. Kurt, as usual, faded into the background, pale and uncertain. But Franz's silence was heavy and threatening. Something had happened to him the minute they'd gotten on the ship. Peter was scared of his unpredictability.

"There may be British soldiers waiting to shoot the first person that emerges from this ship," the commander said. "It is my responsibility to negotiate our surrender. Stay put until I return. If I don't come back, hide in the ship. When you are discovered, just tell them you are stowaways."

Sell turned, climbed up the ladder, and was gone.

"He is not our commanding officer," grumbled Franz.

"We do not have to take our orders from him."

"No one is our commanding officer," said Peter. "We are deserters. I don't think he believed our story about the school for one minute. He could have had us arrested. He could have had us shot."

The six of them waited, listening for any sounds from above. *So far so good*, thought Peter, *no gunshots yet*. He realized he was holding his breath. They were all stonily silent.

Gunter caught Peter's eye. His face was grim.

"What do you think they're doing back at the camp?" Kurt whispered, interrupting the silence in his whiny voice.

"Sending the second best team to the front," whispered Hermann.

"They wouldn't send them to the front if the war is over," said Gunter.

"We're not really sure the war is over," Franz said, looking at Peter.

"What?" said Peter. "You think I made it up?"

"No, I just think that you're so gullible that Commander what's-his-name could have told you any story and you'd have believed it. For all we know, he's out there getting the Gestapo. Seems a bit convenient that he just decides to bring us over to Kiel out of the goodness of his heart."

"It wasn't out of the goodness of his heart. He has to surrender the ship! And he wasn't about to surrender in Denmark." Peter was fuming.

"Shhhh!" hissed Max. He pointed to the roof of the sub.

They went quiet and, in the silence, they heard footsteps above them. Many footsteps, moving quickly. Peter looked at

Gunter. Then he suddenly saw a movement and swung around to see Franz holding a gun.

"What the—?"

"No one is taking me prisoner," Franz growled. His eyes were wild, like a trapped animal. "I took an oath to fight for the Führer and I will go down fighting for the Führer!"

"The Führer is dead!" hissed Peter "And anyone who sees you with that gun will kill all of us, no questions asked!"

Max started to moan softly.

"Jesus, Franz, put it away!" Gunter pleaded.

"Who are you to be giving orders? I'll have you up on a charge of insubordination!"

"Kurt!" Gunter shouted.

Peter turned and saw Kurt moving quickly to the ladder. Hermann had crossed the control room in five steps but Kurt was already at the top.

"Oh, great, now that little shit will tell them," spat Franz. "We're trapped. You've trapped us." His eyes smoldered at Peter.

Suddenly a shadow came into the hatch opening.

"Peter?" Sell's voice came down into the control room. "There's no one here but you don't have long. Time to move."

Peter looked at Franz. Franz held his eye as he put his gun away, into a holster under his clothes. He was amazed that he hadn't noticed the bulge before.

"We're on our way up, Commander," Peter called out.

One by one, the boys came blinking out into the early morning sunshine. They came out into a world of activity and movement.

"We're clearing out," said Sell, "while we can. I've just got a few last things to get from the ship. The Brits'll be here soon. They'll know we've landed. They can have the ship, but they'll have to come find us."

Peter looked around. They were in a large dockyard. There were subs of all sizes moored beside piers. There were munitions littering the port, and warehouses with doors flung open. Parts of engines and pieces of metal and machinery were scattered everywhere. Members of the Kriegsmarine were rushing in and out of small subs, carrying clothes, blankets, food packets, and rucksacks to the shore. Five crewmen stood on the deck, warily eyeing the boys.

The commander narrowed his eyes to look at Franz. "Don't be stupid," he said, "and don't try to be a hero for the Fatherland. There are no heroes anymore."

He turned to look at Peter, Hermann, Gunter, and Max. "Go now. Work your way behind the warehouses over to the woods." He gestured to the right. "You've got to cross the Kaiser Wilhelm canal. There's a bridge. You should be able to get there in a couple of hours." He turned away and started back toward the U-boat. "The British are everywhere, rounding up officers, infantry, recruits. Everyone. Stay off the roads."

They were on the pier when Max suddenly stopped. "Wait," he called to the commander. "Where's Kurt?"

Sell was halfway down the hatch. "He took off. Toward the town," he gestured to the left. "He was moving pretty quickly." With that, the commander was gone.

"We have to find him," said Max.

"Are you crazy?" said Hermann. "Didn't you hear what the commander said? We've got to clear out of here as fast as possible." Gunter and Franz were already taking off at a lope toward the closest warehouse.

"Kurt is part of the team," said Max. His huge face was convulsed by a frown.

"Yeah, well, Kurt left. He knew perfectly well what he was doing. Do you think he'd try to find you?" said Hermann.

Peter wheeled around. "Max, we don't have time. We've got to go!"

"Come on!" yelled Gunter. He and Franz were at the warehouse gate.

"Max, we've got to go," Peter repeated. "Kurt'll be fine!"

Max looked dolefully at Peter. "I'm not fast," said Max. "You know that." Suddenly he turned and started jogging off to the left, in the direction that the commander had pointed.

"Max!" Peter shouted.

"To hell with him," Hermann muttered, and he took off at a sprint toward the warehouse.

Peter watched Max pick up speed. He thought of him running to the safety of the boulder from the factory. He watched as Max rounded a corner and headed down into the town. Loyal Max. Then Peter heard the sound of a jeep and he didn't have time to give it any more thought.

He turned. Hermann, Gunter, and Franz were standing at the door of the warehouse.

"Quick!" shouted Gunter. "In here!"

He raced through the open door. The building was a mass of overturned shelves and broken bottles. The four of them wove their way into the darkness and flattened themselves along the wall.

Peter's heart was racing. He heard the jeep drive down beside the warehouse and pull up to an abrupt stop. It was followed by what sounded like a truck, and then another. He held his breath as the engines were turned off.

There were voices. Authoritative, commanding. Speaking English.

Peter closed his eyes to try to understand what they were saying. His heart pounded so loudly he could barely hear over it. He focused and listened to the English voices, but they were speaking too fast for him. They were shouting but they didn't sound angry. And then he heard the commander's voice.

"First Lieutenant Erwin Sell, commanding officer."

"Lieutenant Conrad, second in command."

And so it went, each submariner stating his name and rank. The English said something and then laughed good-naturedly.

"You can search the ship," said Sell. "Anything of value is out here on the dock. There are no guns, except what is on the ship. Guns are unsafe on a submarine." Peter could hear a wry laugh in his voice. The English were talking quickly again. Then there was silence.

"What's going on?" whispered Gunter beside him.

"I think they're searching the ship," said Peter. He tried to imagine the picture and what the English would find. If they had been five minutes earlier, the English would have found *them*. His heart pounded in his ears, louder than ever.

"Mind if I smoke?" Peter heard Lieutenant Conrad ask.

There was a pause. He imagined the lieutenant miming to an English guard. "Thanks."

Silence again. Peter looked at Franz and was surprised to see a look of deep sorrow on his face. *He's beginning to believe it*, he thought. *The war is over and the British have taken over Germany.*

All of a sudden there was a burst of English. Peter heard the distinct clang of a truck tailgate snapping down.

"Well, at least we get to ride in style," Lieutenant Conrad said loudly. Peter listened closely. He thought he could hear the sound of the submariners being loaded into the trucks. The engines started. Peter couldn't make out any words, but people were still talking. Then he heard the trucks drive back down the road. He listened closely and thought he heard the jeep as well. Then there was silence.

The four boys stood quietly in the warehouse. They waited. But nothing happened. Peter's heart started to slow to a normal speed. They waited for what felt like an eternity before venturing toward the open door. Peter slowly moved around the doorframe to peer out. There was no one. The dock was deserted.

They cautiously crept out of the warehouse. It was eerily quiet. The U-boat sat silently at the pier. Along the pier were the piles of the submariners' clothes. Peter walked toward them.

"What are you doing?" demanded Franz. "We've got to make for the canal."

"This stuff could come in very useful," said Peter. There was a good knit sweater, a strong pair of leather boots, and a warm blanket. No food. But the sweater would be wonderful in the cool of the evening and a pair of leather boots was always a good barter. He began loading as much as he could from the piles onto one of the blankets.

Gunter and Hermann joined him. "I don't know why you're bothering," said Franz. "It will just slow us down."

"Just a hunch," said Peter. "And I think the Brits are going to be busy for a while. Here, this looks about your size." Peter threw Franz the sweater. He'd found a beautiful leather jacket for himself. The idea of being able to barter was so familiar, so comforting that he was soon beaming from ear to ear. "You just never know what you'll find," he said cheerfully.

Peter, Gunter, and Hermann bundled as much as they could carry onto blankets and hoisted them over their shoulders. "Can we get going now?" said Franz impatiently, and they took off at a jogging pace in the direction of the canal. Peter stopped for a moment and looked back. He knew that Max wouldn't have been able to keep up. But he felt badly about the way he'd left, even if he knew that in the end they'd have a better chance, just the four of them. The Hamburg Boys.

Minus Otto.

He turned and caught up with the others, heading for the canal and the road home.

They found a footpath soon after leaving the docks. It wound through a wooded area skirting the edge of the city. It wasn't the main road to the canal, which meant it was safer. Peter thought about Sell. He had no idea how they would have gotten to Germany without him, and he certainly didn't know how they would have found their way to the canal. He hoped that being a prisoner of war wouldn't be too awful.

The spring sunshine warmed their backs. The scratchy blanket bundle began to weigh heavily, and Peter was soon drenched in sweat. They hadn't eaten anything since yesterday afternoon and he felt lightheaded. But there was no choice but to move forward, knowing that ahead lay home.

It was midday by the time they saw the bridge spanning the canal. Peter had thought it would be like the little bridges in Hamburg, where the canals were so small he could cross by jumping from boat to boat. But the Kiel Canal was huge and the water swift. Too wide and fast to swim across. The bridge was long and a train was just chugging across it.

They walked down to the bank, staying hidden inside a grove of alder, and threw down their packs. Franz plunked himself behind the small trees.

"Now what?" said Hermann. Hermann had made the biggest pack of all of them, and he was flushed and sweaty.

"We cross the bridge," offered Gunter, as though talking to a simpleton.

"On the train tracks?" Hermann shot back.

"I'll go see if there's another way," said Peter. Before they could answer, he loped back up the bank and off through the woods. He stayed out of sight, moving from tree to tree, until he had a clear view of the main road that crossed the bridge. One section was divided off for the train, and beside it was a narrow roadway for cars. Only one car could fit through at a time, so there were gates at either end to regulate the traffic.

Beside the roadway was an even narrower pedestrian walkway.

And at the roadway was a guard. A British soldier.

Peter watched for a few minutes, trying to see what the procedure was. He saw a woman carrying several baskets, being jostled by three young children as she approached the guard on foot. They spoke and Peter saw him lift the gate and let her through. He saw her smile and saw the children wave to the guard. The guard waved back.

So he must speak German, thought Peter.

A truck drove up and waited at the gate while the guard spoke through the window to the driver. The guard looked up and across the bridge. He waved to a guard at the other end, lifted the gate, and the truck drove through and over the bridge. Had the guard checked the driver's papers? Peter couldn't be sure one way or the other.

He scrambled down the bank to the copse of trees where Hermann, Gunter, and Franz were waiting.

"There's a British guard," he began. Hermann groaned. "But I think he speaks German. He's alone and looks friendly. I think we can use the evacuee story. We can tell him we got a ride on a fishing boat from Denmark. There's no reason why he'd know anything about the U-boat. And no reason why he'd know about the camp."

"And every reason why he'd take us into custody," spat Franz. "We're the enemy. They're looking for us."

"They aren't looking for four ragged boys in civilian clothes. They are looking for six recruits in uniform. If they are even looking for us at all."

"I don't know what choice we have," said Gunter. "If we want to get to the other side and onto the road to Hamburg, we're going to have to go across."

"There's only one guard?" asked Franz.

"One at each end," said Peter. He looked at Franz's angry eyes. "No," he hissed. "Don't even think about it. We'll have the entire British army on us if you do anything with that gun."

"How many times do I have to tell you, you are not my commanding officer!"

"And how many times do I have to tell you, there are no commanding officers anymore! There is no war!"

"Stop!" hissed Gunter. "We have to do this together or we won't make it. Franz, Peter is right. You've got to keep the gun hidden. We've got a chance if we look young and innocent. We have to get them to believe our story."

"Okay," said Hermann, "but what are we going to say about these?" He gestured to the large blanket packs at their feet.

For a moment, no one spoke. The packs contained their future, everything that they could bargain for to get food, maybe a train ticket home.

"We tell him the truth. We tell him we found everything at the docks when we got off the fishing boat. We offer him something. Cigarettes. Even a British officer can be bought. And we let Gunter do the talking. He looks the youngest and the most honest." Peter looked around. He knew that their future depended on everyone agreeing to the plan. He wasn't entirely sure it would work, but he wanted to believe it. He looked at Franz. Franz looked dubious but he gave a little nod.

"What do I do if he doesn't speak German?" asked Gunter.

"Use whatever words of English you have. We'll all help with some English words, but you'll be the leader, okay? But I really think he does speak a bit of German."

"I hope you're right. All I can remember in English is 'Hello,' 'Goodbye,' and 'Do you speak German?' "

"Well, it's a start," said Peter, hoisting his pack. "Just make sure you don't use our names. Let's go."

They scrambled up the bank to the thickest part of the wood, and doubled back so they could join the main road well out of sight of the bridge. In about ten minutes, they came around the bend and walked straight up to the gate.

Gunter walked ahead of them. The guard stood in front of the gate. He said something in English that Peter couldn't quite understand.

"Speaking German?" Gunter asked in English.

"In a small time," the guard answered in bad German. But he smiled broadly at Gunter. "Where from you are?"

"From Hamburg. We were evacuated to a school in Denmark," Gunter replied in rapid German. "Two days ago, the Danish Resistance came in shooting and we ran away. A fisherman brought us to Kiel. We're trying to get home. To our mothers. In Hamburg."

The guard took some time to think about the words he'd heard. "Denmark?" he asked.

Gunter nodded. *He looks like a twelve year old who's just been given an ice cream*, thought Peter. Gunter began talking and miming at the same time.

"We were sent away from our mothers in Hamburg," he

said with elaborate gestures. "We went to school. Men came with guns. We ran away." He mimed guns shooting, and made a motion of his fingers running. The guard looked at Hermann, Franz, and Peter. They all nodded and smiled, although Peter could see the thin line of tension in Franz's smile. *Stay with us, Franz*, he thought.

"We want to go home to our mothers," Gunter repeated. Every time he said the word "mother," Peter could hear the yearning in his voice. *A good actor*, he thought, *always taps into real feelings*. Peter put on his best homesick face.

"In Hamburg?" the guard asked. Gunter nodded.

"What this are?" said the guard, pointing to the blanket sacs.

"We found things at the dock, in Kiel," Gunter said. He took out a packet of cigarettes and offered them to the guard. "Would you like some?"

The guard took the cigarettes. He lit one and blew out a stream of smoke.

"You to cross. Leave things," he said, pointing to the piles and throwing the match on the ground.

"No!" Hermann burst out. "They're ours." The guard was startled by Hermann's tone and stiffened. His hand moved toward the gun at his side.

"We want to take things home to our mothers," said Gunter pleadingly.

The guard looked at each of them. Peter knew that the moment had been broken. The guard said something in English. Peter thought it sounded like *something, something, won the war*.

"Leave things. Or not to cross," he said in his broken German.

"What, leave them so you can have them?" Hermann said belligerently. Peter put a hand on his arm.

The guard narrowed his eyes at Hermann. "No to carry on bridge," he said icily.

Hermann scooped up his blanket sac and began walking back down the road. Peter could hear him swearing. He certainly didn't sound at all like an innocent schoolboy. He looked at Franz, standing stiffly to the side. Franz didn't have a blanket bag. Presumably he could cross. Would Franz go on his own? But the guard was wary now. Would he search Franz? It seemed impossible not to see the bulge beneath his clothes.

"Let's talk it over," Peter said, taking Franz's arm and leading him away. "I thank you," he said to the guard in English.

The guard shrugged and pocketed the package of cigarettes. Gunter picked up his pack and followed them down the road.

When they finally caught up with Hermann, he was still swearing. "Goddamn Tommy prick! He just wants to pocket all of this stuff himself and sell it off. He knows a good deal when he sees it!"

"Yeah, Hermann, so do we. But how are we going to get across now? That's the only bridge for miles," said Peter. "Would it have hurt you to negotiate a bit? He might have let us keep one bag."

Hermann stopped in the middle of the road and stared at Peter. "Do you remember what it was like in Hamburg last time? It's going to be ten times worse. There'll be nothing. No food, no drink, no work, no clothes—nothing. This is something to start with. We could have traded that pack of cigarettes for enough food for a week, and he just casually put it in his pocket." He picked up his pack again and continued to storm down the road.

Peter, Gunter, and Franz followed a few paces behind, each wrapped in his own thoughts. Peter had been focused so hard on getting to Hamburg that he hadn't really thought about what he'd find there. He'd survived the war and now the war was over. He wanted to start putting his life together. He wanted to try and make sense of these last six years and figure out what "future" meant.

Suddenly Franz stopped. "I think we would all be able to think better with a little food in our stomachs," he said.

"That's an understatement," laughed Gunter. "What are you proposing? A little grass supper?"

"No …" Franz was looking off to the side of the road. His face was scrunched in concentration. Peter looked in the same direction and saw a small farmhouse. A dilapidated barn.

Peter's breath was snatched away as he remembered the farm outside of Bistriz. The softness of Olga's skin. The roughness of the barnboard behind her back.

Gunter stopped dead in his tracks. "Where there is a farmhouse, there might be a farm …"

"And where there is a farm, there might be some eggs …" Hermann had joined them and his eyes looked dreamy.

"What might a farmer trade for a meal? Or for four meals?" said Franz, eyeing their bags.

There was a pause. They could trade cigarettes, but Gunter had given those to the British guard. Their other things—blankets, clothing, the boots—would never entice a farmer.

"A bit of muscle. Farmers always need a bit of help," said Gunter hopefully.

"Schnapps," said Hermann suddenly. "A man will sell his soul for a bit of schnapps." He laughed as they all looked at him, surprised. "And I will sell my bit of schnapps for a meal." He looked at each of them in turn.

"I will sell my bit of schnapps for four meals," he said, swaggering as he headed down the lane to the farmhouse.

Chapter Twenty-Nine

Germany,
May 1945

"He says we can sleep in the barn tonight." Hermann strode back to the group. "I told him the story about the school and the Danish Resistance. He says we must be very brave boys," he said with a laugh.

Peter hated the way the lie sounded in Hermann's mouth. But he knew it was necessary. They couldn't trust anybody.

"Anyway, he said to put our stuff in the barn," continued Hermann, "and make ourselves beds there. His wife will bring us some borscht. He was pretty happy to see the schnapps." Hermann was grinning from ear to ear, clearly proud of himself. Peter had a sudden flash of the old Hermann, the one who was always so angry and competitive, the one who never would have helped another living soul. The months in the camp, working together as a team—it had changed Hermann.

"That's great," said Peter. "Thanks, Hermann."

"Food! God, I'm starving. Thanks, Hermann," said Gunter.

"It will be good to eat," Franz said stiffly.

"But first, he said we should go for a swim. Get a bit cleaned up so we look a bit more respectable. He said the Poles who work on their farm swim in the canal every day. They've got a nice little beach set up. So he said we should put our stuff in the barn, go for a swim and, by the time we get back, there will be dinner."

"Yes!" said Gunter as he raced to the barn.

The barn was filled with loose straw that smelled sweet and inviting. Slats of sunshine picked up the dust motes in the air, and swallows whirled through an open window high above them. They threw their blanket packs down and hurriedly began to rip off their clothes.

A flash of reflected light caught Peter's eye and he looked up. Franz was taking off his drab civilian shirt. The light had caught bright brass buttons underneath.

"What the hell?" said Peter.

Hermann and Gunter turned. They all froze.

Franz was standing there in his full SS uniform.

Franz's eyes locked defiantly onto Peter's.

"You've had that on the whole time?" said Peter. Peter took in the ranked uniform, the holster, the gun.

"It is who I am," said Franz.

"Jesus, you really will get us all killed, won't you," said Gunter.

"I have worked hard," said Franz. His voice rose. "I have trained all of my life for this."

Hermann crossed the floor in two strides and slapped Franz so hard that he spun in a circle and fell to the ground. He picked up Franz's gun.

"And sometimes you lose, Franz," Hermann said steadily. "Sometimes you fight a good fight, but someone else fights harder or better. You can keep on fighting until they kill you. If that's what you want to do with your life. Or you can admit defeat and move on."

They all stared down at Franz. Peter remembered Deiderik slapping Franz in the barracks. Is that all Franz understood? Rank and fighting? How to give orders and how to take them? Was violence the only way to reach him?

"Give me the uniform," said Hermann, palming the gun.

The only sound in the barn was the soft whirling of the swallows.

"It's all I have," said Franz, his voice tight. "It's all I know."

Peter remembered the afternoon in Franz's apartment. He thought of Herr Weber, sent to a work camp for re-training. Franz had given up everything for the Reich, including his father.

Hermann stood very still. He slowly aimed the gun.

"Take it off. Now."

Peter stopped breathing. Hermann stared at Franz. No one moved a muscle. *This is how power works*, Peter realized. With no one in charge, anyone could seize control at any time. Hermann was now in control and Franz had lost his war.

Peter watched as Franz slowly began to unbutton his shirt. He watched as Franz took off his shirt and pants. He watched as Franz followed orders, stripping himself of his rank and transferring his power to Hermann. He stood up in his underwear. He handed the uniform to Hermann.

"Go for a swim," said Hermann. Then he turned and

looked at Peter and Gunter. "I'll be there in a minute."

Franz looked at the uniform in Hermann's hands. "Go," Hermann said. His voice was cold, commanding.

"Come on," said Gunter. "Let's get down there. You're going to freeze, standing there in your underwear. Race you!"

Peter put his hand on Franz's arm. "Come on, Franz," he said.

The water in the canal was bracing and clean. The sharpness of it took Peter's breath away. It broke the spell, and suddenly they were splashing and laughing just as they had done when they were children. Then Hermann joined them, cannonballing into their midst with a mighty yell. Peter allowed himself to believe that maybe, just maybe, they could make a fresh start. Maybe the horrible chaos and confusion of these last six years would melt away like a bad dream.

The sun was starting to set as they left the water, shivering and wrapped in their blankets. Gunter and Franz walked ahead, and Peter could hear Gunter chattering about farms, telling Franz all about their adventures in Bistriz. He turned to Hermann.

"What did you do with it?" he asked.

Hermann looked at him with a grim seriousness. "I threw it into the bottom of the outhouse." He broke into a wide grin when he saw Peter's mouth fall open. "I threw the gun in, too. Then I took a crap. No one will notice any shiny buttons now."

Peter's shock surprised him. An SS uniform, a revered symbol of the Reich, at the bottom of an outhouse? He felt a wave of terror whirl through him, followed by a delicious sense of freedom. He felt the thrill of doing something bad and wrong. And then he burst out laughing.

"Getting shot as a deserter is not part of my plan," said Hermann as he headed into the barn.

The moment they went in, Peter realized something was different. He hadn't paid much attention when they'd changed— they'd thrown off their clothes, dumped out their precious cargo, grabbed the blankets, and run with them down to the canal. He'd been more wrapped up in Franz's uniform than he had with noticing his surroundings.

But the straw was thrown every which way and, as Peter looked, he realized that their clothes were gone. All of their things were gone.

"What the hell?" said Gunter.

"No!" said Hermann, realizing the loss at the same moment. He dove into the straw and began flinging it in the air, searching, digging, to see if their clothes had somehow become buried.

They searched and searched, but only managed to find bits and pieces. Peter found his pair of fancy leather boots and a pair of Kriegsmarine pants. Hermann found a Kriegsmarine shirt. Gunter found a thick sweater.

Just then the farmer's wife arrived at the door of the barn, carrying a tray of bowls filled with steaming borscht. The earthy smell of the beets wafted through the barn. There was freshly baked bread on the tray.

"What happened to our things?" said Hermann angrily. "We had a deal!" he yelled.

The farmer's wife looked pale. She was a tiny woman

with graying hair straggling down from where she'd pinned it at the back of her head. She looked terrified of Hermann.

"I ... I don't know what you mean," she said shakily. "I have brought you your dinner. That is all. Please ..." she was backing away. "Please do not hurt my family."

"No one is going to hurt anyone," said Gunter calmly. "We just want to know what happened to our clothes. Did you take our clothes?" he asked.

"Your clothes?" she repeated. Her eyes took in the scattered straw, their mostly naked bodies, the few articles they'd found.

"We left our clothes here when we went swimming. They're gone. We need them back," said Peter.

"I did not take them. What would I want with your clothes?" she said stiffly. "You have paid us well for the dinner."

"Well, someone took them," said Hermann angrily. "Where the hell are they?"

"Oh," she said with a small gasp.

"What? What is it?" demanded Hermann.

"The Poles," she said. "Just after you came, they threw down their tools. They said they wouldn't work for us anymore. They said the war is over and they were going home." She looked down. "I think they came into the barn," she said.

"And stole everything," said Hermann. "How are we supposed to get home now, dressed as Kriegsmarine? We'll be shot by the first Brit who sees us."

"No, no. They are not allowed to shoot anyone, unless you resist," she said. "They will just arrest you."

"Great. We'll be arrested by the first Brit we see."

"But you are just children. You must tell them about the school."

"Why would they believe us, when we are dressed as Kriegsmarine?" Hermann's face was contorted with anger and frustration.

She paused, thinking. "My husband will write you a letter," she said proudly. She handed Gunter the tray of food.

"A letter?" repeated Peter.

"Yes," she said, smiling with evident relief at her solution. "Yes, he will write a letter and make it look like it has come from your school principal. A letter of transit. To explain why you are traveling home alone. He has very good handwriting," she added.

"A letter of transit," Hermann muttered.

"You eat your soup. I will tell my husband. He will write the letter and say that you are good boys, from good Hamburg homes. I will see if he has any extra clothes that might fit you." With that, she backed out of the barn, still wary and not taking her eyes off them.

Peter looked over at Franz. He was chewing his lip. Peter knew that Franz would rather go down fighting than pretending. But he also knew that Franz wasn't stupid. They were alone, alone in enemy territory now.

Peter hoped that Franz wouldn't ask what Hermann had done with the uniform. He put a spoonful of borscht in his mouth and closed his eyes. The strains of "Summertime" drifted through his mind. For whatever reason, they'd all been thrown together and it was important for them all to make it back together.

Chapter Thirty

Germany,
May 1945

The next morning, the farmer gave them a letter that looked amazingly official. *To Whom It May Concern*, it began.

The bearers of this letter—Franz Weber, Peter Gruber,
Hermann Kramer, and Gunter Schmidt—were
evacuated from Hamburg as part of the Kinderland-
verschickung *program in the fall of 1944. They have*
been under my care at the Gundrun School in Alsen,
Denmark, since then. However, in recent days our
school has been besieged by members of the Danish
Resistance and our fate is uncertain. All students have
been released to return to their homes in Germany.
I have every hope that the boys will return home safely.
 Herr Heinrich Kummer
 Principal
 Gundrun School

The letter was dated May 3, 1945, which was, by Peter's estimate, the day they had left Denmark. It was typewritten and signed with an unintelligible signature. The farmer had used all the information Hermann had given him. It sounded so real. Peter began to wonder if maybe it was true. Perhaps they had been in school. Perhaps they had been given permission to leave.

The farmer's wife saw them off with a still warm loaf of bread and a hunk of garlic sausage. She'd been able to find an old pair of torn work pants and a shirt for Franz. She'd offered one of her own old blouses to Peter. "It's a good color for you," she'd said playfully. But he declined. He'd rather go shirtless than walk back to Hamburg in a woman's blouse. He still had the boots, which, even if they were miles too big, was something. Actually, he thought he looked pretty good in just the pants and boots.

But Gunter accepted the farmer's wife's offer and put on her blue and white checked blouse above his own civilian short pants, which, miraculously, he had kept on when they had gone swimming.

"Thank you very much," Peter said, as they stood in the farmyard, shaking the farmer's hand. "You have been very kind."

"Thank you for the schnapps," he replied. "I'm glad those damn Poles didn't get it," he said with a laugh. "It was very good. I'm sorry about your other things."

"So are we," said Hermann.

"We left the blankets in the barn," said Gunter. "Since we have nothing to carry in them ..."

The farmer's wife nodded. "Are you sure you don't want to stay and work on the farm for us?" she asked. "Now that the Poles are gone, we need help. We can pay you in food."

The boys looked at each other. "No," said Peter. "Our mothers want us to get home," he said, trying to look as young and innocent as possible.

"Ah, you are good boys," she said, kissing each one on the cheek.

Because they no longer had their packs, they decided to try their luck at the bridge again. Fortunately there was a different guard. The new guard, like the last, spoke little German. He frowned at the letter, trying to read it.

"Denmark?" he said. "Why?" he asked, pointing to their Kriegsmarine uniforms.

"We were sleeping in a warehouse on the docks in Fynshav," Gunter said, his story well-honed and practiced. "When we woke up the next morning, all our clothes were gone, stolen. Some of the sailors took pity on us and found us these things."

It's always best to invent a lie based on as much truth as possible, thought Peter.

The guard frowned. Peter couldn't tell how much he understood. He looked down at the letter again. He looked at Gunter, who continued to look up with eyes of innocence.

"Go at," he said, opening up the gate to let them pass.

It took only five minutes to walk across the bridge. Peter looked down on the water of the Kaiser–Wilhelm Canal flowing beneath him. The morning air was fresh and the new leaves on the trees shimmered as they waved in the slight breeze. He felt suspended in time, just as he was suspended in the air.

The sense of peace was broken by the sound of a rifle being cocked. Peter looked up and saw guards sitting in turrets at both ends of the bridge, their guns trained on them. Three soldiers were standing at the far gate. Two had guns drawn and pointed at them. *What the hell?* thought Peter. *The first guard has delivered us into the hands of the enemy.* For a moment he panicked. Should they try to run for it? Head back across the bridge? Jump over the side?

One of the soldiers, the one without a gun, barked at them in English. He gestured.

Gunter took the paper out of his pocket. "I hope this paper will explain, sir." Peter noticed that Gunter's voice sounded high and light. He wondered if Gunter was scared or just trying to sound really young.

The soldier took the letter, frowned at it, and then looked up at them. He asked a question in English.

"We speak only small English," said Peter tentatively.

The soldier looked at each of them in turn, and gestured toward a jeep parked beside the road at the end of the bridge. The two other soldiers lowered their rifles. Peter looked up to the guards in the turrets. Their guns were still trained on them.

"In," the soldier said in English, perching himself on the passenger seat. Peter parroted the word in English. "In?"

"Yes, yes," the soldier said impatiently. A driver turned the key and the engine roared to life, shattering the quiet.

The soldier removed a pistol from his holster and waved it at them. He said something in English that Peter didn't understand and gestured again for them to get into the back.

Gunter, Hermann, and Franz squished together in the back seat. Peter looked at the soldier. He gestured for Peter to hold on to the roll bar along the topside of the jeep. The soldier said something to the driver and the jeep leapt onto the road.

Peter's backside didn't fit in at all. His fingers were clenched onto the roll bar—at every corner and every bump he was sure he would go flying out onto the road. He expected he'd be shot the minute he hit the ground. He tried to turn to look at Gunter's face but it was impossible to see. The noise of the jeep drowned out all possibility of communication.

It was a terrifying fifteen-minute drive that felt more like three hours by the time the jeep pulled up in front of an army barracks. Six low-lying buildings sat behind a high metal fence topped with rolls of barbed wire. *Will they ask questions before they shoot us?* Peter wondered.

The soldier gestured for them to go into one of the barracks. Inside, an officer sat behind a metal desk. He looked up at them and frowned. The first soldier saluted and placed their letter on the desk. He started speaking quickly in English and Peter thought he heard the English word "escape."

"No," Peter said suddenly in English. "No escape. Go home."

The officer looked startled that Peter had spoken. "You speak English?" he said slowly and, Peter thought, kindly.

"Not good," he said. His schoolroom words were starting

to come back to him. When people spoke slowly, he could catch a word or two.

The officer turned to the soldier and spoke a few sentences quickly. The soldier saluted and left the room.

"Tell them we're going home," said Hermann to Peter. "Tell them we live in Hamburg."

Peter looked back at the officer. He repeated, "Go home."

"Going home, eh?" The officer spoke slowly to Peter. "Where's home?"

"Hamburg," said Peter. "We are of Hamburg."

"Hamburg? What on earth are you doing here?"

Peter thought hard to try to understand the question. He understood "what" and "doing" and "here."

"Kinderlandverschickung. School gone. Denmark. Guns," he said trying to make the story as simple as possible. He gestured at the letter sitting on the officer's desk.

The officer shrugged. "I can't read that. It's all Greek to me," he said, smiling.

Peter frowned. Did the officer think they were from Greece? His English words must have been wrong.

"No Greece. Denmark. School."

The first soldier returned with a new soldier, who saluted. The officer spoke to the new soldier and passed him the letter. The soldier read it slowly, his lips moving. He turned and spoke to the officer in English, and Peter made out the words "school in Denmark" and "going home."

"Yes, yes!" Peter said excitedly. "Go home. Hamburg."

The officer spoke again to the first soldier, who turned on his heel and brought four chairs up to the desk. He gestured for them to sit. Peter looked at the officer. "Yes, sit?"

"Yes, sit," said the officer with a slight grin. The officer said something in rapid-fire English that Peter couldn't catch at all. Then the second soldier turned to them all and said in German, "Why are you dressed in those uniforms?"

Peter felt everyone relax. Finally, there was someone they could tell their story to, to explain. Gunter piped up. "We got a fisherman to take us from Alsen to Fynshav," he began.

The translator held his hands up. "Slowly, please!" he said.

"Sorry," said Gunter, and he repeated himself slowly and clearly. When he got to the end of their story, the translator turned to the officer and spoke quickly in English.

The officer eyed them all as he listened to their story. He asked the translator a question. The translator answered him in English. He looked at them and tapped his pencil on his desk. *He doesn't believe us*, thought Peter. *He's going to put us in jail.*

Then another soldier came into the room carrying a tray. On the tray were small cups and an elegant china pot. The officer asked Peter a question but he didn't understand.

"Pardon?" he asked.

The officer repeated the question and Peter understood "do you want," but he didn't understand what he was supposed to want. He eyed the translator.

"Tea," said the translator in German. "Do you want tea?"

"Tea," repeated Peter. He'd never had English tea. "Yes?" he said in English.

"Tea?" Gunter asked him.

"Tea," Peter responded. "They want to know if we want some tea."

The boys all looked at each other. They had heard about the English and their love of tea. Perhaps it was all going to be all right. They were going to have a cup of tea with an English officer. Maybe he believed their story after all.

Chapter Thirty-One

Germany,
May 1945

... and suddenly he's Eugene, and the gun is pointing at me. I know it's Eugene, even though he is grown up now and in uniform. I want to hold him, hug him, tell him I'm sorry. But his face distorts, his mouth opens in a scream and he shoots. I feel the bullet thud into my gut. The pain twists. It burns. I hear myself moaning, but my jaw is locked. And ...

There is a gray light in the room. Sharp pains twist Peter's stomach. He is lying on a flat, hard bunk. His mind whirls, trying to remember where he is and, most importantly, where there is a bathroom ...

It all flooded back. The interrogation, the tea, followed by a meal of strange white bread covered in a black tar called Marmite. He had been starving and had swallowed it down, but the taste was vile—salty, muddy, like decaying meat. Had the British poisoned them? He needed to get to the bathroom fast.

His eyes took in the room. He was on a bottom bunk in a room with four doubles. Peter swung his legs over the side of the bed, sitting up carefully so as not to bang his head on the bunk above. He could hear Hermann snoring above him. Hermann always snored. He slept like a baby even when surrounded by the enemy.

His feet felt the cold floorboards. He crouched over as he shuffled toward the door. He prayed that they weren't locked in.

The doorknob turned and he let himself out into the pre-dawn air. He knew there was an outhouse somewhere, but he couldn't get his bearings and had no idea where it was. His gut stabbed. He stumbled hurriedly to the base of a nearby tree, managing to pull down his underwear just in time before his bowels erupted. He began to shake with the cold and the shock. He squatted until there was nothing left, until he was empty and exhausted. He gathered a few old dried leaves from the base of the tree, thinking to wipe himself, but they were wet with mulch and he decided against it. He pulled up his underwear and covered his mess as best he could before heading back inside to the relative comfort of his British army bed and blanket. He listened to the slow breathing around him and let himself drift ...

In the morning, Peter was surprised to find himself not too much the worse for wear. Apparently the English weren't trying to poison them. None of the others had had any side effects. But they all refused to eat any more of the bread with Marmite, which made the English laugh. Peter was grateful for a steaming mug of weak coffee.

"The captain said I can give you a lift to the main road, the road to Hamburg," said the translator, motioning them to the jeep. "From there it's about a day's march. If you are quick, your mothers will see you home for supper," he laughed.

They drove through the woods, out of the camp. Peter's heart eased as they left the high wire fence behind. They were letting them go, no more questions asked. He could hardly believe it.

The dirt road wound under tall pine trees. Sunlight streamed through gaps in the canopy. Peter felt a huge grin on his face. They were going home.

The jeep stopped at the edge of the wood. A wide road stretched ahead of them.

"Here," said the translator as they stepped from the jeep. He handed them their "letter of transit."

"You might need this. The captain has stamped it, for what good it will do you. Not sure where the next checkpoint is. They'll certainly want you to explain." He looked them up and down.

The four of them made quite a sight as they headed down the main road to Hamburg. Peter strode shirtless but wearing his beautiful leather boots and dusty white Kriegsmarine trousers. Franz wore the farmer's work shirt, threadbare work pants, and bare feet. Hermann wore a Kriegsmarine shirt and a pair of filthy German army pants that the English captain had found for him. "He says you can't walk to Hamburg in your underwear," the translator had explained. Peter suspected the pants had come off a dead German soldier. Gunter still wore the farmer's wife's blouse.

"Thank you," Peter said in English, taking the paper from him.

"Good luck," returned the Englishman in German. He swung back into the jeep and left them in the quiet morning sun.

Gunter ran out into the middle of the road and jumped up and down. "We did it!! They believed us! We're going home!!"

"I don't think they believed us for one minute," said Hermann to Peter. "But there was no point in keeping us there. We aren't exactly a threat."

Peter looked over at Franz. His shoulders were sagged and disillusionment was etched into his face. Peter wondered what there was for Franz to go back to. He'd believed that home was the Nazi Party, and that the Party would last a thousand years.

"Do you have somewhere to go? When we get back?" Peter asked him.

Franz's head shot up. He turned on Peter, his face a mask of fury. "Don't you dare feel sorry for me," he spat. "Don't you dare! You, with your petty little lives, your sentimental nostalgia for 'home.' Yes, go home to your mommas, little momma's boys. Oh, dear, we lost the war, too bad, time to go home." Franz was screaming at him, the pent-up rage of the last three days exploding in the middle of the road.

"You think that the kind Englishmen will serve you tea and toast every day? You think nothing has changed?!"

Peter raised a hand, and tried to interrupt.

"No," yelled Franz. "They hate us more than ever now.

Do you remember before the war, when there was no food, no jobs? Do you remember what life was like? Yes, of course you do, Mr. Black Market. Life was fine for you and your precious momma because you built yourself a little trade empire, and you," he rounded on Hermann, "you were just waiting to take that over and build it for your greedy little self. Everyone out for their own precious skin. Don't you realize that the Nazi Party would have looked after everyone? That there would have been food for us all, all the time? Food, housing, jobs—everything we needed. And now those English bastards will starve us, rape your sisters—even your old hags of mothers—and put us in labor camps, make slaves of us, torture us, and then take away everything! I should have put bullets in all of your heads when I had the chance! My Führer! My Führer! My Führer! Forgive me!" Franz shouted to the sky and crumpled to his knees.

Peter and Hermann stood stock still, staring at him. Franz's vision unnerved Peter. The words had the sound of a premonition. They evaporated like a ghost into the morning air.

Gunter started heading down the road.

"Come on," he called back to them. "Let's get this show on the road."

Peter looked at Franz crumpled on the ground. *Yes*, he thought, *we're a traveling clown show, a surreal parade. I'm just not sure if it is a comedy or a tragedy.* Suddenly Eugene came into his mind. *Eugene loved to dress up*, he remembered. And then he wondered, *what would the war have done to Eugene?*

They'd survived. It was a new beginning, come what may. He turned toward Gunter and the last leg of the journey, the start of the future.

Chapter Thirty-Two

Germany,
May 1945

The walk was long and dusty. Peter's beautiful leather boots were at least two sizes too big and, after a mile, his feet were raw and his blisters were bleeding. He took the boots off and carried them draped them over his naked shoulders, walking in his bare feet.

Franz walked behind slowly, following but never talking.

They'd been walking for about two hours when they crested a hill and saw a bedraggled woman leading a short, skinny horse pulling a small cart. A small boy and a young girl walked beside her. The woman turned back and looked fearfully at Peter, Franz, Gunter, and Hermann. The boy huddled close to her.

"It's all right," Peter called out. "We're just evacuees, heading back to Hamburg."

The family had stopped moving. The woman eyed them. "Where have you come from?" she asked suspiciously. The boy stared back, wide-eyed. The girl, probably about his age, looked off in the distance. Her hair was matted and her clothes torn. There was something strange, a hollowness about her eyes.

Gunter launched into the story of their escape from the "school." *It's becoming the truth*, thought Peter. The woman began to visibly relax. Hermann bent down to the boy. "You want to ride on my shoulders?" he asked.

The boy reached up his arms and Hermann effortlessly swung him into the air.

The boy giggled. "Giddy-up!"

"Neigh!" Hermann trotted off like a big draft horse under the small boy.

"Hey, wait for me!" Gunter took off in a friendly, horse-like trot to catch up.

"Your friend is kind," said the woman. "That is the first time I have heard Gene laugh since we left home." She spoke German with a strong accent.

"Gene?" said Peter.

"Eugene."

They were walking beside the horse, the girl moving mechanically. Franz walked behind the wagon, withdrawn.

"And you," she said. "Do you have a name? A home?"

"Peter," he said with a small smile. "I'm going home. To Hamburg. Where are you going?"

"Sulfeld," the woman answered. "I will turn at the road to Grabau. My grandparents had a farm there. I am hoping there will still be someone from my family who can take us in. We've come such a long way, they must take us in, yes?"

"Where have you come from?" Peter asked.

"Poland."

"Poland! You've been walking all the way from Poland?"

The woman nodded. "The Russians kicked us out. They say Poland is part of the Soviet Union now. They took everything we owned except these scraps of broken furniture and piles of old clothes." She gestured to the cart.

Peter thought back to the day the war started, when Germany had taken back land in Poland. What was it all about? This relentless taking of land. The continuous dispossession of people.

As they walked, they saw more and more people on the road. Most were in rags. By the time they got to the outskirts of Bad Segeberg, the road was a busy thoroughfare of refugees, the homeless and displaced.

"It will be like this everywhere in Germany," said the woman. "We are told to go home but we have no homes. We are beaten, and worse. The Red army ..." She let her voice die. Her eyes flitted to her daughter.

But at least it's over, thought Peter. *Maybe we can make new lives for ourselves.* He desperately wanted time to read, to think, to walk in green forests without having to worry about being bombed or shot at. He felt a sense of relief flood his veins.

But then he stopped dead in his tracks. There was a small group of people by the side of the road. Several were lying on the soft new grass. A few were sitting, staring at the ground in front of them. They were thin as rails, like skeletons, gray skin barely concealing their bones. They wore the striped rags of prison clothes. Like the photograph ...

The woman's eyes followed his. "Their guards have surrendered. They have escaped from the camps."

"The work camp outside of Hamburg? Neuengamme?" asked Peter. He thought of Otto. He thought of Herr Weber, sent to a camp by Franz. A chill went through him. Could one of those creatures be Herr Weber? Otto? Would he recognize them? He started to drift to the side of the road, moving toward them. Fascinated and repulsed.

The woman grabbed Peter's shoulders and roughly turned him to face her. "Don't be stupid," she said with a sudden flash of anger. "There is nothing you can do. Don't you understand that? Nothing. These people are already dead. It is too late."

Peter was shocked at her angry outburst. She turned away from him and turned forward to look at Gunter and Hermann. They were walking hand in hand with the little boy in the middle. They seemed not to have seen the prisoners. He looked at Franz. Franz was still trudging behind, his eyes on nothing.

"If it were not for Gene, I would not care," the woman continued more softly. "Gesa and I, we are nothing. None of this is real anymore."

Peter looked at the girl. She walked like a phantom. He wanted to say something, something that would make a difference. Something that could change what he was seeing in front of him. But the woman was right. There was nothing. There were no words. There was only unspeakable horror that his brain recoiled from grasping. He watched himself walk away.

"When I was little, my best friend was named Eugene," he said. "He drowned just before the war. Is that better?" He asked the question more of himself than of the woman.

The woman was quiet for a long time. "Not better for you. For him …? Who knows? Who can say what his life might have been? He had a good life for the time he had it. His death is not important. It is only how you live your life that is important. Not how long it is."

At the road that led to Sulfeld, the woman gathered little Gene from Hermann and Gunter. The boy meekly assented without argument. Peter wished he had something to give him, but he literally didn't even have a shirt on his back to give. "Good luck," he said, for want of anything else.

The woman looked at him as she led the horse onto the smaller road. "And to you," she said. They began to walk away when she stopped and added, "What is important is that he was your friend. It is your job to keep him alive."

Peter watched as they headed down the road, the girl mutely trailing behind. "Goodbye, Eugene," Peter suddenly called out, surprising himself with his loud voice. "Goodbye, Gesa."

The boy turned to look at him and then turned back to follow his mother, without waving. Gesa made no sign of having heard him.

Peter looked at the road ahead. It was filled with people streaming into Hamburg. Defeat and resignation seemed to hang on every set of shoulders. But Gunter and Hermann stood out like bright sparks. They were deep in conversation, Gunter in his blue woman's blouse, Hermann in his dusty

Kriegsmarine uniform. He thought about how Gunter had been his friend for as long as he could remember, and about how Hermann had been his enemy and was now his friend. And he thought about the Franz he used to know before the war. *What will happen to us now?*

They came around a curve in the road and to their surprise saw a train station. The sign said Ahrensburg. Gunter came running back to him. "Ahrensburg! Can you believe it?! We're home. We're home!"

There were trains filled with people, people hanging out the windows, holding onto open carriages. Trains going into the heart of Hamburg. Peter broke into a run.

Chapter Thirty-Three

Hamburg,
May 1945

The press of people poured out of the train at Rathausmarkt. No one had been collecting tickets or fares—he'd just squeezed himself in and given himself up to the mass of bodies. He'd lost Gunter, Hermann, and Franz in the crowd. He tumbled out of the train and tried to get his bearings.

It was like visiting a foreign city. At first he didn't recognize anything. But slowly, the picture in front of him came into focus. There was the large streetlight in the middle of the square, the one he used to twirl around when he was a child. There was the clock steeple of St. Petri Kirche, marking the head of Mönckebergstrasse. There were the government buildings. The top peaks along the roofs had been shirred off, but the main structures were standing. People were coming and going as though it was a normal working day. They stepped around the bricks, planks, and plaster blocking the sidewalks and made their way in and out of the fragmented buildings.

Peter walked along Mönckebergstrasse. The storefronts were completely vacant. Broken glass lay everywhere and there were several large craters in the middle of the road. He could see completely through the once busy department stores—there were no walls or windows, just outer shells. A pile of metal bomb casings lay at the side of the road. One whole block—Peter remembered there had been a wonderful toy store there—was completely gone. There was nothing left except an enormous pile of plaster, brick, wood, and dirt.

Peter picked his way through the dirt. A group of young nurses in spotless uniforms passed him. They looked out of place as they chatted and laughed amidst the chaos. Women with pinched expressions carrying empty baskets walked by without a word. Old men in ragged topcoats shuffled slowly down the street.

A young British officer in a sparklingly clean uniform was barking orders to a group of bedraggled Hitlerjugend members. They were piling bricks and slowly clearing one small corner of the street. Peter had a moment of panic when the officer looked in his direction. Could he sense that Peter had been in training and had taken the oath? The officer frowned and then turned back to his charges. Peter looked down and realized that, of course, he was drawing attention to himself. He was still wearing the Kriegsmarine trousers, now filthy, and he was bare-chested and barefoot. He no longer had the beautiful leather boots. He didn't know where he'd lost them. Sweat and dirt mottled his chest and arms. He hadn't had a proper wash since his swim in the canal two days ago.

He walked past the Hitlerjugend gang. To Peter's eyes,

the enormity of the cleanup was impossible to conceive. He hadn't thought it could possibly have gotten worse since last autumn, but it had. He felt the same sense of futility that he had felt after the bombing of Klockner, but it was infinitely worse. He could muster no interest in rebuilding the city that had been his home but was now nothing but fragments of walls and piles of rubble.

He turned down Mühren and headed in the direction of the Zoll Canal. He needed to take stock of the city and of his feelings. He was no longer a little boy coming home to Momma. He was a young man starting a new life—whatever that might mean.

His thoughts led him to the hill, the same hill he'd looked down from two years ago when he'd arrived from Hungary. He remembered the horror he had felt then, when so much of the city had been destroyed in the firebombing. Now the destruction was complete. Shards of buildings interspersed the empty spaces. He could see the crumbling spire of St. Nikolai Kirche, but the rest of the church was gone. The Reeperbahn, that used to be an exciting thoroughfare of cafés and nightclubs, was blocked with huge metal girders and bricks forming an anti-tank barrier. He took it all in, but felt no sense of nostalgia or longing. The past was gone. All he had was a small hope that now, finally, there might be a future.

He walked and walked until his bare and bloodied feet led him to the front of his old apartment building. It was still standing, still as exposed as it had been two years earlier. *It's strange*, he thought, *to be comforted by the sight of a ruined house, just because it is a familiar ruined house.* The idea that nothing had changed here since the last time was startling. He was entirely changed. Here was the bomb, still unexploded, by the front door. Here was the plank over the crumbled steps leading up to the door that wasn't there. Here was the hallway, leading down to his old apartment. Here were the starlings swirling in and out of the building, into nests built on the lintels of the doors.

And there was his mother, holding a cake.

"Happy Birthday, Peter."

Chapter Thirty-Four

Hamburg,
May 1945

She stood as still as a photograph, holding the cake out in front of her, smiling.

"I'll make you a cake for your birthday."

His birthday. He was sixteen.

He watched as his mother turned and set the cake down on a crisp white tablecloth. A small vase filled with wildflowers sat in the middle of the table. He watched as she turned to the cupboard and pulled a familiar china plate with red roses around the edge from the middle of a stack. He watched as she cut a piece of the cake and put it on the plate. He watched as she set it on the table, at a place prepared with a silver fork and a white napkin. A piece of birthday cake.

"Oma Ballin said you would be home today."

Peter stared at his mother.

"She is a clairvoyant. She said you would be home on your birthday," she said matter-of-factly.

Peter was still frozen in the middle of the kitchen.

Everything was familiar. Nothing was familiar. With blinding clarity, he realized that it didn't mean anything to him. The idea of home had vanished like waking from a dream. Last time he'd returned, home was all he craved. This time, he realized with a shock, home was a place to leave from.

He became aware of his mother studying his face, expecting him to say something. His mother, standing in their old, ruined kitchen, was holding a cake. *What was the last thing she'd said?*

"Oma Ballin is still alive?" he muttered. Somehow this fact seemed stranger than the fact that she'd said that Peter would be home today.

"Yes," smiled his mother. "Still alive. Still bossing everyone around. She gave me some of the ingredients for the cake, a few things she got on the black market. It's a bit dry, of course. Lard instead of butter. And not much of that. She can't wait to see you. She said you'd come today, and you did."

Peter wished he could smile. He couldn't seem to make his face work.

She turned, filled a glass with water, and set it down on the table. "You might need this," she said playfully. "It isn't up to my usual standards, I'm afraid." She pulled a chair out for him.

"You're so tall. So strong," she went on, cutting herself a slice of cake and continuing to fill his silence. "They must have fed you well in Denmark. Lots of Danish pastries?" She gestured again to the chair.

Peter sat. He took a small bite of the dry crumbs and washed it down with a sip of water. He watched as his mother filled a tub with warm water and salt. He watched as she lifted his feet and put them in. He flinched—the salt stung—but he sat impassively as she bathed off the blood.

Yes, he had grown, and his mother had shrunk. She was small and gray and birdlike in her movements. Her thin hair was pulled back into a bun—she'd clearly made an effort to look her best. But in this demolished city, how could anything look other than destroyed?

She'd made him a cake. She'd used some dried chicory for flavor so the cake was a dark brown color, just as if it had been made with chocolate. It crumbled when he touched it. There were two layers, between them a paper-thin layer of jam. God knows how she had managed to find that. What had she traded on the black market to give him a bit of jam? He remembered when he traded his grandfather's watch for a ham for her birthday.

He knew he should say something, be grateful, be kind. But he felt as though he were peering at her from the bottom of a deep, cold well.

"I have a new apartment near the station. In St. Georg," she said as she carefully patted the wounds on his feet. "I came here because I knew this was where you would come. I knew you would come home. But you can see they've done nothing to fix it. Two years and nothing. I leave our things here and keep it as tidy as I can. I know we'll be able to move back some day. The apartment is really too small, especially now with Emilio."

She was chattering excitedly. He couldn't understand what he was doing here, except that it was his birthday and he was eating cake. "Emilio?" he asked.

She continued to focus on his feet. "Emilio. You'll like him. He's an Italian prisoner of war. He's teaching me Italian—imagine! I met him in the munitions factory where I'm working. Herr Girmann fired me from the photography studio for 'anti-war sentiments' if you can believe it! Anyway, Emilio and the other Italian prisoners all work there—it's the same as when the Russian prisoners worked at Klockner. You remember. He's hoping he can stay in Hamburg once he has been officially released. He's a good man," she added quietly.

The Russian prisoners at Klockner. The skeletal prisoners on the road. Prisoners of war, of conscience, of religion, of race, of sexuality. Were the gates now open wide? Would the streets be filled with released prisoners? Would they turn on their captors?

"Hans left shortly after you. He went to work in a camp. He won't be coming back," she added quietly.

He looked at her blankly.

"You don't mind, do you?" His mother was looking up at him, her face strained with care.

He realized he needed to say something. To play his part. "No, of course not, Mother." He saw relief flood into her eyes. "I am happy for you."

"The apartment really isn't big enough for two," she continued happily, "let alone three, but we'll manage, I'm sure."

Peter let her words sink in. She no longer needed him to look after her. And he realized with a great sense of relief that he no longer needed to worry about her. "That's all right, Mother. I can make a space for myself here." He held up a heavy hand as she started to object. "You said yourself that this is home. I've slept in a lot worse situations. I can stay here and put up a new wall. I'll repair a bit of ceiling."

She tousled his hair in a familiar gesture. "You're quite a grown man now, I can see." He could hear the relief in her voice. "Well, you'll stay with us tonight, anyway." His mother was bubbling with good humor. "I've made us a good turnip soup. Emilio loves my turnip soup!"

And so it was settled. Peter would stay in the apartment and begin to do reconstruction. The building itself was sound. It was just missing walls and a few chunks of ceiling. Miraculously, the plumbing worked—that was something. An elderly couple had moved into an apartment on the first floor and were thrilled to have someone else living in the building. It made them feel safer, they said. Their son had done some rebuilding for them last year when he was home on leave. They hadn't heard from him since. But now the Americans, they said, were helping to fund reconstruction in the city. Slowly, the city was coming back to life.

Peter was content to spend his days alone with a hammer. He mechanically went about his tasks, teaching himself how to put in wall studs, insert lathes, plaster, sand, and plaster some more. In the evenings he'd go to his mother and Emilio for a meal of thin soup and dry bread. Emilio communicated effusively in a mixture of German and Italian, passionately gesticulating. Peter listened and nodded, while his mother fussed around, happy to be looking after her "two men."

His favorite time was late at night, when he'd walk

through the streets alone, in the dark, listening to the sound of his footsteps. He'd reach his dollhouse apartment and feel safe, despite the night bats circling through his open walls.

Summer passed. All through the city, people were shoveling, nailing, plastering. The piles of rubble began to slowly disappear. On the streets, there were fewer and fewer German uniforms and more and more American and British uniforms. American English twanged through the shops, but there was still nothing to buy. Peter's mother was resourceful. Emilio had helped to build her black market connections. But Peter ate her meals without taste, without interest. He couldn't make himself care.

"Peter Gruber?"

A nasal voice broke through the silence of Peter's non-existent thoughts. He looked up from his hammering.

"Are you Peter Gruber?" The American officer spoke in German.

Peter nodded.

"You were in the Altstadt chapter of the Hitlerjugend? You trained in Alsen?"

Peter's heart thudded awake. *Am I going to be arrested?* He had heard that German officers were being tried for war crimes, as if war itself was not the crime. Had he committed a crime other than desertion? Was desertion a crime the Americans could arrest him for?

He nodded to the American. "Yes. I was in Alsen. I left. At the end of the war." He wasn't sure if it was better to say *before* the end of the war or *at* the end of the war. A word might decide his fate.

The American handed him an official-looking paper with an address, date, and time printed on it. Peter's name was on the top.

"You are to report here on Thursday. Bring this paper with you."

The American must have seen something behind the mask of Peter's face. "It's all right," he said, "you are not in trouble. Well, no more trouble than anyone else. But you must report on Thursday. It is an order, the last order to your unit."

Peter spent the next two days even more drawn into himself. He didn't tell his mother or Emilio about the visit from the American. It would be too easy to implicate other people. If he was going to be arrested, he would not involve them. His mother was happy in her new post-war life. Not for the world would he disturb that.

Peter reported at the appointed hour, paper in hand. He entered a large room in a former Gymnasium. Thirty or forty other boys were there, sitting on chairs. Some were chatting in tense, quiet tones, while others were joking with what seemed like false bravado. Peter kept his head down.

He sat alone to wait for whatever would befall him. He ventured a look forward and saw, to his surprise, a movie screen set up at the front of the room. Instinctively, he looked back and saw a projector. A movie? He'd been brought here to watch a movie?

"Peter?" A quiet familiar voice spoke from the chair behind him. Peter's eyes refocused. "Gunter," he said.

Gunter stood up and slid into the chair beside him. Peter hadn't seen him since that day in the spring when they got on the train, the day of the long march. He ventured a look at Gunter and thought he could see his own face mirrored back at him. Two empty masks, with the slightest nod of recognition. Peter wondered if Gunter's cheerful optimism had finally failed him.

"Is ...?" he started to ask, but realized he didn't want to know the answer to the question. He wanted Herr Schmidt to stay suspended in time, pouring coffee.

"Hermann's here, too," Gunter said, his eyes shifting to the back of the room. Peter saw Hermann laughing with a couple of other boys. Hermann looked over and waved good-naturedly. *The new Hermann*, thought Peter. *He learned how to be a friend by not taking life seriously. He'll do well in the new Germany.*

Gunter nudged him gently and pointed to the far corner of the room. Peter barely recognized Franz. He was wiry and his skin had a waxy, yellowish tinge. A twisted snarl of hair hung down in front of fierce, glowering eyes that connected with nothing. *He's mad*, thought Peter with a start. *Insane.*

At that moment, an American officer strode to the front of the room. Although his accent was strong, he spoke fluently in formal German.

"Good evening. The last time you were in a situation like this, you were standing at attention. You were saluting your Führer. But you will never make that salute again. Not here, not anywhere. Your Nazi Party, the party to which you swore allegiance, is now an illegal organization.

"You were young when you joined the Hitlerjugend. You had no choice. Hitlerjugend was a natural progression from your school and your education. You made friends; you trained and learned many valuable skills. You did it all for the good of your country.

"You believed your teachers, your commanding officers, your Führer. You did not question their authority or their actions. If you had doubts, you hid them."

A memory of Gymnasium, of measuring Otto's head, flew through Peter's mind.

"My uncle told me there are people saying these things, using them to prove things that aren't true ..."

The American looked around the room. His face was severe. Peter thought he saw something like hatred in the man's eyes.

"What you are about to see is a documentary about what was happening while you were not asking questions. It is a movie made by American and British liberating forces. We thought we were coming here to liberate you from your tyrannical dictator. But we did not know the meaning of liberation until we walked into Bergen-Belsen, Auschwitz, Treblinka, Dachau, Neuengamme. Death camps throughout Germany, Poland, Hungary, Italy, France, and Spain. Death camps in which your Führer, your commanding officers, and your teachers ordered the murder of six million souls.

"This is what your Nazi Party did. This is what you did."

The lights in the room dimmed.

Peter didn't remember how he got home. He dimly remembered vomiting by the side of the road, while others around him were doing the same. He remembered being terrified of sleep and terrified of being awake. He was aware of being curled in a fetal position, shaking. His mind was a series of electric shocks, sparking and going nowhere. He was beyond tears, firmly held in the fires of hell.

It took him a month to find his future. It started with his worn copy of *War and Peace*. He'd forgotten to get rid of it after he'd come back from Eutin that summer so long ago. The day he'd found it under his old bed, he'd clutched it and rocked it as though he had found a lost child. He let himself drown in the familiar world of Pierre and Natasha.

... Let the dead bury the dead ...

When he had finished *War and Peace*, he knew he wasn't yet ready to surface. He went to Hamburg's newly re-opened library. He gathered books and stories around him like protective walls. He found copies of the Russians that he'd wrapped in a shroud and buried in Eutin. They were no longer banned and he devoured them, finally understanding the humanity behind their words. He read through day and night. He abandoned all pretense of reconstruction. Nothing existed for him outside the books.

His mother came over with bits of stew, trying to entice him to eat, but his brain was working at a fevered pitch, desperate to find something to keep him alive, some way of living with the horror.

Finally, after weeks of oblivion, *The Brothers Karamazov* threw him a lifeline back to the world.

... now go and play and live some of life for me ...

He crumbled. His body wept for the memory of Eugene, for the memory of springtime, of playing in the mud in the canal, of dappled trees, of Olga's hair catching on the barnboard. He held the line and began to pull himself toward the shore.

It was Emilio who told him about the advertisement for workers in Canada.

"Work for the Great Lakes Paper Company in northern Ontario. Passage paid."

He could start in the spring. The Great Lakes Paper Company. Lakes in the north, in a place called Sioux Lookout. A lookout was a place that you could watch the world from and be safe.

He could live in a forest. A place where life would be simple. A place away from civilization. The air would be fresh and sweet. He made a pact with himself: never to let his hands touch a gun again. It was his own personal non-aggression pact. He'd make sure he never again hurt anyone. He could leave the ghosts—Otto, Olga, Franz, and six million others—behind. But he'd take Eugene. Eugene had loved the woods.

He wasn't sure why he hadn't tried to find Gunter before, but an instinct took him to the docks at sunset. As the orange glow began to spread along the water, Peter saw a familiar silhouette sitting on the edge of the ruined dock. He sat down and began to talk to Gunter about trees. If Gunter came with him, they could remember and forget together.

And maybe, just maybe, they could find a way to live some of life for those who couldn't.

Great Lakes. Sioux Lookout. A place where the future might begin.

Glossary

Bund Deutscher Mädel (BDM): The League of German Girls. During the Second World War, it was compulsory for girls ten years old to belong to the Jungmädelbund (JM), or Young girls League. When they were 14, they joined the BDM. As with Hitlerjugend, the BDM was only open to ethnic Germans who were "free from hereditary disease." The purpose of the JM and the BDM was to instill girls with the values of the Third Reich and to train them for their roles in German society—that of wife, mother, and homemaker.

Deutsches Jungvolk (DJ): The German Youth. Usually just referred to as Jungvolk. In 1939 it became compulsory for all boys ten to fourteen years old to be a member of the DJ, but membership was only open to boys who were ethnic Germans and "free from hereditary diseases." Activities such as sports, hiking, and camping took place after school and on weekends. The main purpose of the organization was to teach children the principles of the Nazi Party. Parents who did not enroll eligible children in the program were seen as neglecting their responsibilities to the Reich, and could be charged.

FLAK: The name refers to a type of anti-aircraft gun in use in Germany. It's a contraction of the word *Flugzeugabwehrkanone,* which means aircraft-defense cannon. English adopted the word to mean any kind of anti-aircraft fire coming from the ground.

Führer: The word means leader or guide in German, but it has come to always be associated with Adolf Hitler.

Gestapo: A short form of *Geheime Staatspolizei,* or Secret State Police. The Gestapo was in charge of all areas of the law, throughout the country, but was in itself outside of the law. The Gestapo was feared for their ruthless methods of torture and their arbitrary application of the law.

Gymnasium: A school system for more advanced students. Typically, it is an eight-year program and students must take an exam to enter and be accepted. Gymnasium schools emphasize academic learning and are seen as a preparation for university.

Hitlerjugend (HJ): The Hitler Youth. During the Second World War, it was compulsory for boys aged 14 to 18 to be members of the HJ. Like DJ, membership was only open to boys who were ethic Germans and "free from hereditary diseases." HJ activities took place after school and on weekends. The emphasis was on physical and military training, and the goal was to instill motivation, so that the youth would fight faithfully for the Third Reich and Hitler.

Hort: A program for German children up until the age of 10. Children went after school and on weekends. There was an emphasis on games, outdoor education, and camping trips. Hort is also a kind of kindergarten/daycare.

Kriegsmarine: The Germany navy.

Nazi: In German the Nationalsozialistische Deutsche Arbeiterpartei, abbreviated to NSDAP or Nazi Party. The Party was active from 1920 to 1945. It began as a way to fight communism, but became by the 1930s a party that was dedicated to cleansing the country of anyone who was not a "true" German, that is, anyone who was not an ethnic German or was "impure" in mind or body. The goal was to build a German "Master Race" by exterminating all Jews, Roma, and physically or mentally handicapped people. Homosexuals, Africans, Jehovah's Witnesses, and political opponents were put in labor camps as slaves.

Neuengamme, Bergen-Belsen, Auschwitz, Treblinka, Dachau: The names of several of the hundreds of German concentration camps where Jews, Roma, Slavs, homosexuals, Jehovah's Witnesses, and objectors were interred. They were used as slave labor, but the ultimate goal of the Nazi party was to "liquidate" these "undesirables." Over six million people were killed in the camps over the course of the war.

Resistance: There were many people who fought against the German occupation. Resistance fighters organized to sabotage the Gestapo and the occupying forces. However, the Germans brutally murdered any Resistance fighters that were caught. In fact, towns that harbored Resistance fighters were completely destroyed by the Germans, resulting in the death of thousands of innocent people.

SA: *Sturmabteilung* or Assault Division. The SA were Hitler's private army. Also called "Storm Troopers" or "Brown Shirts."

SS: *Schutzstaffel*, or Protection Guard. SS members were required to profess undying loyalty to Hitler and unquestioningly acknowledge him as their one and only prophet. The SS were combat troops who brutalized and tortured people in the occupied territories, as well as any people suspected of subversion or of impure blood. They eventually held responsibility for all of the death camps.

Third Reich: The Third Reich refers to the period of 1933 to 1945 in Germany when Adolf Hitler was dictator, and the National Socialist (Nazi) party was in power. After Hitler was appointed Chancellor in 1933, he changed the laws so that he was in ultimate control over all aspects of German life. He was, in effect, the law.

Author's Note

Elements of this story are based on the real life of Hans Sinn. Hans was a War Child in Hamburg who went through Jungvolk and Hitlerjugend. At the start of the war, he was the same age as my character, Peter. He was evacuated to Neumarkt and Bistriz, and found himself in an SS training camp in Denmark, from which he escaped in the final days of the Second World War. I owe a huge debit to Hans for telling me his story, and for supplying the photographs that have been reproduced in the book. As painful as it was to remember, Hans wanted this story told in the hope that it might help people to understand how easy it is to warp a child's view of the world.

Hans, like many of his generation, has spent a lot of his life trying to come to terms with the six war years that completely molded his childhood. There is a special German word for this. Vergangenheitsbewältigung: The process of coming to terms with the past.

While this book is set amid real events, the characters in it are fictitious, and any similarity to real names is purely coincidental.

Acknowledgements

A book of historical fiction is hard to write at the best of times, but to write one about a foreign culture is probably madness. But this story came from a first-hand source, Hans Sinn (see Author's Note), and I knew from the moment I heard it that I wanted to try to write it. I have received support and background information from a number of people, but all errors and omissions are entirely my own.

It was extraordinary to have had Hans as a primary source for this story. I have also been very inspired by a number of excellent books, including *Hitler Youth: Growing up in Hitler's Shadow* by Susan Campbell Bartoletti; *Inferno: The Fiery Destruction of Hamburg, 1943,* by Keith Lowe; *The End,* by Hans Erich Nossack; *Hitlerland: American Eyewitnesses to the Nazi Rise to Power,* by Andrew Nagorski; *In the Garden of Beasts* by Erik Larsen; *Gretel's Story: A Young Woman's Secret War Against the Nazis,* by Gretel Wachtel and Claudia Strachan, as well as numerous web sites, podcasts, articles, and internet sources.

A huge debt of gratitude goes to Trish Roach for introducing me to Mainz, Germany, and to Alex Kretschmer who helped me to see the scars that remain. A special thank you goes to Silke Reichrath and Marion Endt-Jones, both of whom read the manuscript for German spellings, idioms, and details of place. I am grateful to the surprising Dr. Robert Chaplin for helping me to understand film-processing techniques from the 1940s.

Thank you to my very first workshop group at Vermont College of Fine Arts, and to Mark Karlins and Cynthia Leitich Smith who were insightful and helpful in their comments on the book's opening.

I would like to acknowledge funding support from the Writer's Reserve Program of the Ontario Arts Council, an agency of the Government of Ontario. I also deeply appreciate the support I have received from Red Deer Press, my publisher Richard Dionne, and publicist Winston Stilwell.

My deep appreciation goes to Penny Hosey, my "grammar goddess" copy editor. Thank you, Penny, for bringing me a step closer to understanding the subjunctive!

This book would not have been possible without the encouragement of my editor Peter Carver. Peter championed this book from the first moment that I started to talk about it. He has been magnificently relentless in his questions, and incisive in his editorial comments. His guidance, wisdom, and unflagging good humor have kept me going through the dark days. Peter, I will always been in your debt.

My mother Laurie Lewis has been stalwart in her support, and patient with my obsession and preoccupation. My children Virgil Alexander, Magdalene Beryl, and Lewis Arthur are my reason for everything. My mother and my children remind me, from both ends of the generational spectrum, that nothing matters more than making the world a better place for our children.

I could not have tackled this book were it not for the love of my life, Tim Wynne-Jones. It was Tim who innocently asked Hans one day, "Hans, did you ever go to camp?" From there, the floodgates opened. Living through this has been hard, but, as you've so often said, it's what we do. Thank you.

Interview with Amanda West Lewis

Photo credit: Matt Miller

What drew you to tell this story?

I went to Germany in 2012 to visit family in Mainz. Mainz is a small, peaceful, diverse medieval city primarily known as the home of Johannes Gutenberg, inventor of the printing press. Eighty percent of Mainz was destroyed during the Second World War. As I explored the city, and saw the evidence of all that had been rebuilt, I began to think about what the war must have meant to ordinary German citizens. But I soon discovered that because of the guilt and shame of the Nazi regime, people did not talk about their losses or their suffering. Then I read *Inferno: The Fiery Destruction of Hamburg 1943* by Keith Lowe. I didn't really know anything about Hamburg except that my neighbor Hans Sinn grew up there, and I was stunned to learn about Operation Gomorrah, the firebombing destruction of Hamburg in 1943. I realized that there was a whole side of the war that I knew nothing about.

Obviously the Nazis were responsible for unspeakable evil. We must never forget the horror of the Holocaust that resulted in the deaths of six million people. But there were millions of ordinary civilians whose lives were shattered by the war. I wanted to know more about their stories.

How important was your encounter with Hans to the writing of Peter's story?

Hans Sinn is a neighbor whom I have known for over twenty-five years. I knew nothing about his history or background until one day about fifteen years ago, when we were sitting together by a lake, watching our children play in the water. The children were singing songs and playing games—the kinds of things kids learn at camp. My husband (writer Tim Wynne-Jones) innocently asked Hans if he had ever gone to camp. Hans replied, with a sad smile, "Yes. Hitler Youth camp." It was quite a shock! He then went on to describe his escape from an SS training camp in Denmark. It was an amazing story, and perhaps even more striking to hear it while we were sitting beside a peaceful lake in Canada.

However, it wasn't until 2012, after I came back from Mainz, that I decided to delve deeper. I began interviewing Hans and spent many hours talking with him about his life before, during, and after the war. I would not have been brave enough to tackle this story without having him as a guide.

Can you say something about the distinction between Hans's real-life experiences and Peter Gruber's story?

Hans told me many interesting facts about his life, and about what it was like for him growing up during the war. I incorporated a number of those facts into Peter's life, and Peter's biography shares much of the same history as Hans's life. For example, Hans had diphtheria as a child and spent weeks in hospital reading the Russians; he had a black market business; he was given his grandfather's watch after his grandfather hanged himself; he was evacuated to Neumarkt and Bistriz, where a gypsy told his fortune. All of these are really unusual and authentic details, so I used them to help me create the character of Peter. There are many elements inspired by Hans's life sprinkled throughout the story. Hans also shared his photographs with me. Seeing them made the story very real for me.

But Hans never gave me any indication of the emotions or motivations that guided him in his youth. I had to build Peter's inner life myself, and so of course Peter is very different from Hans.

I started to discover Peter by thinking about his friends. I think one of the most important elements of a young person's life is his or her relationship to friends. It is through our friendships that we learn who we are. So I created Gunter, Otto, Hermann, and Olga to help Peter discover who he was.

Hans told me that when he was five, he saw his best friend Eugene die in a drowning accident. I think that kind of loss has a huge impact on a young person, and I wanted to include it in the story. I moved the incident forward by five years so that it coincided with the start of the war. Eugene became an important marker for Peter to be able to see how much life he had lived since the start of the war. I think anyone who suffers a loss does this—we live our lives in juxtaposition to those who have died.

Recently a new edition of Hitler's infamous *Mein Kampf* was published in Germany. You quote from this book at times, and also from Hitler's speeches. There are those who say that the book should have remained banned in Germany. What is your opinion of that position?

The Nazis banned and burned books because they didn't want people to think for themselves. They knew that if you let people think, they ask questions. By not asking questions, the horror of the Holocaust was allowed to happen.

If we ban books, we are banning information and knowledge. This can only result in lopsided questions and incomplete answers. I think that only by asking questions can a person make informed, moral decisions. So as hard as it is, I'd have to say that even *Mein Kampf* should not be banned. We must believe in our ability to educate people as to why Hitler's ideas are wrong. More education, not less, should be our goal if we don't want to make the same mistakes again.

In this story we learn how so many in Germany became radicalized through the actions of the Nazi party. Why do you think it is important for young readers in the 21st century to learn about this phenomenon?

Young people are guided by a huge moral compass. They are passionate and desperately want to make sense of their lives. They see injustice, pain, and suffering and they want to make a better world. This is one of the wonderful things about being young—you are filled with hope and idealism. You don't want to hear your parents' old, tired ideas. You want to go out and make things new.

Hitler was able to harness the energy and idealism of the German youth. He made them believe that their lives, which had been very difficult after the First World War, would be wonderful once they embraced their destined future.

Unfortunately, there is a similar scenario being played out today throughout the world. There are many young people living in poverty, hopelessness, and anger. They desperately want their lives to have meaning, but in their despair they have no sense of purpose or belonging. Then a charismatic leader comes along and makes them believe they are needed to be part of a "glorious" campaign to make a new and better world. They become convinced that the world can be changed, or cleansed, through violence. Finally, they have a purpose. They have hope and idealism. Their moral compass has been given a direction. They are supplied with weapons and training, and the results are disastrous.

I think it is essential to look at what happened in Nazi Germany try to understand how easy it is for disaffected and angry young people to become radicalized.

Why did you decide that Peter's dreams were important to the unfolding of his story?

Peter is struggling under the weight of feeling responsible for his mother, when the trauma of Eugene's death separates him from his emotions. He represses his feelings and buries a lot in his subconscious.

But I thought that the reader needed to get a glimpse into what Peter was really going through. Through the dreams, the reader learns more about Peter than he knows about himself. The dreams stop when Peter starts to allow himself to feel his emotions. When he finally begins to work with his subconscious, Peter moves toward a better understanding of who he is.

Not knowing what is happening in the world is a feature of Peter's life, as it was for many of the German people at this time. To what extent do you think it was a deliberate policy of the rulers of Nazi Germany to keep their citizens uninformed?

During wartime, there is often a deliberate policy to withhold information. In Germany, it was illegal to read foreign newspapers or listen to radio broadcasts from other countries. In other words, the only news people were allowed to know was the news that the government wanted them to hear. Ultimately, this was a way to control what people thought. They believed they were winning the war when they were losing. They believed what they were doing was right when it was horrifyingly wrong. There was no voice of dissent to question what was going on. Independent thought was not allowed. No questions were allowed. Hitler's voice was the voice of authority and information. His voice was messianic and compelling. There was simply no other way to see the world.

It was a very effective way to control the population.

But without accurate information, people will resort to rumor. For example, in early 1943, the people of Hamburg had heard rumors that Dusseldorf had been firebombed and destroyed in the same way as Köln. This wasn't true. Dusseldorf was severely bombed, but never firebombed. In the story, I let Peter's mother believe the rumor, although it was, in fact, untrue. I wanted to show that rumors spread fear and uncertainty.

Helmuth Hübener and the U-Boat commander First Lieutenant Erwin Sell are incidental to your story, but they are real historical figures. Why did you want to bring them into the narrative?

This story is set in a real time and place. All of the larger events are true, and they all have an impact on my fictional characters. Helmuth Hübener was a young man whose fight against the Nazis cost him his life. He was only seventeen years old when he was arrested, tried as an adult, and executed. Within seven hours of the guilty verdict he was beheaded. Helmuth was from Hamburg, and his case would have been discussed among young people. I can only imagine how terrifying it would be to know that someone your age was beheaded for treason. It would certainly make you think twice about disobeying orders. I think it helps to explain Peter's reluctance to do anything other than what he is told.

Peter isn't trying to be a hero. He says he is going to survive, and he does. He manages to do so without destroying other people, but he isn't particularly brave. I think it is important to know that there were a few people, like Helmuth Hübener, who showed amazing and inspiring bravery. But I think most of us are more like Peter. We just want to survive.

Peter's escape from Denmark is based on the true story that Hans Sinn told me. Hans escaped from Denmark on a U-boat that went to Germany to surrender. When the war ended, all U-boats were supposed to surrender, wherever they were. U-boat 1102, commanded by First Lieutenant Erwin Sell, surrendered at Hohwacht Bay, which is a small base about twenty-five miles from Kiel. It was being used as a U-Abwehrschule, a training ship, so it might have had a number of one-man subs connected to it. It might have come from Denmark. So I decided to make it the sub that Peter escaped on. For the purposes of the narrative, I have landed it at Kiel on May 4th. The British accepted the unconditional surrender of all German forces in Denmark on May 4, 1945, so I knew that the latest the U-boat could have left Denmark was May 3rd.

Because so much of Peter's life is based on facts, I liked giving him a real ship, and a real commander, to escape with. It is also really fun to do research and incorporate it into your story!

In your previous story about World War Two, *September 17*, the focus is on British children who confronted the terrors of wartime. What connection, if any, is there between their story and that of Peter and his friends in this book?

I was intrigued to learn that German children, like the English, were evacuated to the countryside to be kept safe during the war. Learning about the Kinderlandverschickung made me understand that German parents loved their children every bit as much as the English parents. They struggled with the same issue—how do we keep our children safe while bombs are falling all around us?

However, the main difference between the books is that Peter and his friends are fictional, so I could invent their thoughts and feelings. All of the children that I wrote about in *September 17* were real, so while I could imagine how they must have felt, I had to be respectful of their personal histories.

What became of Hans Sinn, the man whose story provided the basis for Peter's fictional story?

Hans Sinn came to Canada after the war. He lives in a house he built in the woods, where he has dedicated his life to work as a peace activist. He met his wife Marian while on the Vancouver-Berlin Peace Walk in the early 1960s.

Hans was involved with the creation of Peace Brigades International, and over the years has been active in many organizations including the Canadian Friends Service Committee and The Canadian Campaign for Nuclear Disarmament. He worked with dissidents in East Germany to effect the fall of the Berlin Wall. He continues to advocate for recognition of the Armenian genocide, and works with Indigenous groups in Canada to effect social change. Hans

Sinn and Silke Reichrath are co-founders of the not for profit organization: Brooke Valley Research for Education in Nonviolence. http://www.brookevalleyresearch.ca/index.html Part of their mission is to research the long-term impact of war on children.

After the war he made a pact with himself that his hands would never touch a gun again.

Thank you, Amanda, for these thoughtful and moving insights.